KNIGHTMARE

By

Beverley Cann

I dedicate this work to my family whose faith in my abilities gave me the confidence to try something new!

CONTENTS

ACKNOWLEDGMENTS...i
PROLOGUE.. 1
Chapter One... 5
Chapter Two 16
Chapter Three 29
Chapter Four 44
Chapter Five 58
Chapter Six 77
Chapter Seven... 94
Chapter Eight 104
Chapter Nine 114
Chapter Ten 136
Chapter Eleven 146
Chapter Twelve.. 159
Chapter Thirteen 176
Chapter Fourteen... 190
Chapter Fifteen.. 199
Chapter Sixteen... 213
Chapter Seventeen... 231
Chapter Eighteen... 242
ABOUT THE AUTHOR 262

ACKNOWLEDGMENTS

I wish to thank my friend Val MacDonald for proofreading my work, crossing the 'Ts' and dotting the 'Is' and encouraging me to actually finish the book. Also Luke Cann who was my trusted sounding board, who offered his own creative talents giving me a man's perspective. His encouragement was invaluable.

PROLOGUE

S o this was it... retirement.

I glanced at the flowers spilling over the passenger seat as I drove home. So many flowers and their fragrances in the confines of the car were overpowering. I cracked the window. I expected to feel different but it felt like any other drive home after a busy day.

The weekend was as any other weekend but I was sure come Monday morning I would feel a difference. Apart from appreciating the absence of the alarm clock... I felt nothing. Everyone had remarked I must be so excited, relieved, apprehensive, even filled with dread, but I felt quite normal. The weather was cold and wet and didn't really encourage outdoor excursions so I relaxed, watched TV, read books and drank tea. This continued for a while until I realised how easy it could be to turn into a couch potato, so I went to the other extreme.

Appraising my newly painted bedroom, feeling exhausted but rather pleased with myself, I mentally ticked off my 'to do' list. Loo seat fixed, kitchen cabinet fittings tightened, bushes pruned and garden tidied and a thorough spring clean throughout the house. My finances had been put in order and budget planned for 'pension' existence. The car serviced and cleaned, not by me obviously but by some very nice men in the next town who spoke no English and communicated by whistles, hand gestures and smiles and winks.

My conversion from couch potato to cleaning guru also helped shift quite a few pounds in weight which had clung to me for what seemed like forever, not having been helped by the initial retirement diet of chocolate and afternoon sticky buns. This in turn encouraged me to overhaul my wardrobe. Putting out the last bag of clothes on the drive ready for the charity collection I was momentarily tempted to rush out and reclaim it when I saw how empty my wardrobes were, but what was the point of hoarding clothes that no longer fitted?

I continued to reshape my life, walking more, throwing myself into crafts and even joining a choir. Fortunately there had been no audition as it was for 'fun', this being evident when we first started to sing together but it improved with time... slightly.

Of course with more time on my hands I became one of the ladies that 'do lunch'. I sat staring out of the window people watching, a favourite pastime. Today was typical of the last days of winter, dark clothes, grim faces and scurrying steps. I saw my friend Helen crossing the road in front of the teashop and gave her a wave to let her know I had the table already.

"You're looking well," I said as she stooped to give me a welcoming hug.

"Do you think so? Steve took me away for a mid-week break. It was so relaxing, superb accommodation and lovely food. Anyway, first things first, let's order the tea."

We sat and drank our tea and devoured our cream scones, catching up on events since our last meeting. We shared any titbits of gossip and generally enjoyed each other's company. Having worked together for about 18 years we had a lot of history together and had perhaps shared things between us that we hadn't with anyone else. Helen drained the last drop of tea out of the teapot and sat back in her seat holding her cup between both hands. She was looking quite serious.

"What's up then, Evie?"

"What do you mean? I'm fine. I've just told you of all the things I have been doing in the last months."

"Hmmm," she replied, unconvinced. "Something isn't quite right."

I shrugged and attempted a false laugh. "Don't know what you mean." But she knew me too well and saw straight through me.

"You've lost your sparkle. Are you not enjoying retirement? God! You don't want to go back do you?" She looked alarmed momentarily but relaxed when I did laugh this time, shaking my head.

Of all people, Helen was perhaps the one to understand my mixed emotions and help me fathom out what it was that was missing. I didn't know where to start so I just gave a big sigh, opened my mouth and let it all out. My retired friends were really enjoying it and my working friends were counting the days, to me it was just an inevitable progression in life. My body soon acclimatised to different activity but my mind was putting up a struggle.

"It's still early days yet, and you do so much," she pointed out.

"But I do it all for the wrong reasons. If I am honest I do everything out of guilt."

She looked surprised. "Guilt?"

"It seems so wrong to have waited for time to myself and not fill it. I like what I do but I feel I'm just marking time. My crafts which I loved doing aren't that fulfilling anymore, it's like I only really appreciated them when I had to find time out of a busy schedule to fit them in. My reading, I do now just to fill my mind and stop myself from thinking."

Helen placed the empty teacup on the saucer. "Perhaps you need an adventure," she suggested.

I laughed out loud at this. "An adventure, what with my anxiety levels and panic attacks?"

"Oh come on, look at all the things you have done in the past."

"They weren't adventures, they were things thrown at me which I had to cope with."

"…And you coped marvellously," she pointed out. "Look, retirement hasn't panned out for you as you expected. You didn't expect to face it alone, I understand that, but give it a chance. Don't force it, just go where it leads. Give it a bit more time."

She reached across the table and squeezed my hand. Just sharing my misgivings made me feel a little lighter in spirit and I smiled appreciatively at her.

"Or," she said mischievously, "you could look for a man!"

She wasn't expecting a response but I rolled my eyes to let her know what I felt about that suggestion. It had started to rain so we were bidding a brief farewell under the teashop awning when Helen started rummaging in her bag. She pushed a very crumpled leaflet in my hand.

"I saw this while I was away and thought of you. The area is so picturesque it's worth visiting for that alone."

With that she planted a kiss on my cheek and was off, dodging the cars to cross the street. I pushed the paper into my bag and pulled my hood over my head as the drizzle developed into a downpour. I was soaked by the time I reached the car park.

It was later that evening when I retrieved the crumpled paper from my bag.

Wyvern Castle

Costumed event bringing authenticity to your discovery of mediaeval fashion.

Two-day workshop examining the textiles and natural dyes of the Middle Ages and their influence on today's fabrics.

CHAPTER ONE

"Turn around where possible."

"Grrr." I was gripping the steering wheel so tightly my knuckles were white and my hands were sweating. 'Sat-nav' lady had been very helpful on the long drive down, but for the last 15 minutes she kept insisting I turn around. The road was little more than a lane with periodic passing points so her request was pretty impossible. The further I drove to find a safe turning area the further away from my destination I became. To make matters worse the hedgerows either side of me were very high preventing me seeing the layout of the land. I was going to be late and I wasn't far off panic mode.

As I rounded a corner I saw a break in the hedgerow, the daylight was streaming through and I glimpsed a gate presumably to a field, so I pulled off the road and nosed up to it to give me maximum space for reversing. The view caught me quite by surprise. There in the distance rising up from what looked like a village was a tall hill atop of which was a castle. What a relief, at least I now knew in which direction to aim.

The village turned out to be a small town with lots of directions to the castle so 'sat-nav' lady wasn't required any further. The actual road up to the castle was quite steep and I was thankful I didn't meet any of the large tour buses coming in the opposite direction.

"You have reached your destination."

"You don't say," I muttered as I turned into the visitors' car park and crunched across the gravel to the far side where there was a sprinkling of trees. I didn't really have time to sight see but through the trees I glimpsed the ruins of a stone wall. Grabbing my bag I swung out of the car but, turning to lock it, I suddenly felt very dizzy. I gripped the side of the car as a wave of nausea swept over me and there was a buzzing in my ears. I started to breathe deeply thinking that I might have to sit back in the car. I really felt strange; I was bathed in sweat so I grabbed my water bottle and gulped some down.

I had risen at silly o'clock this morning but had consciously eaten breakfast before the journey. Perhaps the anxiety of getting lost had set this off; anyway I drank more water and continued breathing deeply. After a few minutes the nausea and dizziness subsided but there was still a low hum in my ears. Feeling a little less shaky and catching sight of the time on my wrist watch I headed in the direction of the entrance.

The climb to the entrance gate was quite steep. Halfway up on the right was a booth selling entry tickets and site maps. Searching in my bag for my mobile phone to try and find the email of my registration confirmation, I apologised to the lad in the booth.

"Sorry for the hold-up, I have my registration for the course in here somewhere."

My bag was enormous; since I kept all my craft bits and bobs in it, plus my overnight things and personal items. Normally I would have my phone to hand but today wasn't proving to be a normal day.

"It's OK," he grinned, "if you are for the workshop you are on my list and I only have one name left. Let me stamp your hand and then you can come and go as you please."

I dutifully extended my left hand and received a small black stamp of a circle with something inside it.

"Now when you go through the gate," he continued, "keep on till you reach the end of the buildings on your right, take a right turn and go to the end of the block and the workshops will be on your right.

They are the converted stables, you can't miss them."

Bet I can, I thought, but just smiled and thanked him. The daily tourists had started to arrive so I had to weave in and out of a few, but sure enough following his directions I found where I was meant to be. The conversion had been sympathetically carried out so as not to spoil the character of the surroundings, but apart from that nothing else registered as I was still feeling a bit light headed.

"Ah, Evelyn," said a lady in medieval dress who was bearing down on me, "here you are."

She attached a name badge to my chest and steered me into the large airy room. I didn't think this was the time and place to quibble about my name. I had been born into a generation of girls called Patricia, Valerie and Sandra, no one was called Evelyn. I was teased, so moving to a new senior school as a pre-teen I introduced myself as Evie and hey presto, I was one of the crowd.

"I got lost," I apologised, "sorry if I am late."

Every eye in the room was on me, this was not the start I had hoped for. The room was quite large with a huge work table across its width and then two rows of two equally large work benches at right angles at each end. This layout meant that everyone had a good view of the top table and plenty of room to work. Each table had three occupants except the top right-hand side which seated two rather elderly ladies, one of whom was sporting a blue rinse. Well, a good guess where I was heading!

"Oh not to worry, we hadn't started. We are just about to get to know each other."

Mrs 'blue rinse' waved to get my attention.

"Over here my dear, I have saved you a seat."

I sat down and smiled weakly at her. I felt very conspicuous and rather uncomfortable. *Get a grip, girl,* I thought. *This is supposed to be fun and enjoyment which you selected to do, not some sort of punishment you have to endure. Relax.*

I breathed deeply once more and gazed across the room to the opposite table where there were two men and a lady. The younger man who in my day would have been referred to as a hippy or new-age traveller was making some sort of gesture at me. I raised my eyebrows when I realised he was mimicking drinking and he mouthed 'tea' or 'coffee' at me. I mouthed 'tea' back and a few minutes later he put a much appreciated cup of tea in front of me. I was going to like him, I decided.

The two instructors, Meg and Jenny, suggested we go around the room and introduce ourselves and say why we wanted to come to the workshop. The first to speak was Tom, a forty-something history teacher from London. He wanted to bring history alive for his pupils and was hoping to learn as much about the castle as he was the clothes of the era. Next came Fiona, a little plump housewife in her twenties from Suffolk. Apparently she had four children and this was her birthday present from her husband. If she didn't deserve some "me time" I don't know who did and bravo to hubby for realising the fact. My tea-bearing hippy was next. He was a conservationist called Dylan from Wiltshire. He wanted to get back to basics and under his long hair looked to be in his thirties.

I was savouring my tea, it really was the cure for everything and I could feel its soothing powers working when I realised I had missed out introductions from six of my fellow crafters and it was my turn.

"I'm Evelyn from Northamptonshire. I recently retired and as I do a lot of patchwork and quilting I wanted to take the opportunity to discover more about fabric and dyes. As patchwork relies on the use of like materials and good colour combinations for a pleasing finished effect, I thought this a good place to start."

Mrs Blue Rinse stood as if to give a speech. "I'm Margaret and this is my sister Mary." She raised her already penetrating voice a little louder as she referred to her sister giving me the impression Mary might be hard of hearing.

"We have a glorious garden in Devon, many wild plants and flowers, and we would like to see how we can utilise some of them for dying as part of our many hobbies. Don't we, Mary?"

Mary nodded and Margaret took her seat. Introductions completed we were ready to listen and learn.

The morning progressed amiably with Meg and Jenny concentrating on textiles available during the Middle Ages, their properties and availability. This led on to fashion and how some garments and colours were restricted to different classes of people. Colour dyes would be introduced after lunch. We were all surprised lunch was mentioned as none of us had really paid attention to the time, which obviously showed we were engrossed in the subject.

The six participants whose introduction I had missed were apparently a crafting group from somewhere on the south coast. They were friendly but were going to their minibus to devour a packed lunch. So the remaining six of us descended upon the castle tea room and ordered a hearty lunch. I felt so much better than earlier and joined in the group banter. Margaret proved to be quite entertaining. Having been a head mistress which didn't come as a surprise as she had retained and still used her, shall I say, organisational skills and was outspoken on any subject mentioned. This could have proved monotonous but she was so knowledgeable and down to earth that she contributed much to the entertainment factor. I did ask her what career Mary had chosen and she replied quite straight faced that she had worked for the government, but she couldn't tell me what exactly or she would have to kill me.

Tom was engrossed in the site map as he devoured his jacket potato, the rest of us consuming various dishes and commenting favourably about the environment.

"It's such a shame that some of the castle is in ruins, Norman architecture was quite something," he said.

"It still is even in this state," I commented, "it's amazing how such huge sturdy buildings could have been built in the days of so few building aids, did they have scaffolding back then?"

"Yes, of a fashion, but not the metal poles we know today. They also relied heavily on the pulley system for their constructions. The Normans certainly left their mark here and in Europe."

"They were Vikings, you know, Evelyn, isn't that right Tom?"

Tom nodded his agreement at Margaret but couldn't comment as he had a mouthful, so Margaret obligingly continued.

"Vikings weren't all raping and pillaging, well they were but, after many successful raids on the French coast from Denmark, Norway and Iceland, they integrated with the indigenous people and settled. The ethnic identity of the 'North men' or Normans emerged initially at the beginning of the 10th century and continued to evolve over the succeeding centuries."

Having swallowed his mouthful Tom was eager to continue.

"The Normans were noted for their architecture and military accomplishments so when they arrived here in 1066 they made many changes. Saxon strongholds had been mainly wood so the Normans started to replace them with stone as if to leave it in no doubt they were here to stay. Wyvern was built by the Normans although bits were added in later centuries."

"How about we walk the walls?" suggested Dylan. "We can do a bit of sightseeing and enjoy the fresh air before this afternoon's session."

The two sisters politely refused saying they couldn't manage so many steps, so just the four of us set out, although I secretly wondered if I could manage all those steps either. We had been quite sheltered in the tearoom so when we ascended to the battlements we were caught off guard by the strong breeze. We gripped the hand rail and appreciated the glorious panoramic view that greeted us. We could see for miles in all directions. Tentatively peeping over the parapet, the already heady height of the wall was amplified by the deep dry moat immediately below. I turned quickly and concentrated on the structures within the bailey or courtyard. Tom drew my attention to the structure that towered over everything else and explained this was the Keep where all the important rooms were, the great hall, solar, kitchens, even dungeons. We continued on, discovering a beautiful garden behind the workshop and also a very flat grass rectangle running along the second wall we walked. The wind was getting to be quite bracing so reaching the third wall we decided to find the staircase leading down. Just before we did, Fiona pointed over the wall and asked what a particular structure was. To the right was the huge entrance gate and the walk down to the car park. I could see my car nestled near the trees the other side of which were the ruins of a building.

"What would that be, Tom?" she asked.

"Not really sure," he replied, scanning the pages of the site map.

I heard him say something about a priory but after that all I could focus on was the buzzing in my ears and the waves of nausea washing over me. I must have turned pale because I vaguely remember Dylan grabbing my arm, I was so dizzy, and Fiona was patting my face and urging the others to get me down the steps before I fainted. On reaching the bottom I sagged onto a seat and Tom pushed my head between my knees. Fiona had her arm around me and was gently rocking me, telling me everything would be OK.

The four of us were late to the afternoon session. I finally recovered after a bottle of water and some deep breathing. I felt extremely embarrassed and blamed not having a good head for heights for my little episode but I was somewhat concerned this was the second time it had happened. The afternoon was fine and I was completely recovered by the time we were heading for the car park. We were all booked into the local Premier Inn so it was decided to follow each other crocodile fashion. For some absurd reason I averted my eyes from the ruins as I got into my car, only to jump out of my skin as Dylan knocked on the window.

"I was going with Tom but he said after your wobbly this afternoon it might be a good idea to accompany you, that and the fact you are prone to getting lost!"

I rolled my eyes and snorted, but honestly it was nice having him in the car and I was a little touched the way they showed their concern.

*

I felt very positive this morning having slept well, eaten a good breakfast and not having got lost on the way to the castle. Swinging into the car park, I parked as close to the entrance as was possible. Perhaps it was my imagination concerning the trees and ruins having some effect on my dizzy spells, but I was not taking the chance. I leaned on my car with my back to the trees while I waited for the others to pile out of their respective transport.

We were all in good humour which was amplified even more when we were shown into a room bulging with medieval clothing and told to choose an outfit which highlighted a particular station in life or occupation of the time. The knowledge we gained the previous day would, supposedly, aid our selection. I found a full-length blue dress which looked like a wool material. It fitted to the body and then flared slightly from the hips where I draped a braided girdle. This highlighted a matching braid sewn around the neckline. What made me choose this particular dress were the sleeves which fitted to the elbow and then flared out so that one edge almost touched the floor. It reminded me of sleeves on a wizard's robe. I was teased of course with shouts of, "Lady Evelyn, Lady of the manor." I playfully acknowledged their bows and curtsies but soon realised why only the higher ranks with servants to do their bidding wore this type of sleeve. When we set about mixing and using our dyes, I had to roll up my sleeves and pin them behind me to prevent dipping them in the dye baths as I worked.

Placing our freshly dyed material onto drying racks we headed to the teashop for lunch. All twelve of us gathered this lunchtime and it was a cacophony of noise as we munched. The workshop was a success and someone suggested we should have our own WhatsApp group to spread word of any upcoming course we might enjoy and where we could meet up again. We all agreed and set about tapping our phones. Dylan was doing Margaret's for her so I helped Mary with the steps as we were all heading for the Keep to browse as it would be our last chance before we left after the afternoon session.

We strolled arm in arm and chatted easily. Mary explained that one-to-one conversation was acceptable to a point but noisy crowds, high-ceiling rooms and loud music distorted what she could hear.

"It must be very frustrating for you," I said, "and it must be quite isolating too I expect."

"It can be," she agreed, "but mainly it's just my sister and I at home. I have had a good life."

"Mary, may I ask you something? I'm very curious after a comment from Margaret." I hesitated. "She hinted that you were a spy?"

She chuckled quietly. "Oh, that was many years ago."

"You were!"

My mouth hung open momentarily in amazement. She was a sweet, gentle and quiet old lady and here she was telling me she had once been a spy.

"How exciting, was it during World War Two?"

The smile faded a little and she nodded.

"Yes it was, but 'exciting' isn't the word that immediately springs to mind. I look back and know I did the right thing at the time, behind the enemy lines helping our boys, but it was a time of cruelty and grief and poverty."

"Well I think you were very brave. I know I couldn't have been one, I can't think on my feet for one thing."

"The thing to remember is to keep it real, as near to the truth as possible. If you make up too many stories you will be liable to trip yourself up quite easily."

"I will remember that," I said, although I really couldn't think of when I would need that morsel of advice in this day and age. With that, we entered the Keep to browse.

The Great Hall was impressive with high ceilings, tapestries and a huge table almost the length of the hall itself. There were other nooks and crannies, a huge kitchen with a roasting pit and a cordoned-off staircase to the store rooms which I guessed were originally the dungeons. I left Mary on a seat and went to the next floor to see the master bedroom and other smaller chambers but it was the top floor which interested me. Originally it was the solar but now it had been turned into a museum of Wyvern through the ages. Some of the others were already up there viewing the many artefacts on display.

"Evelyn, over here," Fiona beckoned, "there is some very early patchwork that will interest you I'm sure."

I approached a large display cabinet which contained a square cloth of early patchwork. It wasn't large or finished but looked like a work in progress. The colours were faded now but gave the impression that once they had been vibrant blues and greens.

Leaning over to read the description card, I placed my hand on the show case. I shrieked and jumped back cradling my hand next to my chest. It felt as if a huge electric shock had charged through my body and exploded in my head. The pain was so severe I felt I might cry. People had turned to stare so I shook my head and tried to smile blaming a small shock often caused by friction. Fiona wasn't convinced and came to my side concerned that it was something else. I held my throbbing head; I needed to escape this room so I tried to make light of the situation blaming a fast onset of migraine. I fled making some excuse of getting medication from the car and having a power nap.

"I'll be fine. See you back in the workshop." With that I fled, slinging the strap to my bag across my body so I could use both hands to try and steady myself. Every step vibrated my head and the pain became so intense I felt nauseous. *I must get out of the building before I make a fool of myself,* I thought. Stumbling out of the building I headed for the gates but my legs were out of control. My vision became hazy and I gripped the hand rail and practically pulled myself down the slope to the car park. *I must get to my car.* I heard the gravel under my feet but at that moment flung out my hand to find support, leant forward and started retching.

For some reason I thought of the first TV set we had when I was a girl. When it was turned off the picture would collapse into a white spot on a black background. I would sit and stare at it trying to determine when the spot had finally gone. Now my vision seemed to be imitating that TV. If only I could get to...

CHAPTER TWO

I lay face down on the ground: I could taste the soil on my lips. I was cold. Not moving, I listened but all was quiet. Feeling disorientated I tried gathering my thoughts but all I remembered was the car park and then darkness.

Something warm was trickling from my head down my cheek and dripping onto the ground. Rolling my head slightly I tried to lift my hand to it but the merest movement caused my head to explode. Keeping my head as still as possible I slowly crept my hand up and touched something sticky. I withdrew my hand, placing it in front of my one unobstructed eye and opened it slowly. My vision was blurred and the light made me wince. I quickly shut my eye tight and lay waiting for the dizziness to stop but it was too late as the nausea seemed to start in my toes and work its way up.

Someone or something was coming; I could feel the vibration in the ground before I actually heard them behind me. I tried to call for help but it came out as a feeble squeak. I sensed them bending over me but was still surprised when someone roughly grasped my shoulder and none too gently tried to roll me over.

"Stop, stop," I sobbed, "please, my head."

Whoever it was took no notice and tugged even harder, so with what little strength I had I forced my shoulder down toward the ground. My head was pounding and I wanted to be sick. My resistance caused a renewed effort; I heard the heavy breathing and grunts, and then felt a hand grab the fabric and flesh of my hip.

Giving one final heave my body was rolled over and I vomited, after which I retreated to darkness.

I was warm. I felt a pillow beneath my head and a cover over my body. I lay for a few minutes enjoying the warmth and then tried to lift my arm and feel my head. There was a bandage but then I felt someone take my hand and gently pat it before replacing it under the cover. Attempting to open my eyes I was greeted once again by blurred vision and dizziness. I managed to warn that I felt sick before rolling slightly and promptly started retching. The movement started the pain in my head which in turn made me dizzier. I finally lay collapsed on the pillow devoid of energy and the will to live. A cool soothing cloth bathed my face and what felt like a spout or bottle pressed to my mouth. Liquid touched my lips and I sipped cool water and then I retreated once more to sleep.

This process was repeated at regular intervals but for how long I had no idea. Each time I surfaced seemed a little less violent than the time before until on one occasion I woke quite calmly and eventually dared open my eyes. I couldn't focus at first but there were no waves of nausea sweeping through my body this time.

My environment was not as I expected. Instead of a hospital room I saw a small stone-walled room with one tiny window to my left and a wooden door at the foot of the bed. The lighting was the glow from a candle standing on a rough wooden table to my right; this also held a bowl and water vessel. Assuming I was hallucinating or still dreaming, since I had experienced some quite vivid ones, I closed my eyes. Opening them again as I heard the latch on the door, I gasped on finding the same little stone room, this time made to feel even smaller by the arrival of a small robed figure.

The figure was of medium height, slightly stooped and sporting a tonsure. When he turned I was surprised to see he was quite young, with rather prominent ears and a scar across his mouth which disfigured it somewhat. With the stoop I suppose I expected someone older. On seeing me awake he beamed at me; placing the bowl he was carrying on the little table, he clasped his hands together as if giving thanks. His smile lit up his face and for all his unattractiveness his eyes sparkled with warmth and a comforting gentleness.

Realising I was staring I gathered my senses and demanded, "Who are you and what is this place?"

He didn't answer but placed his finger to his lips and proceeded to bring the bowl containing food, I assumed, over to the bed. I asked again but he just carried on and tried to feed me. He smiled encouragingly but refused to speak. This place was strange and I was feeling very frustrated and a little afraid so I pushed away the bowl and with my voice rising through panic I said, "No, no, I won't eat till you answer my questions. Why am I here and not in hospital? What's going on?"

He calmly replaced the bowl on the table and tried to take my hand. I snatched it away but he raised both hands as if to placate me and reached out again. His touch was gentle as he patted my hand. He looked into my eyes as if looking for some recognition on my part and then I realised this was who had tended me during my sickness.

"Oh, it's you. You have been looking after me. You have been so kind, thank you, but please tell me where I am, this is all very frightening."

He frowned and nodded as if in understanding and then held up his finger and disappeared out of the door. He returned a few minutes later with another monk, as that's what I assumed he was, who was older and had rather a more severe face. He smiled but it didn't reach his eyes. His hands were folded in his sleeves and he inclined his head in greeting.

"How are you, mistress? You have been rather unwell."

"I don't really know how I am, where I am, who you are or what has happened. I feel confused. I think I should be in hospital but instead all this," I waved my hands around erratically, "seems to be taking it all too far."

"Too far?" he queried.

The younger monk looked at him full of concern and then back at me with a very weak smile. If the older monk had not been in the room I think he would be back at my bedside patting my hand again.

"Yes, too far. A costumed experience should not include medieval medical care." I was getting very worked up now. "I'm sure I suffered a concussion and as well you know if left untreated can cause life-changing results or even death!"

I was giving the worst-case scenario but after actually saying it out loud it struck home how serious things could have been. Tears weren't that far away so it was taking all my self-control not to start howling like a baby. The elder monk seemed a little surprised by what I had said but nodded and then pulled the little stool from under the table and sat next to the bed. Looking up had caused my head to throb a little so I was rather pleased about this and endeavoured to calm myself ready for what I hoped was an explanation.

"This is Brother Elric," he said, gesturing to the young monk, "he does not speak. He has been tending to your needs day and night since your arrival."

I smiled at Elric with genuine gratitude.

"I am Brother Anselm and I am in charge of the infirmary here at the Priory. You were found in the woods on our boundary in a state of collapse with a head wound. Perhaps you sustained it as you fell, we can't be sure. Do you remember anything?"

I was pretty confused and mumbled something about the car park at the castle and feeling dizzy and how an ambulance should have taken me to hospital if I had a head wound. Brother Anselm frowned and then leaned forward and fixing me with a stare said, "We have cared for you and thank the Lord for your recovery, but think again, do you remember anything else, how you hurt your head perhaps?"

I don't know why he was so intent on discovering the cause of my injury; perhaps he thought I might sue the castle and demand recompense. I shook my head and tried to stifle a yawn.

"I'm so sorry," I apologised, "I seem to get tired so quickly."

"No apology is necessary, mistress; you must work at regaining your strength. Brother Elric, please give our patient her gruel," he ordered and with that gave a slight polite bow and left the room.

Brother Elric took his place on the vacated stool with his usual good-humoured smile and retrieved the bowl from the table.

*

I was recovering my strength but still tired easily. Having woken early this morning I sat gazing out of the tiny window. It was very high up so all that was visible was the sky, but it was refreshing to see something rather than four stone walls. I decided I must broach the subject of my discharge from the Priory, when Brother Anselm knocked softly on my door and then entered with Brother Elric on his heels. They both nodded in greeting and then Anselm approached reaching for my head.

"I believe it's time to remove this," he said, touching the bandage around my head. He started to unwind the cloth.

"Definitely," I agreed, "my head feels very itchy, which must be a sign that something is on the mend."

The last part of the cloth was stuck to the wound and I winced as it was removed. He gently prodded my scalp which was tender but not painful any longer. He seemed pleased with what he saw and I know I felt relieved the bandage was no longer pulling my hair.

"All better?" I asked.

"Externally it's doing very well but I need to find out what has happened in here," he punctuated his statement by tapping my head, "how your memory and wellbeing is coping. I will ask you some questions and we will get a better idea. Is that to your liking?"

"It's fine by me," I agreed. *Finally,* I thought, *progress.*

"What is your name?"

"Evelyn Cross."

"Where have you come from and where were you going?"

"From Northamptonshire to Wyvern Castle."

"Do you know the year?"

"2020."

This answer caused a reaction from both of them. Anselm recovered his facial expression quite quickly but Elric looked completely surprised and looked from me to Anselm and then back to me.

"Do you know who sits upon the throne?"

"Elizabeth."

Once again I got the impression I wasn't saying the right thing and it would impede my chances of getting out of here so to any further questions I vacantly shook my head and said I didn't remember.

They both left and I followed them to the door and listened to see if any comments were being made about me. All was quiet so I made to return to my seat when I caught sight of something under the end of my bed. I gave a tug and out slid my bag. I was so pleased it hadn't been lost in the mêlée. I remember securing it to me when I felt faint but hadn't thought of it since. Sitting on the bed I opened it wide. It struck me that it had been searched. It was usually jumbled but an organised jumble. However, since I still had it I assumed someone had been looking for evidence to my identity or it had generally been tossed from pillar to post and the contents had fallen out.

My mobile phone had no signal so I switched it off. My purse had all my money plus the jewellery I had removed before working with the dye vats. Everything was there so I rummaged to find my cosmetic bag containing a mirror to examine my head. Turning to the light and lifting it up, I shrieked and scuttled back on the bed as if to escape the image. Covering my gaping mouth with my hand I took a second look. The image was the same, I had brown hair. I hadn't had brown hair since my twenties. Currently my hairdresser referred to my colour as silver-grey. I couldn't see any evidence of a single strand of grey.

I was shaking and my stomach was doing somersaults. Looking again I saw very little evidence of bags under my eyes and my jawline was quite firm. Peering closer I could not see a single wrinkle, my skin was smooth and it felt soft and plump. I felt my body. My clothes had been removed, by females hopefully and not the monks, and I had been dressed in a thick robe similar to the monks' garb. It was large and rather shapeless but was lovely and warm. I assumed my days of unconsciousness with no food was the reason for my slimmer shape but now what was I supposed to think? Now that I was concentrating on my body I realised my joints were supple and I moved easily.

I sat staring at myself for a considerable time, dumfounded, until I focused on the silly grin I was wearing. I rather liked the newer version of myself and losing the aches and pains was definitely a bonus. Looking at my right wrist the scar was gone. The scar from an operation had faded with time but now it was gone completely. I racked my brain trying to remember when I had the operation, when I was about thirty I thought. I pulled up my robe frantically examining my left leg. I had been knocked off my bike on my way to work one time and cut my leg. Having only two stitches the scar was small but it was still there. Pacing the floor I was muttering to myself, "When was that, when was that?" I finally decided I was twenty-six at the time. I was numb, here I was a pensioner, but my body was telling me I was aged between twenty-six and thirty. What was happening to me?

The only way to get some answers was to leave this room and see what was outside. I gathered my things and stuffed them back into my bag. I had my shoes but no clothes, still, if the monks could walk around in a robe so could I. Lifting the latch I pulled the door, it rattled but didn't budge. Perhaps it was stuck so trying to make as little noise as possible I gave a mighty heave. I pulled and pulled but it would not open. Eventually I realised I must be locked in, a prisoner, but why? Returning to the door regularly to attempt to shift it bore no results and I was exhausted and more than a little fearful.

I must have dozed because I was awoken abruptly by raised voices somewhere outside.

"I demand to see the injured woman. I have been prevented from doing so for too long." He was annoyed but I didn't recognise the voice. The second voice who I knew to be Brother Anselm was trying to calm the situation.

"This is unwise, she is physically healed but mentally is very unsound. Your questions could confuse her even more and in her condition she could lose her mind completely."

"I have authority to question her. Let me pass."

"Do you really want it on your conscience that you could condemn this poor woman to be locked away for her own and everyone else's safety? While she is a patient here at the Priory she is my responsibility," continued Anselm, "please leave."

"I shall return, Brother Anselm, mark my words."

Pacing my little room frantically trying to think of a way of escape all I wanted to do was weep. I found it hard to focus on the problem in hand which I determined was to secure my escape or risk being locked away as some sort of lunatic. Eventually the door did open and Elric entered with some bread and cheese and a drink. He set them down and meant to leave with no smile; in fact he avoided looking at me altogether.

"Brother Elric," I began, "please stay awhile and keep me company."

He hesitated but then turned to face me still avoiding my gaze.

"Someone came to see me today didn't they?" He nodded. "Were they from the castle?" He nodded again. "Do you think I have lost my mind?" This time he looked up and shook his head vigorously. "Then don't you think I deserve visitors, or to venture outside? Instead I am being held prisoner." He looked around the room uncomfortably as if trying to find an answer written on the wall.

"Brother Elric you are my only friend, won't you help me to escape from here?" I pleaded. He looked quite alarmed and gripped the neck of his robe is if he feared some dreadful punishment. I put my hand out as if to reassure him.

"No, no, listen! I don't want you to leave the door unlocked because then you would be blamed, but if you could get a message to the castle to ask them to return and demand my release again—"

He cut me short with frantic shaking of his head.

"No, listen please. The only person who would have higher authority than the Priory would be my relative." I could tell he was mulling over my idea and before he could dismiss it I continued. "I have no relative at the castle but perhaps someone could act the part to gain my release. It's not actually you who would be lying, I would not expect you to do that." I coaxed as much as I dare; he was my only chance.

Trying to look forlorn which wasn't far from the truth at this moment I asked, "Do you want to see me locked away?"

He looked down at the ground and then slowly at me. His lovely twinkling eyes looked troubled and then terribly sad. Was he sad because he was fighting with his conscience in order to help me, or sad because he knew that he couldn't? I squeezed his arm to try and convey that either way I would accept his decision. He left the room and I heard the bolt being drawn across my only exit. All I could do now was wait.

*

I slept little and this morning my breakfast was delivered by someone other than Elric. When I asked where he was I was told at prayer. So there I sat once more worrying about my fate and now Elric's too. I heard footsteps approaching; I swallowed hard and tensed expecting the worst. The bolt was drawn, the latch rattled and the door opened to reveal a middle-aged, plump and finely dressed woman. She stood staring at me and then her face took on a disappointed and somewhat sad expression. She clasped her hands and brought them to quivering lips, turning to Brother Anselm, and exclaimed, "She doesn't recognise me. She doesn't remember her Aunt Hilda."

As Anselm bent to reply, she was not a tall woman, I glimpsed Elric behind him and some relief lifted my low spirit. He was wide eyed and almost willing me to join in the charade. 'Aunt Hilda' was obviously my cue.

"Lady Hilda I did try and prepare you regarding her mental state."

But Anselm had no time to continue as I stood and said, "Aunt Hilda?"

"Niece," she exclaimed, holding out her arms. "Come let me embrace you."

I didn't have to pretend to be relieved and joyous because that was exactly how I was feeling. We met in the middle of the tiny room hugging one another, both having tears in our eyes. Mine genuine and hers part of a superb Oscar-winning performance. I did manage not to get completely absorbed in the moment and lowered my head to whisper in her ear, "Evelyn Cross, my name is Evelyn Cross."

She stood back to look at me, gripping the tops of my arms fiercely and continued, "I have been so fearful of your safety, you are long overdue." Turning to Anselm she directed her next comment to him.

"Evelyn is recently widowed and I am her only living relative, so I told her to come to me and I have secured her a position at the castle sewing. Why did you not send word that she was with you and save me such grief?"

Not allowing him to answer, she returned her gaze to me with some disapproval. "Child, where are your clothes?"

Anselm hovered trying to make some amends for her displeasure. "Mistress Evelyn was in a poor state when she arrived so we fetched two women from the village to remove her soiled clothing so that it might be cleaned."

Hilda looked past him and saw Elric at the door and shaking her hand in dismissal ordered, "Fetch them." He in turn bobbed his head and scurried off.

"She will recover well with my company and God forbid, if she doesn't I will be there to care for her."

It was obvious she meant to take me with her; she was such a whirlwind of authority everyone just stood back out of her wake. Clasping my hand she headed for the door where Elric proffered my bundle of clothes.

"Robin," she summoned her escort who was a tall young lad,

"take the bundle and Mistress Evelyn's bag to the cart." With that she marched out of the room with me in tow.

I briefly thanked Brother Anselm for his hospitality and care as he followed us to the little cart waiting outside. Robin handed me onto the front seat followed quickly by Lady Hilda. As he walked around to take his place in the driver's seat I barely had time to thank Elric for everything he had done for me. I emphasised 'everything' and he inclined his head in a bow of thanks. His eyes were twinkling so I knew he understood my meaning. With a jolt we set off and Hilda leaned close and whispered not to speak until we were clear of the Priory.

I sat happily squashed between the two of them on a board obviously built for two, a safety measure I concluded to prevent me from being removed back to the Priory, and breathed in the fresh air. The cart took a little trail through the trees toward the castle. When we emerged I marvelled at the view. We were already on high ground but to my right on the summit sat Wyvern. No longer in ruins or showing the weathering of a thousand years it sat majestically, the pale stone gleaming in the sunlight. Two soldiers in livery stood either side of the gate and a flag was flying over the battlements. Either side of the approach road were crude wooden abodes, some with smoke coming from a chimney and others with an open fire outside the entrance. People were going about their business and animals wandered about while others munched away in pens. There was no sign of a car park, just a tiny village in the shadow of the castle trusting in its protection.

I felt an icy shiver run down my spine, all the joy of leaving the Priory evaporating. This was not a costumed event. I wasn't in a coma or some sort of suspended consciousness reverting back to memories of the last thing I experienced before my bump on the head. What I was seeing was real, the stuff of fantasy and fiction writing, of people transported back in history. I loved historical romances and had dozens on my Kindle to enjoy at my leisure when the high tech and hustle and bustle of life proved stressful.

"What's real, my dear?" asked Lady Hilda.

I must have mumbled something aloud unintentionally. I was flustered and didn't know how to reply, I obviously couldn't tell her the truth or what I had begun to think was the truth or she would have me locked away as a lunatic thinking Brother Anselm was right all along.

"I'm so muddled with all that has happened of late and I don't know how long I was injured and at the Priory. I feel that I have lost track of time."

Robin skilfully turned the cart to start the ascent to the castle gate. It was narrow and passing another cart coming in the opposite direction would have caused problems, but there were just pedestrians who moved to the side to let us pass, some nodding in respect to Lady Hilda.

"Well that is to be expected," she sympathised, patting my hand reassuringly. Whatever time it was I had at least observed that it was an era of hand patting.

"It is springtime," she continued, "springtime 1195!"

CHAPTER THREE

I was draped over the side of a tub choking out the water from my lungs. Panicking, I tried to gulp in mouthfuls of air which just caused me to choke even more as water gushed from my nose and mouth onto the paving slabs. Eventually after a few successful gasps I clung to the rim of the tub and dissolved into tears.

*

Passing through the castle gates in the little cart more people seemed to stare and a couple of children pointed at me until their mother pushed them behind her skirt and shushed them. I was obviously a spectacle and as I tried to sink into my robe I realised I stank. Hilda and Robin were pressed against me on the seat and I felt embarrassed.

"Lady Hilda," I ventured, "I really need to bathe. Would that be possible?"

She looked at me, particularly where my hair was still matted with blood and gave a little nod. On the steps of the Keep which rose to a significant height in front of us, was a young girl who on seeing us came running over.

"Milady, all went as planned?"

"Yes Maggie, quite an adventure." Then indicating me, she said, "Mistress Evelyn would like to bathe, go and prepare if it is possible."

Maggie bobbed her head and left in double time. Meanwhile, Robin encouraged the horse to continue its journey to the rear of the building where I smelt a definite aroma of food. My stomach rumbled but first things first. Hilda sent Robin into a little building adjoining what I later found out to be the kitchen. He returned quickly telling us it was possible to proceed.

On entering I discovered that this was a bath house and Robin had been sent ahead to ascertain if it was vacant of men. It was quite an ingenious setup built adjoining the kitchen, in particular the bread ovens which warmed the stone wall and the bathing water. There were two wooden tubs separated for modesty's sake by curtains, one of which was being prepared by Maggie and two other young serving girls. Lady Hilda left me at this point, giving Maggie instructions to escort me to her bed chamber when my toilette was complete. A little stool was set next to the tub that I might step into it which the three girls were waiting for me to do. I realised they had no intention of leaving and that I must cast aside my robe and modesty and allow myself to be washed and scrubbed by them. My self-consciousness soon evaporated as the lovely warm water washed over me. The tub was lined with sheets to protect one's more delicate places and I was directed to sit or move as necessary so that I could be thoroughly washed. Maggie gently washed my hair trying to avoid my wound and after the other girls had rinsed my hair with clean water they were dismissed.

Maggie left to bring clean drying linens so I tried to juggle my position so that I could soak until her return. The only way I could lay back and submerge my shoulders was by bending my knees almost to my chin which I just about managed to do and then closed my eyes and relaxed in the luxury of warm water.

I heard soft footsteps and assuming it was Maggie paid no mind. Suddenly an arm was hooked under my knees pulling my legs from the tub causing my upper body to disappear below the water. I tried to grasp the sides of the tub to pull myself up but I couldn't reach. I endeavoured to hold my breath as I struggled but water was already in my mouth and I began to choke. Kicking fiercely I thrashed about in the water. My lungs were burning but still my legs felt like they were held in a vice and I was weakening with my frantic moves. I released the air from my lungs in a stream of bubbles, water rushing in through my mouth and nose to replace it. I felt myself going limp just as the grip on my ankles was released.

Everything was vague after that. Arms pulled me up in the tub. Someone was hitting my back and I could hear scuffling and shrieks. Maggie was calling my name and giving instructions. I could hear a man's voice too but I was so weak it was taking all my effort to get air into my lungs. I felt the three girls drag me out of the tub and wrap drying linens around me followed by a cloak the hood of which was pulled up over my head and face. One of the serving girls grabbed my roll of clothes and the other two half dragged and half carried me up what seemed to be an endless flight of cold stone steps. Finally I was thrust through a door and sat on a stool. Everything was a blur but as I was hustled from the bath house I remember glimpsing Robin lying motionless on the floor with blood tickling from the corner of his mouth.

"What has happened?" cried Lady Hilda, shocked at our entrance.

"Someone held Mistress Evelyn's head under the water and tried to drown her," said one of the girls who immediately received a poke in the ribs from Maggie and told to hold her tongue.

"Maggie, is this true?"

"Yes, milady, and she would have been had it not been for young Robin."

"Oh my goodness," said Lady Hilda, pouring something into a goblet which she then wrapped my cold hands around and ordered me to drink. Doing so I coughed and spluttered but I could feel the liquid warm my insides so continued to sip but more carefully this time.

The girls wasted no time and started rubbing my skin briskly with the linens which not only dried me but seemed to encourage my circulation and bring me back to my senses. A clean white shift was put over my head and pulled down over my body almost to my knees. I felt my woollen stockings stretch over my freezing toes and fastened above my knees with garters. As one of the maids shook out my gown something dropped to the floor. Picking up my briefs and holding them at arm's length she looked quite alarmed and asked, "What is this?"

Trying to look as casual as possible I took them from her and hurriedly put them on much to the amazement of my audience. "Latest fashion," I quipped and buried my face as far as it would go into the goblet.

"You may go now," Lady Hilda ordered. "Take the wet linens. Maggie, stay and dry Mistress Evelyn's hair."

"Ladies, thank you so much for everything you have done for me today," I said, addressing the three serving girls. "I really appreciate your services."

Seeming rather surprised they gathered the linens and bobbed a curtsy to me, beaming as they left. Maggie wrapped my hair in dry linen and tried to squeeze as much water out as she could. I had visions of many a 'bad hair day' without my hair dryer. Beginning to feel human again I decided to engage in conversation to prevent dwelling on what had just happened.

"You have been so kind too, Lady Hilda. Your actions at the Priory were superb."

She placed her hand on her breast and smiled modestly but I think she was rather pleased with her achievement. We chatted as Maggie wrestled with my hair and I soon realised that Lady Hilda bore little resemblance to 'Aunt Hilda' as she had a gentle, calm manner and a genuine care for those around her regardless of their station. She agreed to call me Evelyn.

"Your hair is very short, mistress," Maggie began, but I saw Lady Hilda give her a warning look. All the females I had seen had long braids hanging from their headdress so my chin-length bob was quite the exception. I just nodded, not wanting to discuss the subject but rummaged in my bag for my comb. Maggie had detangled my hair so I quickly divided and started plaiting it, weaving in the hair from one side of my head as I went. Maggie watched with great interest and proceeded to weave the other side. She did a much better job than I and then pinned the resulting ends at the back of my head. Next she took a stiff band of linen and secured it around my head. It felt uncomfortable at first but I had noticed that all females except the very young wore some form of head covering, so to blend in I needed to do the same. A veil was then attached to the band. It was quite simple, I was pleased to say, as the one Lady Hilda wore rather resembled a nun's wimple and must be very restricting.

Maggie gathered up the last wet linen and went to leave just as there was a knock at the door. Maggie opened it and then turned to Lady Hilda and announced Sir William DeLacey. Hilda nodded and Maggie opened the door wide allowing Sir William to enter, then closing it behind her as she left.

Sir William was striking and I hoped I heard 'Wow' in my head and hadn't uttered it allowed. He was at least six feet tall with a slim athletic body. His long boots were black. His leggings and tunic were black with a black leather doublet over the top. He wore no head covering and his hair was black, swept casually off his face and laying on his collar at the back. His face was fair with a strong straight nose, high cheekbones and black lashes. The only colour about him was his blue eyes. He would have been handsome if he didn't wear such a serious expression on his face. If he was in the movies he would definitely have been cast as the bad guy.

His left hand rested on the hilt of a sword and there was also a dagger attached to his belt. Rather a lot of weaponry for a social visit, I thought, however Lady Hilda seemed particularly pleased to see him and crossed the room to greet him; in turn he took her hand and bowed over it. His face softened briefly as he said, "Your rescue mission was a success, well done, milady."

She beamed and turning in my direction replied, "Indeed. Let me introduce you. This is Mistress Evelyn Cross, Evelyn this is Sir William DeLacey."

I wasn't sure if I was meant to shake hands or curtsy but attempting to rise to do the latter, Sir William gestured for me to remain seated.

"Mistress Evelyn please do not rise on my account, you have had a distressing morning. I hope I find you much recovered."

There was the merest of smiles but his manner seemed genial so I replied that I was a little more myself. Lady Hilda indicated to her chair behind him and she discreetly crossed the little room and perched on a bench at the foot of the bed. Sir William repositioned his sword and sat relaxed across from me. I, however, was not relaxed at all. I rather felt I was about to be cross examined and I had no notion what to say.

"I had endeavoured to speak with you sooner but was prevented from doing so."

I recognised his voice from the Priory. "I believe I heard you when you came to the Priory, it would have been refreshing to have a visitor. The monks nursed me back to health which I truly appreciated, but I did feel they were a little overprotective."

"I am sure, but if you feel well enough now, we could talk. Perhaps together we can discover why and by whom you were attacked."

I nodded and smiled but inside I was panicking again. How much should I tell him? In fact what should I tell him? I wanted to get back home but I didn't want locking away as a lunatic. Suddenly I pictured Mary from the workshop and how we had strolled along discussing the finer points of being a spy. 'Keep it real,' she had said, 'don't stray too far from the truth.'

"Perhaps we could start by discovering how you came to be in the grounds of the Priory. Where did you travel from?"

"I came from Northamptonshire," I began.

He interrupted me with an unexpected question. "You are familiar with the castle at Northampton?"

I sensed he might be testing me, checking that my story was true so I racked my brains searching for any scraps of history or geography that might aid my story. I was in trouble; history in particular was not my strong point. I studied science and most of that hadn't even been discovered in this present time.

"No, I have never visited Northampton, I was closer to the castle at Rockingham, but I lived in a small village for most of my life, this is my first venture into the world."

"And why is that?"

"Well, the story that Lady Hilda told the monks was very close to the truth. I am widowed and I am looking for a position sewing."

His eyes were totally expressionless and didn't leave my face. There wasn't the slightest hint he believed me or thought it a pack of lies. He did raise his eyebrows as if encouraging me to give a fuller explanation after commenting that perhaps there were closer places to look for sewing than Wyvern. I could tell he was dubious as to my education too as I didn't come across as a peasant or servant. *Oh!*

What would Mary say? I wondered.

"My mother was a seamstress and taught me her trade. She would take me to the local manor houses when she was called upon to sew new garments. I played or had lessons alongside the children of the house. As I grew I worked alongside my mother. I met and married a carpenter from the next parish; unfortunately he became ill and died. The lord of the manor said I must leave our cottage as it needed to pass to another worker from his estate. Since I sewed for his family he offered me lodging at the manor. The position was not a success," I continued, "and I knew I must leave the place."

"That was a very big step for a woman all alone in the world. Why could you not stay?" asked Sir William.

"I could not provide all the services expected of me."

"By the lady of the manor?" queried Sir William.

"No," I replied, "by the lord of the manor."

I turned to Lady Hilda and said, "It was at this time I cut off my hair."

I heard Hilda gasp softly as she grasped my meaning. She seemed to think my story believable but did Sir William? He looked very thoughtful.

"Surely you needed preparation and help in your undertaking."

"I had help, Sir William, from his wife. Understandably she did not want me in the manor. She gave me some supplies and I accompanied her one market day and joined a band of pilgrims heading south. That is what I have been doing, travelling, sewing when I can, but always with bands of pilgrims, never alone. That is how I came to Wyvern."

There was a silent pause after I finished. I waited with my heart in my mouth. Had I sounded plausible? Did they believe me?

"That explains your arrival to Wyvern, but not why you were found on Priory land. Did you accompany the pilgrims to the Priory?"

"No Sir William, I remember standing before Wyvern, but I had no intension of visiting the Priory," I started, and then went on to explain what had happened after that, right up to the point of leaving to come to the castle this morning. I did say that Brother Anselm thought it likely I had hit my head falling but I was found in a small clearing and after the subsequent events of today I now thought it unlikely.

"And why is that?" Sir William's questions were short and to the point. He was polite and listened intently to my story, but gave me no encouragement or additional information to be sociable. Perhaps I was overthinking his demeanour because I couldn't describe what I believed might have happened to me and wasn't very good at concealing my anxiety. Was he allowing me to give him the facts in my own words, or ramble on giving me sufficient rope to hang myself? My arrival, a woman alone, was suspicious.

"A random act of violence is perhaps not uncommon, but for it to happen twice in so short a time is not a coincidence. I believe the attack this morning was an effort to quieten my tongue as a provision against me recognising my initial attacker."

Sir William nodded his head slowly, I hoped in agreement.

"I have been informed that for the intervention of Robin the outcome might have been entirely different. He saved my life. How is he? The only thing that remains vivid in my mind is of him lying on the ground bleeding."

Sir William was quick to reassure me. "Robin is recovered. He is a sturdy lad, quite capable of looking after himself."

"So why was he lying on the ground unconscious?" I realised that the way I had asked this question verged on sarcasm. If it was, Sir William graciously overlooked it and replied that Robin had stumbled over the stool as he was dodging a blow from the attacker and hit his head on the bath stand of the other tub. He rendered himself momentarily unconscious during which time the assailant made his escape.

"Did he see who it was?" I asked hopefully.

"No, he was hooded."

My disappointment must have shown on my face as I was feeling rather unsafe in this environment.

"Mistress Evelyn, please believe me when I assure you I will do my very best to find this man. Your safety is paramount, but I must ask you to never be alone and do not leave the castle."

With that he rose, gave a slight bow to me and Lady Hilda and left.

"How strange," I said to Lady Hilda. "He isn't very talkative is he? I expected more, perhaps his view of the attack or even some idle chit chat to put me at my ease."

Hilda laughed softly. "He is very economical with his conversation. He takes note of details and people's actions. I don't think I have ever been present when he indulges in 'idle chit chat', but I admire and respect him, he is a very fair-minded knight. Now my dear why don't you have a little rest? I will stay with you. Soon we will have to attend the Duke and Duchess in the grand hall for our meal and sometimes it can be a very drawn out and tedious occasion."

With that she took up her sewing and returned to the chair Sir William had vacated. I lay on the bed having removed my head dress first with some difficulty and was surprised how weary I felt.

I dozed until I was gently awakened by Hilda telling me we must go down to eat. We both adjusted our clothing making ourselves tidy and Hilda helped me with my head gear. On reaching the Great Hall I was surprised how it reminded me of the workshop with the long table across its width and two parallel rows of tables running down almost the whole length of the hall. The place was abuzz with loud conversations, each battling to be heard above its neighbour. We were seated quite a long way down the hall but the top table was still visible. It was very crowded and I was jostled and nudged by my neighbour, who was a rather large lady. She regularly turned to me good naturedly and beamed with a mouthful of rather brown decaying teeth. I attempted to return her smile, acutely aware that deodorant was yet to be invented.

When no more bodies could be squashed into the hall everyone hushed and stood as a grandly dress man and his lady took their seats at the top table. He signalled for us to be seated and almost immediately the hall was flooded with servants carrying platters of food. The top table was served first with the better dishes of meat, fowl and game. By the time we were served there was some fowl left and huge pies steaming in front of us. There were surprisingly few vegetables but I managed a spoon of cabbage and some purple red lumps which were apparently carrots. Large loaves of bread were plentiful and Hilda cut off a wedge for both of us. Everyone seemed to have a little knife about their person which was produced to aid with their eating. Not having one, I had to make do with the spoon which was provided. Our goblets or beakers were filled and everyone tucked in. I wasn't particularly hungry but tried to show good manners and eat and compliment the food.

As soon as I took a few mouthfuls of whatever it was in my beaker it was refilled. I concluded it must be alcoholic as my cheeks began to flush and to my surprise I began to relax. Hilda gave a running commentary of our hosts the Duke and Duchess of Plessey. The Duke, Richard, was tall and 'well made' with brown hair and a jovial manner. He was in deep conversation with Sir William who was seated next to him. Apparently they had fought together on many occasions and were good friends. Richard would periodically gaze at his wife who looked little more than a girl. She was small and fragile and her beauty was marred by a sickly grey pallor and dark circles beneath her eyes.

"Is she unwell?" I asked. "Poor girl isn't eating and looks to be suffering."

Hilda leaned closer and in a whisper said, "She is with child for the second time. She lost her first baby before it even drew breath and with this one cannot stop being sick. Duke Richard is beside himself with worry but all attempts at easing her vomiting have been unsuccessful."

I sat contemplating the state of medieval medicine. What could be given for her suffering, or any suffering for that matter? I dreaded to think what remedies the poor girl was having thrust upon her. God forbid bloodletting was being used, which seemed to be the cure for everything. The physicians of this era based everything on the balancing of the bodily fluids or 'humors' to maintain good health.

I was totally lost in my own thoughts so when I finally abandoned them and glanced back to the top table; I was startled to see Sir William staring at me intently. I looked away, embarrassed, and acted as if to eat another morsel from my plate. Looking up again, I saw he was still staring, so feeling a little flustered turned to Hilda.

"Has the Duchess tried ginger?" I asked.

"Ginger?"

I made as if I was engrossed in conversation as I was rather flushed from William's attention, or the wine, I wasn't sure.

"I have heard ginger is very beneficial. Take a bowl of fresh water, not water that has sat for a time," Wine or ale was the main drink, I had noticed, probably due to water having innumerable germs present. "Boil it for quite a few minutes," I continued, "and then cover and set aside to cool. When it is warm, take fresh ginger and grate into the liquid. Add some honey and then the mixture needs to be sipped."

Hilda listened intently and to prevent me giving into my curiosity to see if William was still looking in my direction I asked, "Does the Duchess eat oatcakes?"

Hilda frowned and then shook her head.

"If the oats are ground to fine flour and then made into very thin wafers, the sickness can be kept at bay by nibbling on them."

I drank deeply once more and gave into my curiosity. When I directed my gaze back to the top table I saw Robin leaning over William's shoulder and speaking into his ear. When he looked up he saw me and for some absurd reason, probably the wine, I gave a little wave. He smiled. William seeing his expression looked over at me just as I was beckoning Robin to come over to me. He looked bemused and raised his hand in dismissal and nodded at Robin who started heading in my direction.

This was the first time I had taken note of his appearance and understood why William had said he was capable of taking care of himself. He was easily as tall as William but still had a youth's wiriness. His hair was a muddy blond, somewhat untidy, reaching his collar. His lashes were light and framed hazel or green eyes, I couldn't tell. He gave a polite bow to me and then Hilda and all of a sudden I realised I hadn't a clue what to say to him.

I took a deep breath and smiled, trying to look composed as I could see in my peripheral vision William watching, still looking bemused.

"Robin, I understand I owe you a debt of gratitude. You came to my rescue and at your own cost. How is your head?"

He gave a dismissive action with his hand. "I am perfectly well, mistress."

I lifted my hand to my own head and gave it a tender rub.

"Well speaking from experience I can state that head wounds can be very unpleasant."

He grinned and said, "I have a hard head."

"Well you acted like a true knight in shining armour coming to save me."

"A knight I am not but I hope to be one day."

"You will make a fine knight," I reassured him, "but for now you are my champion."

Not thinking, I offered him my hand to shake. He was slightly taken aback but then stepped forward, took my hand and raised it to his lips. The gesture was very brief but I was touched by his gallantry; he bowed to Hilda and retreated.

Hilda was rising from her seat. The duchess was retiring which apparently meant other ladies in the hall could also leave. I was a bit wobbly so Hilda and I climbed the steps arm in arm like a couple of giggly schoolgirls. I liked Hilda and she seemed to have taken me under her wing.

We shared her bed and I thought I would sleep soundly but sleep evaded me. I could hear Hilda's slow rhythmical breathing and I tried not to wake her, but I was restless and feeling a little unwell. I realised I needed a bathroom and quickly, but of course there was no such luxury. There was a night soil pail in the room; however, the way I felt I was reluctant to use it.

I carefully crept out of bed into the freezing cold and felt my way to the door and then along the passage trying to find the garderobe. It was further than I remembered and my stomach was churning. I felt too ill to be afraid and stumbled on. Eventually I found it; I hitched up my night shift and collapsed onto the very primitive loo.

Feeling hot and clammy promising never to drink again, I lost the entire contents of my stomach one way or another. The stone wall was cool on my forehead but now my teeth were chattering and I felt terribly weak. Waiting for the waves of nausea to pass I clung to the wall groping my way back in the direction I had come.

Feeling I wasn't going to make it I paused, propped against the wall when, in the darkness I heard the scrape of metal on stone. 'Never be alone,' I had been warned. Trying to suppress the terror I tried to run but I was running blind. There was a crack of light ahead so I aimed for it and gasped in relief when I realised it was Hilda's room. In my hurry I hadn't closed the door properly and as it stood ajar the glow from the spluttering nub of candle lit my way.

Once inside the room I grabbed the wash bowl and crawled back into the bed trying not to disturb Hilda with my frozen body. I lay in the dark hugging the bowl feeling like death and began to cry. I was over 800 years from home. I didn't speak the way those around me did and I didn't understand their way of life. I missed modern conveniences I had grown up with, not least of all medicine. Here, women were second-class citizens who were reliant on men who could use or abuse them at will.

I had nothing and no-one and I wept until another wave of nausea racked my body. This is how my night passed until exhausted, I must have fallen asleep.

CHAPTER FOUR

The noise of battle was deafening. The horses thundered about the field, the soldiers roared with every clash of swords and even the arrows whistled until they thudded into their respective target. It was mesmerising. I stood transfixed until with no warning my arm was gripped and I was spun around finding myself nose to nose with Robin.

*

I awoke very late this morning. A single shaft of light penetrated the high narrow window of the chamber. The bowl I had cradled most of the night had been removed, cleaned and now stood on the table. My surroundings no longer smelt of a sick room which is more than I could say of myself.

A servant girl jumped up out of Hilda's chair and greeted me cheerfully.

"Ah, mistress, you are awake at last. Lady Hilda told me to sit with you but not to awaken you. She said you had a poorly sleepless night. How are you feeling, mistress?"

I felt drained, weak and a bit grubby. My eyes felt swollen and my head ached a little. I attempted to sit up and the servant girl came rushing over to assist me.

"I feel rather delicate." Then looking at her, I said, "I recognise you but I'm afraid I don't know your name." She was one of the girls who had bathed me on my arrival, the rather chatty one.

"I am Avis, mistress. Lady Hilda was called to the Duchess this morning so I'm here to help with your toilette and dressing. I have some water waiting for you to wash and your dress is brushed and smoothed."

She helped me from the bed and ushered me to the bowl where she had put fresh drying linen. There was a small screen in the room so I placed it around me as I still suffered from modesty. She seemed oblivious to my worries and darted behind the screen and whisked off my night shift. Thankfully she then went about her duties making the bed while I took the opportunity to bathe all over. I felt fresher definitely as she went about dressing me. She was very efficient and once clothed motioned me to the stool so she might dress my hair. This seemed to be her cue to strike up a conversation. I didn't mind, she was quite sweet and with her chatting away hardly stopping to draw breath, it meant I had to make little effort and could take time to gather my thoughts. I still felt desolate but fortunately the physical symptoms had left me.

"Mistress, no wonder you feel poorly after putting up with the things you have suffered since you got here. I think you are very brave to stay on with all these terrible things happening. My goodness, we are all fearing for our lives but it seems he wants you dead."

Avis was sweet but totally tactless and not having Maggie here to jab her in the ribs as she had before, carried on assuming I knew what she was talking about.

"Who wants me dead?" I asked.

"Why, the murderer, mistress, the one killing all the people. He had only killed men before but after he went after you we are all scared in our beds."

I was shocked; thankfully Avis was behind me and couldn't see my look of horror. I tried to use a calm voice and find out as much as I could.

"How many is it now?" I queried casually.

"Must be about four I think but that doesn't include the ones he dug up."

I felt as if all my breath had been sucked out of me. I couldn't speak and I grasped my hands together so that she couldn't she them shake. She fastened my veil and cheerfully proclaimed she was done and that my appearance was much improved.

"Lady Hilda asks that you stay in the castle either here or the Great Hall until her return."

I nodded and thanked her for her help. She gathered the wash things and linen and was halfway out the door when I called her back.

"Avis, where might I find Sir William?"

I tried to keep the shock from my face but I could feel it being replaced by anger. We had sat and discussed my attacks and no mention was made of murder. Someone in his position, friends with the Duke, would know about this and nothing was said. No warning given, no acknowledgement that the two things might be connected.

Avis popped her head back around the door. "He will be on the practice field, mistress; most of the men start their day there." With that, she bobbed a curtsy and was gone.

I didn't know my way about the castle but through sheer determination I found my way out. I remembered the wall walk with Tom, Dylan and Fiona and the large rectangular field along one of the castle walls and thought that would be a suitable clearing for training but I was disorientated and didn't know which way to turn. On the left in front of me was the stable block so I started to march along its length until I came to a smithy. The blacksmith pointed me in the right direction and told me to follow the noise. I stumbled a few times but my fury spurred me on and I soon heard the din. I was completely taken by surprise at the volume of noise. Practice it may have been but it all seemed very real.

I scanned the field looking for William but it was hopeless, it was when I stepped forward once again that I was spun around and was confronted by an incredulous Robin. Manners were forgotten and he had to shout to make himself heard.

"Woman, what on earth are you doing?"

Shaking off his hand I shouted back, "I want to speak to Sir William."

I turned intending to carry on with my mission, he spun me round again.

"This is not the time or place to speak to him. He is with the Duke and you are not allowed on the field."

"Well he will have to make time."

We proceeded to have a scuffle but he clung on.

"Mistress, you will be hurt," he pleaded.

It was obvious he didn't want to hurt me and loosened his grip slightly. Of course I used it to my advantage and turned toward the field. I was stopped in my tracks, however, as a galloping horse and rider were bearing down on us and it didn't look like they intended to stop. I think the horse wanted to continue but the rider reined him in and stopped too close for comfort. I gasped and stepped back into Robin who steadied me. The horse was restless and pranced about but the rider handled him well and soon brought him under control. It was then that I saw it was Sir William and he didn't look at all pleased.

"What are you doing on the field?" he demanded.

"You lied to me!" I shouted.

He looked startled. "I have never lied to you."

"Yes you have, you lied by omission."

He frowned and I felt a bit stupid. How could you lie by omission? It didn't make sense but I was in too deep now. His horse was restless and William was trying to calm him while listening to my accusation.

"Omission?"

"Yes." I was getting breathless from shouting. "Murder!"

"Sir," interrupted Robin as he pointed to the field. Another rider was approaching at a much more sedate pace and from the looks on William and Robins' faces I deduced it was the Duke. I was angry at William but it was not my intention to cause him trouble or lose face so I shut my mouth tight and lowered my head inspecting the ground intently.

I heard William give a huge sigh and then he looked over my head to Robin and said calmly, "Escort Mistress Evelyn to the Great Hall and wait there with her until I am finished. Restrain her if necessary."

He turned his horse and trotted to meet the other rider. They both halted and exchanged words. The Duke looked in my direction and I saw him nod to William. Well that made a good first impression, I don't think! Some of the soldiers had stopped fighting and had watched the spectacle and now stood staring at me. Robin took my arm and I shook it off. One of the soldiers laughed at him and shouted, "Is she too much for you to handle, laddie? Pass her over to a real man; I'll sort her out for you."

All his comrades laughed but Robin remained silent. He went to take my arm once again but before he could I rounded on the solder and standing as tall as I could I looked down my nose and said, "Grow up. Act your age, not your shoe size." I'm not sure he understood what I said but he knew it was derogatory. He went off, muttering under his breath with his comrades using him as their means of amusement this time.

We started toward the castle but after a few steps I needed to stop and catch my breath. The adrenaline which had coursed through my body during the confrontation with William had drained away leaving me weary and dehydrated. I was cold too, visibly shaking and my teeth chattered. I took a deep breath and started once again. This time I did not shake off Robin's hand as he gently gripped my elbow and guided me towards the main building.

The Great Hall was perhaps one of the warmest rooms in the castle thanks to braziers strategically placed down its entire length. It was no surprise to learn that it was a favourite congregation point. Whether it be to make plans, eat, spread gossip, flirt or keep warm, this was the place to be. Along the length on both sides were little alcoves which offered a modicum of privacy and shelter from the draughts which were still present even with the warmth. With most of the men on the practice field there were plenty to choose from and Robin sat me down in one opposite a brazier.

"Mistress Evelyn, will you promise to remain here while I fetch your cloak?"

He looked baffled when I shook my head.

"Its fine, Robin, I don't have a cloak for you to fetch. All I have is what you see." I lifted my arms to emphasise the point.

"So you were robbed when you were attacked?"

"I really don't know," I replied and changed the subject quickly. "There is one thing you could do for me as a very great favour. Could you stop calling me mistress? I hate the term. My name is Evelyn."

He made to protest but I carried on quickly.

"If you need to refer to me in public and etiquette demands it then you may, but just talking between ourselves call me Evelyn. Lady Hilda has agreed and if she has surely you can too. It's ironic really; I hated my name when I was younger and only answered to Evie but now it is my greatest wish that people call me by my name. I have no title so please."

I tried to use a pleading face and we both laughed. He excused himself and went to the large table at the top of the hall. All the others had been cleared away and stacked at the bottom of the hall ready for the main meal later. He returned with a large beaker and a slab of bread which had been drizzled with a little honey. He proffered the drink and I was a little reluctant but knew I needed to take on liquids.

"I'm not sure this is a good idea after last night," I said.

"It is very weak," he encouraged, "and it will warm you."

I took a drink and it was refreshing and after a while I felt a little warm glow in my chest. Robin perched next to me. I still had no knife so asked him to cut the bread in half. I didn't realise how hungry I was until I took the first mouthful. The bread must have been from today's batch as it was still soft. I offered him the other half as the original piece would have made a good door stop, and after some urging he took it and devoured it like a hungry dog. We munched in silence; I took another drink and then offered it to him. I could tell this wasn't the way things were done here but by this time I didn't really care.

"Tell me about yourself, Robin. What is your role in the castle?"

He sat up proudly and declared, "I am Sir William's squire. I have been with him since I was 10 and he has taught me well. He is a good master and I follow where he goes including into battle."

That surprised me and I asked what he did in the battles.

"When I was younger I tended his equipment but for the last two years I have fought beside him. I still tend his equipment though." He smiled and I could see he felt his worth and was proud of his abilities.

"How old are you, Robin?"

"I will be sixteen this summer."

He spoke like some seasoned veteran. We chatted on for some time and it became very relaxed between us. I was still cold but the watered down ale had helped to warm me a little. I thought back to earlier and my stomach flipped.

"I am in trouble aren't I? I mean with Sir William, heaven forbid probably Duke Richard too."

Robin shrugged and then looked over my shoulder.

"Well, we will soon find out."

Sir William had just entered the hall and Robin rose to greet him. They stood some way off so I couldn't hear what was being said but I didn't need to guess. Their conversation lasted some time then Robin left and William started walking toward me. I rose and my knees were shaking, my mouth was dry and I was more than a little anxious. He paused and then headed for the refreshment table and returned with two goblets. He didn't look angry but he wasn't smiling either, his face was expressionless. He carried himself well, confident and upright. The closer he came to me I regretted my earlier actions, but then I thought I did have a valid point and decided to pursue it.

He stopped directly in front of me so I curtsied. He proffered the goblet.

"Evelyn," his voice was quiet, "I may call you Evelyn?" he asked.

"Yes, Sir William, I preferred that you did."

He opened his mouth to speak again but nerves caused me to jump in and I gabbled at some speed.

"Please accept my apologies for our previous confrontation. It was not my intention to draw attention to us and cause you embarrassment. I was focusing on my own feelings of frustration and anger and gave no thought to the affect my behaviour would have. I'm dreadfully sorry."

I finished a little out of breath and waited for his response but

Robin reappeared and William turned to him and nodded.

Robin was carrying something over his arm and when he shook it out I could see it was a cloak. He moved forward and began to drape it around my shoulders. I was startled and said, "Robin, this is not mine."

The cloak was dark blue and closely woven so that it was thick and warm. It had a lining which was soft and luxuriant to the touch. Robin ignored my protest and fastened the clasp at my neck. A large hood draped down the back and at the front were two slits for the hands to pass through. It was beautiful and so warm. I had not been warm since entering the castle. Perching atop a hill the wind was strong even for springtime and the castle was full of draughts. I was accustomed to central heating and my clothing, although a fair copy of the fashion was not fit for purpose. I had noted that women and indeed the men too, dressed in layers dependant on the weather. My attire consisted of a thin shift and a dress which was minus the underskirts necessary for warmth. I stood momentarily basking in the warmth and comfort.

I looked at Sir William about to protest but he could see my dilemma and said, "Please Evelyn, use this cloak until your clothes taken in the attack can be found or replaced. I feel responsible for your safety and welfare whether it be from injury on the practice field or catching a chill."

There was a slight smile on his face. This was a different William from the one I had encountered before. This William was gracious and caring and his face softened with his smile. He was in fact quite handsome.

"Shall we sit?" he continued. "And we can discuss what is troubling you. Perhaps you would feel more comfortable if Robin remains."

All three of us sat and Sir William looked at me expectantly, he obviously wanted me to set the ball rolling. I took a breath to compose myself and purposefully looked him in the eye. My knees may have been knocking but I wanted him to see I needed to be taken seriously.

"It has come to my attention that there have been numerous murders at Wyvern. I was attacked twice and yet you didn't think it important to mention this to me. Perhaps there is a connection, perhaps there is not but for my own safety I think it important that I should have been made aware of the facts."

So far so good, I thought, but then for some reason I imagined that maybe Sir William was just humouring me. There was no outward appearance that this was so, perhaps my confidence was waning and given the period in time I feared that as a mere female my concerns would be deemed irrelevant.

"I'm not an empty headed female; I can cope with the truth."

Oh dear, wrong choice of words, said in haste regret at leisure.

"You are far from an empty headed female, from the small amount of conversation we have shared I deem you to be quite astute and forthright. I do feel you are keeping something from me but we are newly met and perhaps given time you may share your confidences. My concern for keeping quiet was solely not to cause you more worry. You are a stranger here; you have suffered physical assault and had no one to turn to. I had hoped you would find a friend in Lady Hilda and once you were stronger I would have enlightened you of the reason you needed chaperoning at all times. It seems you are impatient and have forced my hand."

He added the last comment quite seriously but he quirked his eyebrow and his eyes reflected the light giving the impression of a playful sparkle. There again that could have been wishful thinking on my part.

"Now that I have forced your hand please tell me what is

happening here. I find coping with fear of the unknown far more stressful than anything you might tell me."

"I am not totally sure of that in this instant but if you will assure me of your confidence I will proceed."

I nodded eagerly and William drew closer so that he could speak softly. Robin looked about, noting who was close by and if they could eavesdrop; being satisfied all was secure he too drew closer. William took a long drink from his goblet and then placed it down beside him. Subconsciously Robin and I did the same and then waited, watching William's face intently. He hesitated, gathering his thoughts and then said almost apologetically, "Things had already progressed when we arrived."

"When you arrived? Is this not where you live?"

"No," William continued. "I have a manor house some distance from here. Robin and I came when Richard, the Duke, sent word to me. He was concerned about the turn of events and having not been able to find the solution requested that I come and try to discover what was happening. I would act as a guest but use my visit to explore, unhampered, different suspects."

"Like a private detective?" I interrupt.

"A private detective?" Robin asked, never having heard the term.

William looked equally confused. How was I going to explain this so as not to look out of place in this environment?

"Yes. A private detective is someone other than the local law enforcement who is hired to discreetly investigate a certain situation: to work undercover so as not to alert the perpetrator."

Robin grinned and was quite impressed. William nodded his head slowly looking very thoughtful.

"I like that title. That is what Richard requested I do."

We all smiled and nodded our approval and then William continued.

"A body was found of a man with a knife wound the length of his chest. He was laid at the edge of the Priory land. He was on his back with his arms crossed over his chest as if ready for burial. A few weeks later the same thing happened. A man was laid on his back with his body ready for burial this time with a wound to his stomach. The third time it happened, the body stank and was already bloated. There were no wounds but the body was once again laid ready for burial."

I was a little confused. "It's not usual for murderers to take the victims to a churchyard for burial."

"Well there lies the mystery," William continued. "None of the men had been murdered. Each was a man from the village given last rites and laid to rest on his death."

"You mean someone had dug them up, mutilated them and then left them at the Priory for reburial?"

"It would appear so. It was then that I received a message from the Duke to pay a visit. I was pleased to do so as he has been a comrade in arms and a friend for a considerable time. It was agreed that the reason for my visit would remain a secret between the three of us. Later, after your arrival we extended our confidence to Lady Hilda so that she could befriend you and aid in your protection."

I was a little disappointed and it must have sounded in my voice as I mumbled, "Oh. I thought Lady Hilda had befriended me because of her caring nature and concern for me, not because she was ordered to as part of your plan."

"Lady Hilda was chosen exactly because she is a caring person and totally trustworthy. Her husband was one of the previous Duke's knights and she attended Richard's mother as a lady in waiting. She has known Richard since he was a child and he has great affection for her. Trust me, Evelyn; her friendship with you is genuine."

I felt a little reassured and gave a weak smile, composing myself to hear the rest of the tale.

"Very little happened after that and life carried on much as normal until a body was found in the wooded area between Wyvern and the Priory. The victim lay where he fell on his back with his chest ripped open. This was murder, for it was one of the young village lads. It happened once more shortly after to another male villager. Both were laid to rest alongside the other victims on Priory land.

"Extra guards were posted and everyone told to always keep with others, on no account be alone. There were no clues to the murders. We exhausted every possibility and then another body was found. This was a guard found just outside the castle wall, left in his own blood, where he fell."

William shook his head slightly as if in defeat and gave an audible sigh as he added, "Then you were attacked."

I gave a little shiver but couldn't help being a little intrigued. I was an avid reader and loved a good murder mystery. I had never been as close to murder as this or nearly part of one, but already I was mulling over the facts. I remained silent for a while and I think the two of them thought I was trying to recover from such a bloodthirsty tale. They both were startled when I said, "Your murderer is getting bolder. He made do with dead bodies to carry out his depravity but then graduated to fresh kills from the village. His confidence or blood lust increased and he targeted castle staff and then ultimately attempted to murder his first female, me. Perhaps his aim is to choose nobility for his next victim."

William and Robin exchanged glances and then looked at me. William looked a little uncomfortable, perhaps because he had had no success unmasking the villain. He didn't appear the type to be defeated, more likely frustrated at his lack of success.

"You said the bodies were mutilated," I queried. "In what way?"

Robin was reluctant that I should know the gory details and exclaimed, "You don't need to know that, Evelyn, 'tis a grisly business to be sure."

William disagreed and said, "Evelyn is now our confidante and if she needs all the facts for better understanding then we are duty bound to tell her. Also she may appreciate how dangerous it is to go wandering about the castle especially at night."

I could feel my face flush as William fixed me with a stare. Had it been him who made the noise on my hasty visit to the garderobe during the night? Oh dear, it hadn't been a quiet ladylike visit and I had looked positively awful. Another less than positive impression I had made. I swallowed with difficulty and concentrated on my hands fidgeting in my lap. William knew his point had been made.

"On all the bodies except one, various parts of the innards were taken."

I wrinkled my nose in distaste. "Whatever for?"

William shrugged slightly.

"There are many rumours amongst the villagers, none of them pleasant. Some say for Devil worship or witchery, others have even suggested for consumption!"

My jaw did drop at this remark.

"I don't believe cannibalism is the reason." William was quick to lay my fears to rest. "Taxes are high and the people do suffer. King Richard's need for more funds to finance his Crusade in the Holy Land falls heavily on the peasants; however, Wyvern is a close community and pulls together. Duke Richard endeavours to be a fair landlord."

I remembered the food served in the hall the previous night and wondered what his definition of 'fair' was, but I knew I must not make waves and draw attention to myself, especially with my inclusion into the trusted few!

CHAPTER FIVE

Isat on the bed in Hilda's chamber staring at my canvas bag. I had retrieved it from under the bed where it had been concealed since my arrival from the Priory. Inside was everything I owned, my total worth. There was so little, nothing for my survival, yet some of these few possessions could spell danger for me now.

*

William, Robin and I had stayed together well into the afternoon. Finally warm, wrapped in the cloak which even now was draped around my shoulders, I was in no hurry to leave the Great Hall where the three of us sat in earnest conversation. By the time we took leave of each other I felt I knew them both a little better and felt safe in their company. I liked William who discarded his stern look to reveal a composed, calm manner which from time to time allowed a smile to grace his features. He always seemed to be in perfect control, capable but willing to listen. Watching his interaction with Robin I saw a great partnership and realised that although to me Robin was a young lad he was in fact a capable and seasoned soldier. He was William's right arm and I had been wrong to treat him as a youth of my era. In his time, boys were expected to mature early and unfortunately die much too young. I saw very few old people which was to be expected, I suppose; life was hard, the environment harsh and it took its toll.

After having demanded to hear all the facts regarding the murders I was shocked at how grisly they had been. No drugs, internet or video games to blame here, just pure evil. I had started to overthink the details. Were the victims still alive when their organs had been ripped from their body? Would there be a third attempt on my life to finish the job started on my arrival?

I swallowed audibly and William encouraged me to drink from the goblet. He paused, but continued when I nodded that I was recovered. We had discussed the motive at length but not come to any conclusion. The soldiers of the garrison under Duke Richard's command were on high alert and William and Robin had been quietly investigating in the background, but all leads had been exhausted. There really wasn't any pattern to the killings apart from them all being male, that is until my attack. If it was blood lust killing, everyone was at risk. I suggested that devil-worship rituals incorporated young virgins, so I was led to believe, not that I had ever had anything to do with that and was purely making my statement based on movies I had watched. Obviously, I kept that fact to myself.

I did emphasise my concern regarding witchcraft though. I knew from history that many women had been accused and put to death unjustly. Fear of the unknown caused many to point the finger. Often it was based on a woman's knowledge of herbs and plants used in healing. William had raised his eyebrows when I declared that plants were the root of modern medicine but he didn't pass comment. I reigned myself in but did add that the power of suggestion and group hysteria could cause a great deal of trouble. Trial for witchcraft never ended well using trial by water; if the accused sank she was innocent, if she floated she was guilty. It was thought witches floated because they had renounced baptism when entering the devil's service. Regardless, she would then be put to death for witchcraft, either way the accused ended up dead.

It was this suspicion of the unknown that had prompted me to retrieve my bag and examine the contents. I had thought someone at the Priory had rifled through the bag or at least gathered up and replaced the contents that may have fallen out, but nothing was ever said. I would be foolish to leave anything to chance now.

William had offered to escort me to Hilda's chamber when we finally disbanded. He had politely knocked the door to see if Hilda was within. Receiving no answer he entered and searched the room then returned to me on the threshold when he had found no-one. We stood staring at one another; I wasn't sure what to say and began to feel a bit flustered when he continued eye contact. Finally I thanked him once again for the loan of the cloak; in truth I would have been very reluctant to relinquish it. He took my hand and my pulse raced when he said, "The colour blue suits you very well." He then lifted my hand to his lips briefly.

"Take care, Evelyn, and bar the door until Lady Hilda's return."

I felt like a giddy schoolgirl and finding my mouth refused to work I nodded my head in assurance I would obey and fled into the room. I barred the door after which I heard his footsteps retreating down the corridor. Well! I wasn't expecting that reaction to him and realised I was wearing a stupid grin on my face as I foraged under the bed in search of my bag.

Having smoothed the bed cover I tipped my bag upside down so that the entire contents spilled into an untidy heap. It was my intention to separate the items into three piles; one of items that were dangerous as they were obviously not of this time, one of innocent items and the last pile, items that perhaps I could use surreptitiously. Sorting proved difficult and frustrating as I was unable to be decisive and this was hampered further by the sheer amount that had accumulated over time.

The dangerous pile had obvious things like my mobile phone,

keys, money, bank cards and wristwatch. The safe pile only had my jewellery so far and even so I worried that the settings were so different and delicately fine compared to that worn by the ladies of today. I sighed as I inspected the remainder of the pile. My cosmetics were fairly safe but unfortunately all were contained in plastic tubes and cases, even my comb was plastic. There was a pile of papers: the printed handouts from the craft workshop, several sheets of songs I carried so that I could study the lyrics for my next choir meeting, an old shopping list and several coupons. I had seen no paper since my arrival and I'm sure it would be parchment if I had. Even my sewing kit was suspect, especially the scissors and tape measure.

I had quite a good supply of paracetamol since I had bought several boxes when I started suffering at the workshop and an almost new tube of throat lozenges; I'm not even sure where they came from. I had a ballpoint pen, a couple of safety pins, a purse-size perfume spray and quite a bit of fluff and tissues. There was a swatch of material demonstrating the dying we had been trying on the course and a neatly folded shopping carrier bag I always carried to accommodate any spur of the moment purchases. Unfortunately it had NEXT printed across it.

I gathered the dangerous pile and put it inside the carrier bag having turned it inside out first so that the logo was less visible. There must be somewhere to hide this in the room; unfortunately there was little in the way of furniture and no loose stone or wood anywhere concealing a little hidey-hole. Eventually I settled for the bed which was so heavy it was impossible to move. Between the carved headboard and the stone wall was a small space, the result of the ornate carving. I repacked my plastic carrier to make the bundle as small as possible and after much wriggling and pushing managed to secrete it between the bed and the wall.

Returning to the remaining pile, I took the swatch of fabric and my sewing kit and thought I would sew a simple pocket or purse to suspend from my girdle to allow me to carry a few little items. Hopefully in time this would include a few coins but that was a problem to solve later. I pulled the little stool up to the table on which the candles stood and poked a spill into the almost dead embers of the brazier to light one of them. It wasn't easy sewing by candlelight but I worked away and realised I was quite happy finally having something to do. The little purse was very basic but when I unclasped my girdle and slipped it on it didn't look out of place and I was relatively pleased with the result.

Selecting a few items I placed them in the purse: the remaining jewellery I wasn't wearing, my little scissors, a strip of paracetamol from one of the boxes and the safety pins. After washing my face and hands I took a single squirt of moisturising cream and smoothed it over my face and hands, after so long it felt quite luxurious. I smeared the merest hint of lipstick onto my dry lips with my finger and then dabbed a little fragrance on my throat. My toilette complete, I gathered my belongings into the canvas bag and concealed it back in its hiding place beneath the bed.

I felt pleased with my achievement and removing my veil I tossed it onto the bed and gave my head a vigorous rub. It felt so good to be unrestricted so I pulled out my bag once more and taking the fragrance spray liberally coated the brush Maggie used on my hair. Brushing my hair with gusto I toed the bag back into its place beneath the bed. After several minutes I stopped mid-stroke as there was a knock at the door.

"It is me my dear, Hilda."

I unbarred the door to a very weary-looking Hilda followed closely by Maggie who steered her to her chair. Hilda gave a little groan of relief as she sank into the chair; meanwhile Maggie turned her attention to the brazier which was barely alight. She gave me a sidelong look and I realised she wasn't impressed that I had almost allowed the fire to die. I apologised, feeling rather embarrassed but she just nodded her head as she stoked the embers to life. Turning my attention to Hilda I knelt beside her and rubbed her hand.

"What's wrong, Hilda, are you unwell?"

She smiled weakly as she replied, "I am so very tired. The last few days have been very hectic and I am not as young as I once was. Would you mind if I supped in my chamber this evening? Will you be able to go to the Great Hall alone?"

"I wouldn't dream of leaving you alone. We will sup together and I can keep you company. It will be like a girlie night to ourselves."

She chuckled at this, shaking her head at my strange expression, but squeezing my hand she seemed to like the idea. I wasn't sure if I was still in Maggie's bad books so very hesitantly asked if she would bring me some supper on Hilda's tray. My misdemeanour already forgotten, she assured me she would and disappeared out of the door.

Hilda settled herself in her chair; she already looked improved, and noticed my little purse.

"Why that is very sweet, did you sew it?"

She examined the stitching and nodded with approval.

"Yes, I quite enjoyed being industrious and it is practical even if it is rather empty. I realise I need to get myself organised, actually I was hoping you would help me."

"I will help you in any way I can, what is it you need?"

I hesitated, not knowing quite how to phrase what was on my mind.

"I am sadly lacking in garments, especially undergarments. I have a ring that I would like to exchange for coin; do you know how I go about this? I know very little about life here at Wyvern and fear I could be taken advantage of."

Hilda nodded in understanding but was unable to give advice, after all she was a lady and I imagined had never been in my predicament. At that moment Maggie returned with a tray laden with various dishes which smelt very tempting. I helped her clear the table so that she could unload the tray. As we busied ourselves making up the dinner plates Hilda tactfully asked her if she knew where I could sell my ring. She shook her head and then turned to me and quite earnestly suggested I not do it myself but find someone I could trust.

"Mistress, I don't think you would get a fair exchange, you being a lady and a stranger to these parts."

I knew she was probably right and was a bit disappointed but put on a brave face and said, "Oh well, a nice warm underskirt will have to wait."

I took my meal back to my stool which I had pulled away from the table nearer to Hilda. Maggie gave Hilda hers, bending to say something in her ear as she did so. Hilda's face brightened and she exclaimed, "Why yes, I had forgotten all about those, there may be something."

I was a little puzzled as Maggie went to the end of the bed where there was a trunk draped with an embroidered cloth and used as a bench. I had often sat on it as I wrestled with my knitted stockings. She lifted the lid and peered inside.

"Spread the items on the bed so we can inspect them after our meal," instructed Hilda.

She gestured that I ate, which I did as I watched Maggie remove various garments and shake them vigorously before laying them on the bed. I detected a faint aroma of lavender; the contents of the chest had obviously been packed away very carefully. I was so curious but I could tell from Hilda's demeanour that I was expected to finish eating before exploring the items. Maggie having finished unpacking poured us both a drink. Hilda would not be rushed so I resigned myself to wait patiently and eat; this was no hardship as I realised I was truly hungry.

Maggie returned the empty dishes to the tray ready to take them to the kitchen. She left the wine. Hilda looked so much better than when she had first returned and Maggie seemed quite happy to leave her in my care. Having pointedly stoked the brazier she bobbed in Hilda's direction and left with the laden tray.

I pulled my stool next to Hilda and refilled her goblet. She seemed to have returned to her good-natured self and I was quite content to sit beside her and wait for her to start a conversation, which she did after a few more sips of wine.

"I was lady in waiting to the Duchess Cicely, the present Duke's mother," she began. "She prided her appearance and was always immaculately dressed, with so many gowns. I had a fair hand at sewing so whenever a gown needed mending or altering it was my task, she would allow no other to touch it. Her clothes were good quality and beautiful and expensive too, of course. The Duke would shake his head in exasperation but indulged her because he loved her very much. She was not a wasteful woman, however, and when she decided an item could no longer be worn she passed it to me to alter for another person or purpose.

"The original recycler," I said. "Reuse, remake, repurpose," I added when Hilda hesitated.

"Yes exactly that, nothing was wasted. When she died her best gowns were passed to other ladies in the castle but I still had all the worn items: It was too painful to cut them for repurpose, her death hung heavy on my heart, so Maggie carefully packed them in the trunk. Go and look, my dear, and see if there is anything that could be of use. Judging by your little purse you are quite able with a needle and thread."

"Oh Hilda, won't it upset you to see them cut and used?"

She shook her head. "No, Evelyn, time has passed and it would give me pleasure to see them put to good use."

I approached the bed slowly, almost afraid to touch the garments which obviously meant so much to Hilda. On top of the pile Maggie had laid an underskirt, it was worn and the seam was ripped but it was linen and soft to the touch. I spun around to Hilda holding the garment to my waist. We both looked pleased until I looked down and saw that it was short. The women of this time were on average shorter than those of my time. It didn't help that Cicely was shorter than average whereas I was taller.

"No matter, Evelyn," Hilda said, undeterred, "I am sure there are others which could be used to create a false hem."

Encouraged, I searched the pile and found three in all. Another linen one had lost the drawstring at the waist and the third was a pretty dyed bluish green.

"I could mend the linen skirts and put false hems on them using the dyed material," I exclaimed. "That will be ideal since my dress isn't as long as I like and the underskirt will show below it, covering my ankles better."

I was warming to this task and returned to the pile. I found one shift, once again a little short but this wouldn't show as it was worn under the dress. I examined some dresses which were woollen and lined with linen. Cicely being of higher rank could afford this luxury. I put my selected items to one side and began carefully packing the gowns back into the chest. I was quite excited to have a project especially one that would provide that extra source of warmth.

Hilda watched contentedly as I busied myself. Colour had returned to her cheeks and she was quite relaxed.

"You are going to be very busy, my dear. I have some thread which you may use."

"Thank you, Hilda, I can't wait to make a start."

I smoothed the bed cover and was about to return to my stool when there was a gentle rap at the door. If it was Maggie she would have entered after knocking but the door remained closed. Hilda and I exchanged glances; she gave a slight shrug to indicate she had no idea who could be there. I approached the door which I realised was unbarred; William had told me repeatedly to take care and be vigilant in staying safe. I didn't open the door but called out, "Who is there?"

"Robin," came the reply.

I realised I had been holding my breath in anticipation so gently exhaled and opened the door.

"Mist... Evelyn," he began. "Are you well?"

He seemed a little tongue tied but then continued.

"You and Lady Hilda were not at dinner. Sir William has been occupied with Duke Richard so I knew you were not in his company and I was afraid something was amiss."

I was quite touched he came to check on us and smiled, assuring him we were both alright. He hesitated and then made to leave when I had an idea.

"Actually Robin I was just thinking of you."

He looked surprised. "You were?"

"Yes, come inside."

He looked from me to Hilda and seemed reluctant to enter. I realised that perhaps it wasn't the 'done thing' for ladies to invite males into the bed chamber but I just grabbed his sleeve and gave a gentle tug so he crossed the threshold. When I barred the door he looked a bit apprehensive so I linked my arm in his and drew him further in the room. I pulled another stool from under the table and placed it alongside mine. Hilda was looking confused but graciously smiled at him and trusted that I knew what I was doing.

I sat down and since our arms were still linked he plonked down beside me. We were in close proximity and I heard him inhale as he brushed against my hair. He had obviously caught a whiff of the perfume I had used on my hairbrush. It was then that I realised my hair should be covered but it was too late now so the best thing to do was get down to business.

"Robin, I need some coin," I began. "I have a ring which I can sell but have been advised not to attempt this myself. Could you help me? Do you know how to go about this? Or perhaps William could be persuaded to intervene on my behalf. I know you would both ensure I receive a fair price."

"I will do whatever I can, it may take some time but I will do my best," he replied after sitting quietly thinking for a few minutes.

I hugged his arm and said, "Oh, thank you so much."

The decision was, which ring to sell. I couldn't part with my wedding ring and my engagement ring was quite different from those worn now. I had a little gold knotted dress ring which wasn't worth a great deal so it had to be my eternity ring. Rootling in my purse I finally found the ring and presented it to Robin on the palm of my hand. It was a plain gold band with diamond chips encircling it around the middle; I hoped it would not arouse suspicion.

"It is very pretty, are you sure you want to part with it?"

"There are other things I am in need of, Robin; best put its value to good use. Do you have any idea how much it is worth?"

Robin pursed his lips and shook his head. "I know nothing of jewellery except I cannot afford it. Do not worry, Evelyn. I will get as much for it as I can."

He rose to leave ready to set about his task. I walked to the door as he took his leave of Hilda, unbarring and opening it. He hesitated as he turned in the doorway, looking at the ring and then at me. Did he suspect something? I couldn't tell. I thanked him once again and tried to give him my best dazzling smile and closed and barred the door.

For the first time since my arrival I felt positive. I was trying to take control of my life and I felt I had made a few good friends. I sat with Hilda and the evening passed pleasantly as we discussed the best way of going about my sewing project. Maggie returned to help Hilda get ready to retire and then busied herself preparing for the morning. As she made to leave, Hilda called her back.

"Bring Avis in the morning to assist Mistress Evelyn with dressing and her hair. She will be joining me when I wait on the Duchess."

"Yes milady," she said and scurried off.

I barred the door and then sped across the cold floor and jumped into the bed beside Hilda. It was cold in my shift and I pulled the covers under my chin. I was to attend the Duchess, well that was going to be an experience, that's for sure. I prayed I would not make a spectacle of myself for Hilda's sake as much as my own.

*

Hilda and I sat quietly sewing; we had come to the solar after a very hurried breakfast. It was a large chamber at the top of the keep and I remembered it as the museum when I had first visited Wyvern. It was lighter than other chambers in the castle having two openings to each internal recess complete with window seats. There was no glass but some kind of oiled material which let light in but kept out the wind. It was quite pleasant and I understood why the Duchess would prefer to spend her days here. Several other ladies were present, most of whom were very young like the Duchess and they were chatting amongst themselves.

It was sometime before Alice arrived and we all stood in greeting when she finally came through the door. She was such a small little figure and really wasn't showing any physical sign of being pregnant, although she had a pretty wrap draped around her so it was difficult to tell. She was still pale but I was pleased to see that the dark rings around her eyes had disappeared. She comfied herself in an armchair with several pillows and placed her dainty feet on a footstool. Once she was settled we resumed our seats and waited for her to speak.

One of her ladies in waiting drew a little table next to her so that a second could place the tray she brought in on it. The tray contained a bottle and goblet and a platter covered by a cloth. The lady poured some liquid into the goblet and passed it to Alice who accepted it graciously and then indicated she wanted something under the cloth. She took a small wafer and nibbled on it, it was then I realised she had decided to use the suggestion I had passed on to Hilda regarding ginger and oatcakes helping with sickness. Indeed Alice looked quite content sipping and nibbling. I don't know if the remedy was the reason her sickness had abated or if the sickness had reduced because she was further on in her pregnancy. It could even have been the power of suggestion, either way I was pleased she was feeling better.

She chatted with her ladies, looking at their handiwork and was very interested when items being stitched for the long-awaited baby were proffered. Eventually her gaze settled on Hilda and I.

"Lady Hilda, I see you have brought Mistress Evelyn to join us today."

Hilda rose and approached the Duchess and I followed suit. I had no notion of the etiquette expected of me so whatever Hilda did I copied. When she presented me to Alice I bobbed a curtsy and waited for her to speak first. She replaced her goblet on the table to give me her full attention and when she spoke her voice was light and girly but nonetheless welcoming.

"Mistress Evelyn, it is a pleasure to finally meet. It would seem I owe you my thanks."

I wasn't sure how to reply so smiled in acknowledgment.

"The remedy you passed on to Lady Hilda has been very beneficial," she gestured to the oatcakes, "and far more palatable than many other so-called remedies I endured to quell the sickness."

"I am pleased you are feeling better, milady," I said quietly because I had no proof the ginger and oatcakes were the miracle cure and felt a little guilty at taking ownership.

"I tire so easily and feel quite weak more often than I care to," she continued and gave a pained sigh which caused the younger ladies to flock around her and coo like a cote of doves.

"Milady you are weak because you have eaten little for some considerable time. It's now time to expand your diet to include nourishment for you and the baby."

Some of the ladies registered shock that I should be so forthcoming but Alice leaned forward in her chair, showing interest.

"What do you suggest, Mistress Evelyn? I am fearful of starting the sickness again."

"I quite understand but if you avoid spicy food that will help. Try to include lots of vegetables, especially green ones, and fruit in your daily meals. Oatmeal for breakfast is fortuitous for helping… bodily functions."

"Oh," she replied, moving back in her chair. Was I wrong to mention bodily functions? If I was Alice was very gracious and smoothed over the pregnant pause by drawing attention to my needlework, which maybe wasn't so good since all her ladies were stitching items for her whereas mine was for me. Lady Hilda, ever watchful came to my aid explaining quietly so as not to embarrass me in front of the room, that all my belongings had gone astray during my attack. Everyone heard but I think it was Hilda's way of warning off any gossiping among the younger less mature females.

Alice was quite concerned. "You were left with nothing. Oh my goodness, to be in such a situation?"

She obviously had never experienced having only one piece of clothing and seemed genuinely concerned. She examined my stitching and appreciated what she saw and encouraged me to continue. The day continued pleasantly. I was eager to finish my stitching so sat quietly working away listening to the others entertaining one another. By mid-afternoon Alice said she was feeling fatigued and wanted to rest. She disappeared through a partition which separated part of the large solar for use by the noble pair as their bed chamber. Her departure signalled our dismissal so Hilda and I decided to take a stroll within the castle walls. Returning our needlework to Hilda's bed chamber I gathered up the cloak and draped it around my shoulders. Passing through the Great Hall I looked about hoping to see William but he was not there and I felt a hint of disappointment.

Out in the fresh air Hilda and I strolled arm in arm casually watching life going on around us. We passed the forge where we were greeted by a blast of hot air, quite pleasant in cold weather but unbearable in the summer in such a cramped space. Around the corner was a leather craftsman busily working and we stopped to watch, fascinated by his skill at cutting the leather so accurately to any size or width. He did it effortlessly and we were both fascinated. He then went on to stitch two pieces together and I crept forward so that I could get a better view; the aroma of new leather was wonderful and I put out my hand to touch the shiny hide. When he looked up I hesitated, thinking he didn't appreciate such close scrutiny but he smiled.

"Tis a lovely smell, mistress, the new leather."

"Oh it is," I replied, "and you work it so skilfully. May we watch?"

He seemed pleased we were showing a keen interest and told us to gather round while he stitched. He demonstrated how he would make a hole in the leather with an awl and then a corresponding one in the second piece of leather. Taking a needle, one in either hand, he would pass each through the hole from opposite directions, in effect double stitching, making the join very strong. The holes were evenly spaced and the stitching impressively even.

"Your stitches are more even than attempts of many ladies I have known."

"Thank you, mistress," he beamed. "I have been doing this for many a year. My hands have seasoned to it now."

He held out his hands which were strong and I could see the fingertips were hardened and calloused.

"Hands of a true craftsman," I declared.

He seemed flattered and modestly inclined his head.

"Thank you for the demonstration," Hilda said, "it was most informative."

We both turned to continue our stroll when I felt something under my shoe. Looking down I saw the smaller strips of leather that had been trimmed and allowed to fall to the floor.

"May I have several of these strips?" I asked, bending down to retrieve a couple.

"Mistress, they aren't big enough to be of any use to you."

"On the contrary, the narrower the better," I replied.

I sorted through the scraps looking for something the width of a shoe lace but all seemed to be too thick or too short. I sighed in disappointment.

"Here, mistress, tell me what you want and I will cut it for you."

I explained what I wanted, so taking one of the thicker scraps he deftly pared it so narrow I held my breath thinking he would cut his fingers.

"That's marvellous," I declared, taking it from him and winding it around my fingers so that it would fit in my little purse. Bidding him farewell we continued on our walk. Hilda looked at me, raising her eyebrows. "Another little project?"

The walk had been so refreshing, the sights and smells had really awakened my senses so I was quite buoyant on our return. We rested and then tidied ourselves ready to go to the Great Hall for supper. It was busy but I could see from my seat some way down the hall that no one was seated at the top table as yet. Hilda noticed my frequent glances and asked, "Waiting for anyone in particular?"

"Not really," I replied, but Hilda gave a knowing smile and was about to make a further comment when the guests arrived and started to take their seats. There were far more than usual, it seemed the Duke had many visiting knights and the table was quite crowded but I saw William take a seat at the end of the table separated from Richard for once. The Duke and Duchess arrived, the latter looking refreshed after her rest. She was a pretty girl and looked quite charming when she was smiling. William looked quite severe once again but spoke with his neighbour. The food arrived on cue and the noise was a crescendo as everyone jostled for a helping.

As the meal progressed I couldn't help but keep glancing at William who was totally oblivious to my presence. Why should he notice me? After all, I was nobody, definitely no one of his station. I gazed into my cup and gave a disappointed sigh. As I raised my head I realised he was staring at me, his face softened and he smiled and then he raised his goblet in salute. I raised mine in returned and knew

I had a silly grin on my face which I didn't have any control over.

I was so engrossed in the moment that I had not heard someone approach from behind and I almost jumped out of my skin as a head was thrust between Hilda and myself. Hilda's hand went to her breast which was a little gesture she favoured when surprised, or sad, or ill or any change of her normal composure that needed emphasising. I gave a little shrill and my wine spilled on the table.

"Robin, you startled me," I admonished. "You did that on purpose."

"No, my lady, I wouldn't do that."

He was trying to look innocent but his mischievous grin gave him away. I could see William trying to cover a chuckle with his hand.

"How are my two favourite ladies this evening?"

"Don't try and flatter your way out of it, Robin."

He pretended to be hurt, but Hilda and I subconsciously scooted up on the bench so that he could wriggle in between us. We both had a soft spot for this lad but would never let on. He had no plate so cut a slab of bread and ladled the stew on top of it. He devoured it ravenously and when Hilda and I watched open mouthed he looked puzzled.

"What?" he exclaimed. "I'm growing I have to keep my strength up."

"At that rate you will measure up to Goliath!" Hilda said dryly.

We supped together, comfortable in each other's company. After a while I felt a hand on my thigh. I thought I had imagined it at first but then I felt it again. Surely not Robin being so forward. I checked his cup to judge how much he had consumed, not that much. When it happened again, quite insistent this time, I turned to face him about to put him in his place. I stopped as he open his eyes wide and nodded down to my lap. Yes, his hand was on my leg but clutched in it was a little leather purse. I covered it with my hand and felt the chink of coins. I moved to raise it up and take a look but he guided my hand back under the table.

"Best you count it back in your chamber," he said quietly. "There are lots of prying eyes here."

I was surprised. "You sold my ring already? My goodness, that was quick."

He gave a knowing wink and released the purse into my lap. It felt quite heavy.

"Put it somewhere safe," he whispered, "don't carry it all about your person."

"Robin, thank you so much, where did you sell it?"

He just shook his head and smiled making it clear he wasn't about to tell me. I squeezed his arm affectionately.

"Once again you come to my rescue, my knight in shining armour."

I was teasing him but what I said was very true. He smiled and bidding Hilda and I goodnight disappeared into the crowd.

William managed to disentangle himself from the knights on the top table briefly to escort Hilda and I to our chamber. This was the part of the day I enjoyed although this particular evening he apologised for not being able to stay and chat.

And so the days continued, sewing with the duchess, strolling with Hilda and when possible spending time with William. I felt quite contented for once and my thoughts of returning to my own time seemed less pressing.

CHAPTER SIX

Alice was hysterical and had locked herself in her chamber demanding two burly soldiers guard the door. As we attempted to enter the solar two equally large soldiers barred our way, ordering us to go and wait in the Great Hall and not to leave the castle. They were grim and assertive and not the type to argue with, so Hilda and I meekly turned and back tracked to the steps. We gave each other a confused and worried look, not knowing the reason for this but did as we were told. I felt very anxious and shaky and was praying this had nothing to do with yesterday's incident.

We had been sitting with Alice as was our routine; I joined in some of the chatter now that I knew the ladies a little better, when Alice complained of a headache. She looked tired and as time progressed became quite quiet. One of her ladies disappeared and returned with her physician. He was not someone I felt I could warm to. He was extremely thin with a sombre face and rather a large nose. I remembered thinking to myself he rather resembled a vulture but took little notice of him until he produced a bowl with the intension to bleed the Duchess.

I had stood quickly uttering a gasp and dropped my sewing to the floor.

"You are not going to bleed her, surely?" I said.

"I most certainly am. The Duchess' humors are out of balance, they need to be restored to promote good health and relieve the pain in her head. Who are you to question my methods? I have been

77

physician in this household for many years."

He moved forward with the bowl as the rest of the room stared open mouthed at me for speaking out, but I was not deterred.

"Milady do not allow him to do this. You have been eating and doing everything in your power to keep you and the baby well. Letting your blood will make you weak and deprive the baby of all the nutrients, I mean goodness you have consumed to make him strong."

The physician waved me away in dismissal and made to carry on. The Duchess hesitated and then raised her hand to stop his advance.

"Mistress Evelyn has given me sound counsel so far, perhaps she is right."

Oh my goodness, he started to shake with rage.

"What can she know about medicine, a mere woman? Why, I doubt she has even produced children herself."

The Duchess looked at me and I knew what was coming.

"Have you experienced carrying a child, Evelyn?"

The answer to this question could be very complicated so I just shook my head. The physician who I later found out was called Master Hook, sneered at me as if having made his point, but Alice kept her hand up preventing him proceeding.

"Do you have a remedy, Evelyn, that is a little less invasive?"

I got the impression Alice had a distaste for bloodletting and her expression was willing me to say I could help. I was facing a dilemma. I had some paracetamol in my purse which were capsules so I could easily shake the contents into a drink, but how would I explain this to a room of onlookers? I was so determined that Alice not have to endure a useless procedure that I nodded.

"I think I will try Mistress Evelyn's remedy first, Master Hook, if you don't mind."

He was furious and his mouth worked like that of a goldfish, unable to find words to express his fury at being dismissed. He turned and stomped out of the room giving the merest of bows. Now I was in a predicament and wasn't sure how to proceed, but I knew I must be confident, well, look confident at least.

I rummaged in my purse on purpose and managed to remove two tablets from the strip without giving a clear view of what I was doing. Proceeding to the little table beside her chair I took Alice's goblet and poured a very small amount of liquid in the bottom. It was easy to separate the capsules keeping my hands over the casing, and sprinkle the contents into the goblet. I swirled it for a short time to allow it to dissolve and then offered it to Alice. She looked dubious and her ladies took a sharp intake of breath. I waited but still she hesitated so I swilled the contents once more and then gulped down the mixture. All eyes were on me, but when I didn't writhe in agony or drop down dead I heard a united exhaling of breath and took it as my cue to prepare another draught which Alice consumed with no complaints; she did pull a rather unflattering face regarding the taste so I refilled the goblet and told her to drink.

We returned to our sewing and within 20 minutes she was chattering and laughing happily, that was until the door opened and a procession of men walked in led by the Duke, followed by a very haughty-looking Master Hook who was still carrying the bowl.

Richard approached his wife and took her hand gently and raised it to his lips.

"My love, I understand you refused Master Hook's ministrations to aid you with your malady. You must promise me you will take care of yourself and our child."

He looked at her so tenderly and she gazed into his eyes; they were certainly a love match. It was then I noticed that William was one of those attending the Duke and he was regarding me with a stern look.

My face became very hot and I wanted the floor to swallow me. However, for the first time since my arrival at Wyvern I had been able to offer some small service which had been beneficial and had prevented the Duchess having to endure what I considered a useless barbaric procedure. To my surprise I was ready to stand my ground and speak up for what I believed was right, so I pulled myself up straight and clasped my hands in front of me to stop them shaking.

"My lord," Alice began, "Mistress Evelyn said being bled could make me and the baby weak."

If I didn't know better I'm sure she was batting her lashes at her husband who was totally under her spell.

"You know how I dislike being bled," she crooned, "and Evelyn mixed me a draught and I feel so much better."

She certainly looked the picture of health and she literally glowed when she smiled. Richard was convinced and kissed her hand once more. Turning to Master Hook he gestured to Alice.

"See, she is improved, no worries."

Richard left the room followed by his entourage, Hook however stayed long enough to give me a hostile warning look before he departed.

*

Hilda and I entered the Great Hall which was crowded mostly with the females of the castle, who mingled, speaking in hushed tones looking around anxiously. Something serious was definitely amiss but no one offered an explanation and avoided eye contact with us. As we went further into the hall I saw Maggie and Avis on the fringe of the crowd so I touched Hilda's arm to draw her attention to them. Avis was sobbing uncontrollably and Maggie was trying to console her, pulling her close and gently stroking her back. Hilda was full of concern and rushed to their side sitting next to Avis and circling her arms around her shoulders. I could see that Maggie too was crying but was desperately trying to control her emotions.

"My dears, what ails you so?"

"Rose is gone," wailed Avis.

"Where has she gone?"

Avis was unable to speak so Hilda looked to Maggie for an explanation.

"Who is Rose and where has she gone?"

Hilda was caring but was quite firm in her questioning of Maggie who swallowed hard and with great self-control tried to give a clear account.

"Rose worked in the kitchen; she was from the village and with child."

Maggie swallowed again and wiped her eyes on her apron, I placed my hand on her shoulder for support and after a moment she continued.

"This morning her body was found in the ditch just outside the castle wall."

It was too much for Maggie who broke down and started to weep again. I was shocked, as was Hilda and we tried to comfort the serving girls. We had both been lulled into false security thinking, hoping, praying that the murders had ceased. I vainly hoped it was an accident but with all the commotion it was obvious it was a foul deed. There had been other murders but none of them had caused this reaction. I looked at Hilda who returned my questioning look.

"Maggie," she said gently, "what happened?"

The poor girl looked wretched but she managed to whisper, "She was sliced open and the baby was taken."

I recoiled in shock, covering my mouth trying to stifle a shriek as did Hilda. I saw the colour drain from her face and I put my hand out to steady her in case she fainted. I felt sick to the stomach and was very unsteady myself but Hilda was made of sterner stuff and quickly regained her composure and gathered all three of us to her to comfort and mourn together.

That's how we stayed until there was a commotion at the door and a group of soldiers entered the hall. Richard and William were not with them, instead they were led by a burly older knight who barked orders at us.

"The Duke is with his lady giving comfort at this time so you must all answer to me. You will not leave the castle, you must not be alone and if you have any information you will pass it directly to me."

He looked slowly around the hall and I could see people visibly shrink under his gaze. He wasn't particularly sympathetic to the upset the gruesome act had caused but it was clear his intent was to find out who had committed the act one way or another. His methods were not going to be as quiet and discreet as those used by Richard or William. With Richard indisposed I was surprised that William was not leading the investigation but then he had been working in the background so far so perhaps that was where he preferred to remain.

The soldiers left the hall and I asked who the knight was.

"Oh, that is Sir Godfrey."

The way Hilda said his name gave the impression she was not partial to him but I dropped the subject when she suggested we all go to her bed chamber so the girls could mourn quietly and we could give comfort and strength to one another.

We spent the day together quietly allowing Avis and Maggie to come to terms with the death of their friend. I was shocked and disgusted by the brutal manner in which she was killed and it took an age before I stopped shaking. We were clustered around Hilda's chair perched on stools, so close it was easy to lend a comforting arm or to hold a hand for support. Hilda encouraged them to talk of Rose and after a while Avis and Maggie reached the point where they could say 'do you remember when…' or, 'Rose was very good at…' It was therapeutic and a soothing balm orchestrated by Hilda who remained composed and such a strength for us all.

Evening had arrived and Maggie rose and went to the brazier and gave it a poke but it was totally out. She sighed and then turned to us and suggested we should eat and she could fetch some hot coals to start the fire again. Hilda would not allow her to go alone so Avis volunteered to accompany her.

"Hilda you were so comforting to the girls," I said as I noticed her slump into her chair on their departure. "Few would allow serving girls the luxury of taking time to grieve as you did. Your kindness and consideration was much appreciated by them."

She smiled weakly and shook her head, she looked tired and only managed to repeat, "Wicked, wicked."

We ate a sparse meal but it was sufficient as none of us had a great appetite. Maggie and Avis tidied the dishes and offered to help us ready ourselves for bed but we declined. I could help Hilda and after promising to stay together for safety they prepared to go.

Heavy footsteps were approaching and then there was hammering on the door. We all started and before Maggie could reach the door to open it someone pounded again.

"Open up!" a male voice shouted gruffly and as Maggie unbarred the door two armed guards marched into the room pushing the door fully open, almost knocking Maggie to the ground.

"What is the meaning of this?" demanded Hilda as she rose from her chair.

"We are here to arrest Mistress Evelyn Cross," said one of the guards none too politely as he and his fellow guard crossed the room and pulled me to my feet from the stool. They were rough and gripped my arms tightly pulling me toward the door.

"Let her go," cried Hilda, "you cannot do this."

"Yes we can," came the reply. "Sir Godfrey's orders."

I was terrified and started to struggle but the grip on my arms tightened so painfully I allowed myself to be dragged along. Trying to look back to Hilda I saw her with her hand covering her mouth and a look of horror on her face.

"Find William," I screamed.

I soon stopped struggling when I realised the enormity of what was happening; my legs shook and buckled as we descended the stairs and I realised we were heading for the dungeon. The guards said nothing but continued to support me although not so brutally now that I had stopped wriggling. We went down one floor from the Great Hall and stood on a landing whilst we waited for a scruffy individual carrying a large bunch of keys to approach from the stairs presumably leading to lower levels.

"Who do we have here then?" he said standing far to close and breathing very unpleasant breath in my face.

"She is a pretty one," he leered, taking another step closer so that our noses almost touched.

I turned my face and grimaced hoping one of the guards would pity me.

"She is to stay on this floor away from the men, Sir Godfrey's orders, and leave her alone, none of your dirty little games."

The gaoler stood back feigning a hurt look and then shuffled over to a heavy wooden door secured by a large lock. He sorted through the bunch of keys finally selecting the one which would unlock the door. He turned and mockingly giving a low bow and chuckled as he said, "Enjoy your chamber, milady."

The guards pushed me over the threshold and the door slammed. I felt panic and fear, the cell was tiny and claustrophobic and I felt hot and clammy. I was breathing faster and my heart was pounding, my stomach twisted in pain and I fell to my knees retching in dry heaves. The sweat was rolling off my face along with tears; I was totally out of control. This continued for what seemed like an hour but in fact was much less. Finally as I gulped in mouthfuls of air my body started to settle and shiver with cold after sweating so much.

I stayed on the ground to recover myself trying to remember my relaxation exercises I had used in the past when anxiety struck. I couldn't concentrate so I began talking to myself, quietly in case I was in earshot of the gaoler or other prisoners. I kept repeating to myself not to be negative and eventually decided to try and find something positive in everything around me. Given my situation it would prove difficult but what else could I do?

Standing, I faced the door, it was sturdy and bolted but the top third had a window cut in it replaced with bars. There was a torch on the wall outside my cell and when it was lit the glow penetrated the cell so that I wasn't totally in the dark.

I turned ninety degrees to the left to see a solid stone wall. I reached out and it was dry to the touch, health wise this was very beneficial, and pushed against it was a long bench. It wasn't very wide but if I was careful I could lay on it preventing me sleeping on the floor.

Once again I turned and faced a solid stone wall but right at the top where it met the ceiling was a grille to the outside. I couldn't reach it but it let in fresh air and I could see if it was day or night.

The final wall offered very little but I saw an old bucket in the corner. I peered in and to my relief it was empty. Bathroom facilities, I assumed. As cells went I suppose it was acceptable, much better than those further underground I thought. The little exercise made me feel calmer and more in control and I decided this was the manner I needed to survive this ordeal. I sat on the bench and looked to the door, my ears straining to catch any sound of someone approaching. Surely someone would come and inform me of my crime or question me. I waited and waited.

*

I awoke to a very narrow shaft of light coming through the window. I ached from balancing on the bench but I had slept a little during the night. I was desperate for a bathroom and grimaced when I realised all I had was the bucket but needs must. I approached it gingerly after listening at the door to make sure no one was about. I had only just finished and returned to the bench when the gaoler appeared and unlocked the door. He was holding a dish and beaker which he unceremoniously slammed on the floor. He was about to say something when I quickly piped up, repeating in my head, *Positivity, positivity.*

"Ah, good morning to you, is this breakfast? I'm starving."

I smiled and tried not to sound sarcastic and it had an effect because he just stood there totally taken aback by my good humour. He opened his mouth to say something but thought better of it so he closed the door, not slamming it, and peered at me through the window. I fetched the food and sat back on the bench. Smiling, I thanked him and gave a little wave which startled him and he left shaking his head.

The food looked most unappetising and didn't smell much better. I think it was oatmeal but it was cold and had formed a grey shivering mass and after three mouthfuls I had to put it to one side. I thought the drink would be water but it was the very weak ale that was usually served in the hall. It filled my stomach. I placed the dishes next to the door and tried to glimpse if anything was happening; all was quiet on my floor but I could hear some banging coming from below. My positive thought for this morning was that I was fortunate to have been placed in this cell. It was a little cold but it was dry and I could tell by the grille that it was a bright day.

Surely I would see someone today. The time dragged by and I found myself pacing back and forth like a caged beast at a zoo. With great resolve I sat down and started rummaging in my purse where I found my little plastic comb, probably not a good idea to have about my person but it offered a few minutes of activity. I removed my veil and the pins from my hair, it still wasn't long enough to do anything constructive with but Maggie and Avis had both shown great skill in tidy creations. I however was sadly lacking in this talent especially having no mirror and my few minutes of activity turned into at least half an hour. Finally smoothing down my veil and shaking the skirts of my dress I was tidy if not as clean as I would like.

Sitting on my bench, inactive, allowed the anxiety to creep in and I started to worry why I was here and feared what would happen to me. William must know I was here, why hadn't he come? My stomach had started to tie itself in knots and my breathing was becoming short and shallow. I needed something to distract myself, so I rummaged in my purse again and found the leather string and some blue strands of thread which I started to braid and knot together. The light wasn't good so I really had to concentrate and strain to see the thin materials. It worked; there were definitely more knots in the string than in my stomach.

I heard movement in the passage, quiet steps but definitely coming my way, even so I still jumped when a form blocked my window.

"Evelyn, are you there?"

I jumped up and took hold of the bars and looked out of the

window hoping to see William but felt a little disappointed when I saw Robin's concerned face.

"Where is William?" I asked and it was Robin's turn to look a little disappointed.

"He was called away to his manor on personal business. He knows nothing of the murder or your arrest."

"When will he return? Surely I'm not suspected of murder."

My voice had come out as a high-pitched squeak and I gulped and breathed deeply to try and bring it under control. William was my only hope of getting out of here and now he wasn't even at the castle.

"I do not know when he will return, that is why he bid me remain to watch over you."

He looked down and hesitated, he obviously thought he had failed at his one task. My heart melted a little for him.

"Neither of us thought anything like this would happen. Why am I here? What have I supposed to have done?"

"Evelyn you have been charged with witchcraft."

"What?" I gasped as I reeled backwards.

"Yes, you are accused of using witchcraft on the Duchess."

It took me a minute to gather my senses. I knew I had taken a risk but Alice had recovered from the headache and was well when I left her. What had changed to bring about my incarceration?

"Is the Duchess well?" I asked nervously.

"She is very well, but since the last murder everyone is nervous and Sir Godfrey means to get results."

"But what has the draught I made have to do with murder?"

Robin shrugged. "I think Sir Godfrey is paying attention to anything that is amiss in the castle hoping something will present a clue to what has been happening. I also think someone may have whispered in his ear!"

"You mean Master Hook?"

"Well, he did lose face a little and a man of his standing may wish to retaliate when he is suffering with wounded pride."

"Surely the Duke doesn't believe him."

"The Duke is concentrating on the Duchess; this child is very important to them both and in the absence of William, Richard just passed the problem to Godfrey."

"But," I spluttered anxiously, "no one has been to see me or question me or even inform me of my crime."

"Perhaps that is a positive thing, Evelyn, if Godfrey has placed you here out of harm's way to deal with you later, it allows more time for William's return. He will stand for you and Richard listens to him, they are great friends."

I smiled weakly. I hoped he was right, I knew he was trying to cheer me. I returned to the door and gripped the bars with both hands.

"I don't like it in here, Robin."

He saw the fear in my eyes and coved my hands with his own and gave them a squeeze.

"I will not desert you, Evelyn, and Lady Hilda will try to come to you, be strong."

He put his hand inside his doublet and produced an apple and large chunk of bread. They were too large to go through the bars so he cut them in half and carefully passed them to me. He made to leave and I grabbed his hand, the solitude of the cell with nothing to occupy myself would drive me crazy. He squeezed it gently and then was gone.

As expected time dragged slowly, eventually I heard movement and from the shuffling and jingling of keys I thought it was the gaoler, even speaking to him would relieve my solitude. Standing, I cleared my throat and summoned my positive, cheerful voice.

"Hello, is that you, gaoler? I wondered if you are not too busy, may I have a drink?"

He didn't answer but shuffled along and then peered into my cell. Smiling, I repeated, "If you are not busy may I have a drink?"

"I am busy."

He turned to leave so I tried to engage him, talk to me, anything.

"Yes, I suppose you are kept busy and having to go up and down, up and down the stairs must be very tiring. I imagine some of the prisoners can be very unpleasant. Does Sir Godfrey come and inspect them every day? Only I wondered if anyone would be coming to explain why I am here."

He turned and looked at me and with a sneer.

"Sir Godfrey comes when he wants to come. Think yourself lucky he hasn't been to see you, witchcraft is a stretching offense."

"Stretching?"

He made as if a noose was around his neck and pulled a grotesque face when he jerked it above his head pretending to hang.

"Of course that's only if you admit to being a witch, if you don't they will toss you in the pond."

He must have seen my smile falter because he chuckled.

"Now if it's murder." He sucked his teeth and shook his head, I knew he was goading me and trying to get a reaction. I refused to rise to the bait.

"Oh I don't think it will come to that. Can you honestly see me chopping up people? I'm not very strong and the sight of blood does make me feel rather weak."

"Hmmmm," was his only reply and he set off down the corridor.

I returned to the bench and tried to lie down. I thought about what he had said and fear started to creep over me. It wouldn't go away; there was no distraction so I started practising my relaxation technique. The next I knew I had woken with a start after falling to the ground. I was confused at first, looking around me, eyes wide, until I remembered where I was but still sweating and breathing rapidly. The nightmare left me shaken, dark shadows digging bodies out of the ground, cutting them up and selling them by the bag full. The dark shadows counted the coins gleefully and then went on to the next grave.

The dream seemed so vivid and it had scarred me. I sat on the bench gripping the edge with both hands, back pressed against the cold stone wall. I was totally alert, nervously straining to hear any noise, fearful of the shadows and what the future would bring. *William, why aren't you here?*

Most dreams are forgotten before even getting out of bed, nightmares take a little longer to fade, but what I had dreamt stayed with me all day, every detail vivid and gruesome. It was with a half-hearted 'good evening' that I greeted the gaoler as he unlocked the door of my cell and placed my meal on the floor. He hesitated, expecting some kind of comment but all I could muster was a brief smile. He left and locked the door and then gazed through the window.

"Being locked up getting to you, is it mistress?"

He didn't say it too unkindly much to my surprise, so I smiled and nodded my head and replied. "Yes, a little." He gave what sounded like a snort but didn't reply with any cruel taunt and shuffled off.

Sometime later I heard footsteps, soft and padding on the flags, and relief flooded through me when I saw Hilda peering through the bars. I ran to her and tried to grasp her hand. She looked concerned but brightened when she saw I was unharmed. Tears started rolling down my cheeks and she crooned softly trying to comfort me.

"Oh my dear Evelyn, I have been so worried for you. I have tried to get an audience with Sir Godfrey but he has no time for me. I know no more than Robin told you this morning. Take heart, once the Duke and Duchess hear of your plight I am sure they will order your release."

I nodded eagerly as she tried to stroke my face but I felt pessimistic. With William absent and the nightmare still hanging over me I felt less than positive.

"Any news of William?"

She shook her head.

"He could return tomorrow or be away a month, there is no telling. Family matters do not run smoothly or to plan."

"What family does he have?"

Hilda hesitated but was then interrupted by the gaoler who made it quite clear she was overstaying the few minutes he had granted her.

"Stay strong, my dear, I will try and come tomorrow."

I feared sleeping thinking the nightmare would return but eventually dozed. Again the dark figures appeared, this time abandoning grave digging in favour of murder. Coins changed hands and then dismembered limbs and organs danced before my eyes. I must have called out in my sleep for when I awoke, once again on the floor, the gaoler was peering into my cell telling me to keep the noise down. When I didn't respond he repeated himself and added that he could come in and hold my hand! His expression was not one of concern so I assured him I was quite well and for him not to worry.

After he left I hauled myself up onto the bench, bathed in sweat and breathing rapidly. Obviously recent events were colouring my dreams which were so realistic and unnerving. There was no way I wanted to go back to sleep so having finally calmed myself I set about reviewing my dreams logically. Someone had once told me that dreams were like a computer rebooting and throwing out lots of facts. Whether that be true or not perhaps my dreams were my brain trying to make sense of the murders.

I sat until dawn mulling over the pictures in my mind's eye. Was someone paying for these murders to take place? That seemed so unlikely in this day and age, people were too poor to hire a hit man and for what reason? The victims were some of the lowliest in the village. I could think of no common denominator connecting the victims. And who were these shadow figures committing these awful crimes? They were like historical versions of Burke and Hare! I sat bolt upright.

"Oh my god!"

CHAPTER SEVEN

My cell may be small but I had plenty of exercise pacing back and forth this morning. Since realising I might have stumbled onto a motive for the murders, I was restless and impatient for a visitor. I hoped Hilda would visit and get a message to the Duke; he would surely listen to her if only out of respect for her service to his mother. Robin could inform William if he had returned, either way hopefully it would result in another line of enquiry. I realised I would need to take care who I shared my theory with for in my current situation it might be viewed as the ravings of a mad woman.

Breakfast arrived; at least this morning the porridge moved around the plate, but I could only stomach two mouthfuls. I managed to greet the gaoler cheerfully endeavouring to conceal my agitation.

"This food doesn't improve with time does it?" I ventured as I lifted a spoonful and allowed it to slide back on to the plate with a plop. "What did you have? Something tasty I am sure?"

"Same as you, mistress."

"Really?" I was very surprised. "How on earth do you survive on this mush?"

The gaoler snorted. "It's regular meals, more than some get."

I had forgotten how poor some of the locals were and regular meals were a luxury but how they could eat this on a regular basis surprised me.

By the time Robin's face appeared at the window I was practically hopping from foot to foot with impatience. It must be late morning by now and I had got to the point of doubting his appearance.

"Where have you been? What has taken you so long?" I blurted out, dispensing with any pleasantries.

"Evelyn I have to sneak in here past the gaoler and I do have other duties to perform."

"Bribe him with food."

"Pardon?"

"Bribe him with food."

"…With food?" He looked confused.

"Yes. The poor wretch has the same slop that is served to me so he would appreciate a decent meal. Anyway, that's not important right now; I think I have a motive for the murders."

Robin went to speak but I interrupted again.

"We may not have much time, come closer."

He came close to the door and put his ear to the bars so that I could speak softly, preventing anyone from hearing; no one was about but I didn't want to risk it. I had been so eager to pass on my theory that I hadn't given any thought to how or what I should say, after all, the event I was referring to hadn't happened yet. I took a deep breath and just hoped it sounded plausible.

"In Scotland there was a physician who wanted to further his knowledge of the human body. He wanted to see how the body was constructed and how it worked in detail so that he was more able to treat his patients. He was allowed to use the bodies of dead prisoners and suicide victims but his thirst for knowledge meant he needed more bodies. To solve this problem he employed two men who would keep watch at the graveyard and when a new body was laid to rest they would return at night and dig it up."

Robin listened in disbelief but kept quiet so that I could continue.

"Their names were Burke and Hare and they were quite

disreputable characters. Soon people became suspicious of the grave robbing and would guard the graves, thus depriving them of quite a good income for the physician paid them for the bodies. The bodies needed to be fresh so not wanting to lose their income they turned to murder. They killed some sixteen people before they were caught."

I stopped for breath and looked at Robin who was staring at me wide eyed. He didn't speak right away and when he did whispered hoarsely.

"Do you think this is what is happening here at Wyvern?"

"I don't know but there are so many similarities. The first three bodies were dug up, the third one not being desecrated because it was already decomposing. All the bodies were cut open and various organs removed. You have to admit it is a possibility."

Robin shrugged. What I had said had shocked him, not the blood and gore because he had fought in battles, but the way the victims had been used like joints of meat.

"You must pass on my theory, Robin; we have to stop these murders somehow."

He nodded slowly. "Yes but who to tell? Duke Richard hasn't been seen since the last murder and William has not yet returned. I do not know how receptive Sir Godfrey would be to your theory."

I saw his dilemma. "I don't think it wise to tell him. Do you think Hilda could gain access to Richard through Alice?"

Robin gave a heavy sigh. "Leave it to me, Evelyn, I will try my best."

He turned to leave and then returned feeling in his doublet for the food he had secreted away for me. As he passed the food through the bars I touched his hand and smiled at him. I trusted him and knew he would do all in his power.

The next person I saw was the gaoler who brought my evening meal. I had worried all afternoon about what the reaction would be regarding my theory or if it had even been passed on. I was weary but roused myself and greeted the gaoler cheerfully. He paused and nodded in acknowledgement before he left, his resting face far less ferocious than usual. Could he be softening towards me? Wishful thinking perhaps?

I pushed my food around my plate, it was totally unappetising but I knew I had to eat to keep up my strength. I heard the jangle of keys and thought the gaoler was returning sooner than usual to retrieve my dishes. He unlocked the door and stood aside for two cloaked figures who entered and paused until he left and relocked the door. As their hoods were removed I saw Hilda and Avis beaming at me. I was so relieved and pleased to see them both that I embraced them and could feel tears forming in my eyes. Human contact at last, it was wonderful and I didn't want to let go. Hilda too had moist eyes but she disentangled herself and pulled me down on the bench.

"Now come along, Evelyn, we do not have much time, we have a plan for your escape."

"What?" I almost shrieked and Hilda put her figure to her lips.

"We must hurry." Avis removed an old blanket from under her cloak and shook it out, while Hilda removed her cloak and gestured that I stand so she could place it around my shoulders.

"Milady I wish you would let me stay, this is no place for you to spend the night, and anyway I am closer to the Mistress' height."

I stood listening with a look of horror on my face.

"Do you mean to change places with me, Hilda? I won't let you, you will be terribly uncomfortable and liable to get into trouble and be punished."

She shushed me and carried on arranging the cloak. I tried to protest once again but Hilda held up her hand to silence me. She looked stern and determined and I could see arguing with her was pointless.

"Now listen carefully to the plan, all you need to do is keep your mouth firmly shut. I will lie on the bench and Avis will cover me with the blanket; the lighting is poor so the gaoler will see a body sleeping and hopefully not realise it is not you. You wear my cloak and pull the hood well over your face. You may need to stoop a little as I am much shorter in stature than you but Avis will position herself between you and the gaoler. Robin is chatting to the gaoler while he eats a very good supper we supplied to bribe him for this short visit. Robin too will shield you from view. The gaoler will see one prisoner asleep in the cell and count three visitors leaving."

Hilda was a little breathless after divulging the plan but I think that was due to nerves regardless of how confident she appeared. I did as she bade even though my stomach was knotted with fear. Avis pushed me to the darkest corner of the cell and then helped Hilda take her position on the bench.

"Oh Hilda, what happens when you are discovered? I can't allow you to take that risk."

"It is decided, Evelyn. Hopefully Robin will have hidden you away by the time of my discovery and then I will rely on my relationship with the Duke and Duchess to see me safe. We must pray for William's speedy return."

The familiar jangle of keys announced the gaoler's approach. Hilda faced the wall and Avis pulled the blanket up to her chin and then carefully balanced on the edge of the bench as if comforting her, and as the door was unlocked and pushed open Avis started as if to soothe her.

"Mistress don't fret, this will all be in the past soon. Sleep now and you will feel refreshed in the morning, especially with this blanket to keep you warm. We will visit again if we may and Lady Hilda will continue to partition for your release."

With that she tucked the blanket around Hilda and stood to leave. I followed with shaky steps and as we emerged from the cell Avis and Robin stood close to the gaoler obstructing his view. I held a cloth that Avis had quickly pushed into my hand, up to my face as if wiping away tears. Robin kept up a constant chatter with the gaoler who seemed much pleased with his tasty dinner and before I realised, we were climbing the steps from the dungeon and taking a back passage out of the Great Hall.

We crossed the courtyard heading for the main gate and as we did so several other serving girls joined the group. They were chattering but I stayed silent and tried to stay in the middle of the group. I had no idea how we were meant to leave the castle or where we were bound but I had faith in Hilda and Robin and meekly followed where I was being led.

At the gate we were challenged by the two sentries on duty. Robin calmly stepped forward and announced it was his turn to escort the servants back to the village. This duty had been instigated since the last murder in an attempt to keep the servants who didn't live on the premises safe after their day's work. The guards stood their ground, peering at us in the failing light. It felt as if it was taking longer than necessary and I could feel myself shake.

"Come on, you men, you are just envious of my task of taking so many lovely ladies home of an evening."

He gave a mischievous smile and then winked; a couple of the girls started to giggle and the guards stepped aside to let us pass. As we walked down the hill towards the village a few comments followed but they weren't repeatable and then the guards laughed.

We walked casually through the village and as we did so the girls peeled off to their appropriate cottages. Avis was the last to go but I was worried as I knew she lived in the castle.

"Don't worry, mistress. I will stay with one of the girls until the morning. I will be safe as I hope you will."

I gave her a hug and thanked her, she had taken a great risk helping with this escape and I was touched by her willingness and bravery in doing so.

Robin and I ducked behind a barn on the edge of the village.

"We must wait here until it is completely dark and the guards have changed watch."

We stood by the wall and then Robin bent and patted the grass to make sure it was dry.

"Let's make ourselves comfortable while we wait."

I was still overcome by what had transpired and sat quietly hugging my knees. Robin sat beside me plucking at the grass and releasing it to the slight breeze.

"Whose idea was this, Robin?"

He grimaced and then said, "Well it was sort of a joint effort really. I told Lady Hilda everything you had told me. She was fearful for your safety if the accusation was made and said we must set you free. She wasn't prepared to risk Sir Godfrey dealing with the situation so," he raised his shoulders and shrugged, "here we are."

"I admit Sir Godfrey is somewhat gung ho but he isn't a bad man, is he? And surely Richard would have the final say in the matter?"

"I'm really not sure. Lady Hilda is usually very wise in her judgement but there is history between the two of them which may cloud it on this occasion."

"History, what sort of history?" I asked quite intrigued.

"When Lady Hilda's husband died Sir Godfrey wanted to take her as his wife. He asked many times and every time she refused him. He didn't take it well."

Robin peered around the side of the shed; the light was fading fast but the guards hadn't changed watch yet. He sat close and the warmth of his body was comforting for my stomach was knotted tightly in fear.

"Why would you all do this for me? You have only known me for a short time yet you are willing to risk so much."

He looked bemused and then said quite simply, "We like you, you are our friend."

I was emotional and could feel my throat close and tears spring to my eyes so I tried to look busy fishing around in my purse. I brushed away the tears and then found what I was looking for and held it up.

"You are my friend too; all of you are, so here is your early birthday present."

He looked surprised and pleased but then frowned.

"Thank you ermm… what is it?"

I laughed. "It is a friendship bracelet. I made it for you and you tie it on your wrist and wear it for as long as we are friends."

He seemed to like that idea and proffered his wrist so that I could tie it on.

"Which hand do you fight with?" I asked.

"Both of them."

"Which do you eat with?"

"Both of them."

I sighed and rolled my eyes. "Stop teasing, which hand do you write with?"

He held up his right hand, so I pushed it down and tied the bracelet to his left wrist.

"I have put it on this wrist so that it doesn't get entangled with anything," I explained. "I think it will be fine, it's a close fit."

He held up his wrist and peered at it but it was dark by now and he couldn't really see it very well, so I suggested he examine it in the morning. Peering around the corner of the shed he was satisfied it was time to make a move.

He pulled me to my feet and I made myself ready.

"Where are we going?" I asked.

"To the Priory."

I recoiled. "You cannot be serious; I don't want to go back there, it was hard enough to get away the first time."

"It is the safest place."

I stood rooted to the spot so he tried to give me a gentle pull.

"Evelyn, the monks took great care of you before and have agreed to give you sanctuary until William returns and attempts to sort out this problem. Please Evelyn, think about it, you are near to us and with people you already know and cannot be removed from the Priory without the Prior's permission."

He did make sense but I had a foreboding about the place, however I begrudgingly agreed. With that he took my hand and quietly started to lead me through the wooded area. I couldn't make out the way but he had no problem and pretty soon we approached the Priory from the rear. We skirted an enclosing wall until we stopped at a small side gate which had been left open for us. Pushing our way through we were met by Brother Elric who locked the gate after us and beckoned us to follow him. We kept away from areas where the other monks gathered and eventually entered the priory by a side door.

I was pleased to see Elric who was wearing his usual welcoming smile but I froze as Brother Anselm came around the corner. His hands were in his sleeves and his expression was serious, but as he reached us he bowed and gave us a cordial greeting.

"Thank you for helping us, Brother Anselm," said Robin.

"She will be safe with us, have no fear."

He held out his arm gesturing that I follow him but Robin remained where he stood.

"Go ahead," Robin encouraged. "I will try and bring news to you if there are any developments."

I didn't want to go, I would rather be with Hilda and Robin where I felt safe but they had done so much for me. I knew I must not let them down. I nodded eventually and after a nervous smile I turned and followed Brother Anselm down the corridor.

The room I occupied was not the one I had before but it was identical in appearance. Brother Anselm told me I must keep my presence secret and not be seen by the other monks. He did say I could have access to the chapel at certain times and there was also a little garden hidden away out of sight which would be at my disposal. My meals would be brought to my room. With that he bid me goodnight and left.

Sitting on the bed I felt a little lost and very anxious. I wondered if I had exchanged one prison for another and on impulse I went to the door and lifted the latch. I breathed a sigh of relief for it was not locked as it had been before. I worried for Hilda left in my cell, not the most comfortable place for a lady such as her to stay and then I worried she had been discovered. What would happen to her or any of the others when the escape was discovered? I don't know if my surroundings were the influence but I prayed fervently that my friends remained safe.

CHAPTER EIGHT

Days turned into weeks as I waited for news from Wyvern. At first I was in a constant state of anxiety, but now I approached each day with the thought that no news was good news. The days had seemed so long that I asked if I was permitted to help with the chores to pass the time. It was difficult as I needed to keep my presence from the Brothers and they were everywhere. The Prior was aware that I dwelt at the Priory; after all he had needed to give his permission for my stay. Brothers Anselm and Elric were the only brothers who officially knew but I was sure several other brothers did also having stumbled upon me by accident. They never acknowledged me and discreetly turned their heads as if to say, 'if I don't see you, you are not here'.

Any sewing was no longer sent to the castle but given to me instead. I helped in the infirmary drying herbs and any other little job I could do. Brother Elric followed me like a little puppy and showed me what was needed; even Brother Anselm softened a little and gave me instruction. I did feel secure but I still worried about my friends at the castle.

It had been a warm day and in the late afternoon I retreated to the little garden which had become a familiar haunt. It was hardly a garden, just a bench against the wall of one of the outbuildings facing the perimeter wall. Meadow flowers grew against the wall and I had weeded to give them ample growing space and watered them frequently now that the dry summer weather had arrived.

As I relaxed I heard rustling on the other side of the wall, it was nothing out of the ordinary as various animals often investigated the undergrowth; it was their home after all. The rustling continued and I noticed the leaves on the tree nearest the wall started to quiver and then shake vigorously. With no warning a dark figure sprang from the lower branch skimming the wall and with great agility landed on my side. I was startled and sprang up, backing against the wall, covering my mouth with my hand to smother a gasp. Had I been discovered and someone was here to whisk me away to the castle or even worse, was this the murderer?

The stranger recovered from his leap and lifted his head to look at me.

"William!!!" His name came out as a hoarse squeak. I was rooted to the spot, words failed me. He was tanned from the sun but there was a pallor to his skin and dark smudges beneath his eyes. He looked very weary but he managed to smile as he said my name in greeting.

"When did you return? How did you know I was here? Are the others safe?"

Regaining my power of speech the questions rolled out of my mouth and he put up his hand to quiet me and then walked over to the bench and bade me sit. We occupied opposite ends of the bench, turned slightly to face one another, our knees almost touching. I had prayed for his return but now he was here I felt strangely shy and embarrassed about things that had occurred in his absence.

"Robin told me you were here," he began but immediately I interrupted.

"Is he safe?"

"Robin was imprisoned the day after your escape for the part he played in it. The Lady Hilda and Avis were also arrested but they have been locked in her bed chamber and Maggie sees to their needs."

"How long has it been? I have lost track of time being here."

"It has been three weeks."

I stood and started to pace back and forth. I felt wretched for their incarceration and clutched for an idea, any idea to set them free.

"I will go back, turn myself in so that the Duke will release them."

"Evelyn, please sit and calm yourself, it is essential we talk through the events so that I understand completely what has happened. Even with your return they would remain under arrest, the deed is done. Perhaps the only thing we can do is clear your name and find the murderer."

Reluctantly I sat down and tried to calm myself. Regardless of how I felt William seemed to be the one needing rest and reassurance.

"William you look so weary and troubled," I began. I wanted to know what ailed him but knew I should not pry. I hoped he would tell me but if he didn't then I had to wait until he thought it appropriate to.

"The journey back took longer than I expected, I did not arrive till well past midnight only to find Robin in the dungeon and you missing."

I was sorry to have been the cause of this but I think there was more to his appearance than that. William was renowned for his calmness and ability to take most things in his stride. I thought perhaps his visit home was more likely to have been at the root of his troubled appearance.

As if to stop my thoughts and any further questioning on my part William looked at me quite earnestly and said, "Now Evelyn you must tell me of all events since my absence, Robin had little chance to explain anything as the gaoler came almost immediately and banished me. Since your escape the security has improved somewhat so you must tell me all and do not omit any detail."

I took a deep breath and then with a calmer steady voice I began to explain my murder theory but William shook his head.

"Evelyn you must begin at the beginning, you have been charged with witchcraft, have you not?"

I was frustrated, my twenty-first-century brain thought the whole charge idiotic, but my twelfth-century being knew that the allegation was taken very seriously and if found guilty I would be executed. I recounted the incident as accurately as I could emphasising that I had consumed the exact same medication before administrating it to Alice so that she would be confident I was not trying to do her harm. Her headache disappeared and nothing more would have been said if Master Hook had not fetched the Duke.

William listened intently, questioning me about the medicine. Here I stumbled at first but eventually decided to tell him that I brought it with me from home where someone had made it for me because I suffer from headaches on occasion. This way I could plead ignorance as to its content and he seemed satisfied with my explanation. He nodded his head thoughtfully and requested I give an account of the murder theory. Once again I kept my story as close as I could to the Burke and Hare episode in Edinburgh, well, as much as I could remember, trying to emphasise the similarities between those events and the ones at Wyvern.

He sat motionless for a time when I had finished recounting my tale, staring into space, his eyes moving rapidly as if replaying in pictures what I had said. Eventually he looked at me with a spark of interest in his eye.

"This is definitely something to investigate," he said.

"You must tell Richard and Sir Godfrey before there is another murder; there is no time to waste."

I was quite excited now but was crushed when a look of horror came to William's face and he shook his head, saying, "This we cannot do."

"What! William… you must, why not?"

He could see I was upset so leant forward and gently laid his hand on mine.

"My dear Evelyn do you not see? Charges of witchcraft have been levelled at you, more than likely by the Duchess' physician who feels you have infringed upon his authority. Now you suggest the murders have been committed by someone trying to gain medical knowledge of the human body, macabre as it seems a physician perhaps?"

It dawned on me what he was saying.

"There is only one physician at the castle so Master Hook would automatically come under suspicion. Given the situation it might be seen as a vendetta on your part to try and discredit him, at best you simply would not be believed."

I sat motionless on the bench; I knew William had a valid point but now my hopes of this awful situation ending were crushed. I was so engrossed in my own thoughts that I did not notice Brother Anselm appear from around the corner until he stood before us. He gave a slight bow and spoke directly to William.

"Sir William, I was not aware of your return or this visit to the Priory."

"Brother Anselm," said William, rising to his feet and returning the polite pleasantries, "I did not wish to draw attention to my visit and entered the Priory as discreetly as I could."

He looked at the wall and Anselm followed his gaze and the corner of his mouth twitched slightly.

"Just so," he replied.

William continued, explaining that he felt obligated to ascertain my safety and understand what exactly had taken place. He thanked him and then said that he needed to return to the castle before his absence was noted.

Anselm nodded in understanding and was quick to reassure him.

"Fear not, Sir William, we shall guard Mistress Evelyn well. May I suggest you leave by a little less physical method?"

He motioned to the wall in the distance where the little gate Robin had used to bring me here was situated. William nodded in agreement and I stood to accompany them. Anselm walked ahead and William strolled by my side.

"Be brave and careful, Evelyn, I promise I will do all I can."

He smiled gently and I melted. I hoped he was right and really didn't want him to leave but he left me on the path and walked to the little gate where Anselm was unbarring the exit. They spoke softly and I could not hear what was being said but at one point William shook his head and then bowed it, looking to the ground. Anselm raised his hand and I thought he was praying because he made the sign of the cross over William, who then turned, smiled and was gone. My heart was heavy at his departure and I walked in silence back to my little cell, next to Anselm who was silent and appeared to be in deep thought. At my door he bade me farewell and said that Elric would bring me some supper shortly.

I had been very excited at William's long awaited return and had enjoyed his short visit. My pulse had raced and the smile refused to leave my face. Naively I had assumed he would make everything right, until he had pointed out the revelation of my theory was not that simple and my immediate return to the castle was not possible.

Alone I sat on my bed quite forlorn and anxious. Things had taken a downward turn since my arrival at Wyvern and I saw no improvement in the near future. I doubted I would get much sleep tonight and I was correct for by morning I had slept little and what I had was fitful. I did not feel at all refreshed or any calmer and was thankful that some mending had been left by my door so that today I could work quietly in my room.

I found it hard to concentrate on my work and my stitches were far from even, causing me to unpick them several times. With no distractions my imagination went into overdrive and the anxiety for the safety of my friends and indeed me reached fever pitch. My appetite was poor and I pushed my food around the plate. I began pacing in my room trying to control my fears but to no avail, sleep would not be my companion tonight. Time passed and eventually there was no light coming though my little window, it must be well into the night. I wasn't tired but I lay on top of my bed cover and tried to quieten my mind.

Someone was calling my name. I must have dozed and was dreaming, but then I heard it again and this time someone was shaking my shoulder.

"Mistress Evelyn, wake."

It was Brother Anselm who stopped shaking me when he saw I was beginning to wake. His voice was little more than a whisper but there was urgency in his tone.

"Come, Mistress Evelyn you must rouse yourself, come quickly, soldiers are coming from the castle. Make haste, you must hide."

I slipped off the bed quite shaken, scrambling to find my shoes.

"Leave nothing behind," he ordered as he retrieved my cloak from a hook, "there must be no sign you have been here."

I stumbled around dizzy from standing up too quickly. I had fallen asleep in my clothes and had no other belongings so I nodded to him and he peered out of the door and then beckoned me to follow him. He was surprisingly fleet of foot when he needed to be and appeared to fly down the corridor with me trying my best to keep up. It was dark but he was familiar with the way and I was too confused to notice where we were actually going. In the distance a torch burned in a sconce and we headed for it. I was totally disorientated so it was encouraging to see a glimmer of light beckoning us.

Anselm removed the torch and held it high to illuminate our way. I was breathless through exertion and fear so he hesitated a moment so that I could catch my breath. He moved aside to expose a small archway with steps going downward.

"Take care, mistress, the steps are very steep."

He turned to lead the way and I grasped his hood to steady myself. We descended to a corridor, the only lighting being our torch. My heart was pounding and I strained for noise that someone may be following. We passed two doors and then stopped right at the end in front of a small locked door. Anselm placed the torch in a sconce and fumbled with a bunch of keys until he found the right one. The door creaked open and he ushered me inside. It could hardly be called a room it was so tiny, it was more of an entrance hall leading to a locked door no more than six feet away. By the door was a bench which he gestured to. I sat and he wrapped the cloak around me for warmth.

"Wait here and make no sound. I will return as soon as the soldiers have gone."

I dumbly nodded my head.

"You will leave the torch won't you?"

He shook his head. "I cannot, the glow from it will show beneath the door."

He departed, closing and then locking the door. Any glimmer of light disappeared as he walked away and I was left in total darkness. I could feel my lower lip begin to quiver as I shrank into my cloak. The darkness was overpowering with no sound so I closed my eyes in fear, all I could hear was my blood thundering in my temples and ragged breaths escaping my throat. I stayed like that for some considerable time, my breathing not returning to normal but definitely improving so I slowly opened my eyes, peeping through my lashes at first and then fully when they had become accustomed to the darkness. I could vaguely make out shapes; I was in what was little more than a cupboard much smaller than my first impression. If I reached out my hand I could almost touch the opposite wall. To my right was the door I had entered by, to my left was the door which was locked and apart from me and the bench nothing else. It was quite cool; I was sure I must be underground so assumed this was the storage area. There was a faint smell, perhaps something had spoiled and gone off. I sank further into the cloak and prayed I would not be here too long.

My prayer was not answered and the night dragged on, my fear turning to impatience. I rattled the door to make sure it was locked, it was. I tried the other door, also locked. I slumped onto the bench once more, it was getting a little stuffy and for a moment I thought I might suffocate but putting my hand to the bottom of the door I could feel a slight draught seeping through the crack.

Did it really take this long for the Priory to be searched? Why on earth would the soldiers come in the middle of the night? Perhaps William's visit had been discovered and he had been questioned and eventually my whereabouts discovered, but still, it must be morning by now.

Eventually there was a noise on the other side of the door. I held my breath in anticipation as there was a jangle of keys and then the door opened slowly. Brother Anselm stood in the doorway and I exhaled loudly in relief. I stood and made to leave the room but he held up his hand to prevent me.

"Wait, mistress, it is still unsafe, you must remain where you are for a little longer."

"What?" I screeched and Anselm put his finger to his lips and looked around furtively.

"Some of the soldiers are still here. The master at arms was suspicious at not finding you so posted a guard by the gates when he left. You must remain here until they leave to ensure your safety."

I made to protest but Anselm ushered me back to my bench.

"It is for your safety. Patience, my dear," he tried to soothe me but I wasn't happy.

"Here, I have brought you something to eat."

"I'm not hungry." I knew I was sulking but being restrained in the tiny room was more than I could bear, it was even smaller than my prison cell had been.

"Just a little longer, please. Here, at least take this drink, I have put honey in it to keep up your strength."

He placed the beaker in my hand and smiled encouragingly.

"Perhaps you will eat the food later but drink up, you must stay strong."

I begrudgingly took a sip and it did taste very nice so I took another mouthful which seemed to please him. He slowly closed the door and I heard him turn the key. There was little I could do so I drained the beaker of its contents which were warm and sweet.

I suddenly felt incredibly tired, so much so that I had difficulty keeping my eyes open. My head nodded forward until my chin rested on my chest and the last thing I heard was the beaker clattering onto the flagstones.

CHAPTER NINE

The darkness was palpable. I lay in total darkness, cramped in a confined space. I tested the limits of the space by trying to move my feet, which I could not and moving my arms away from my body, I could not. I felt the panic rising and tried to lift my arms to reach in front of me. I hit my knuckles on something hard. I gasped in terror, I was in a box. I wriggled my arms with great difficulty until they rested on the lid. I pushed but nothing happened. The terror welled up and I started to scream and scratch at the lid. I sobbed and soon I had difficulty breathing. I tried to gulp in the air knowing that pretty soon there would be no air left to breathe.

I was hysterical and eventually my hands collapsed on my chest and I gasped, exhausted. Now my screams had abated I thought I heard a scratching on the outside of my prison. Fearing rats I hesitated, but even in my confused state I decided rats were better than suffocation and proceeded to scream afresh.

Suddenly the lid slid sideways and a head peered over the side. It was dark but having been in total darkness my eyes adjusted quickly and I saw a rather grubby face with dark eyes and hair staring at me. His stubbly chin rested on a dirty frayed shirt collar around which was tied an equally soiled stock, the ends of which were tucked into a well-worn jacket. I'm not sure which of us was the more surprised. He pushed a battered hat back on his head and scratched his scalp.

"This is a braw fresh specimen," he exclaimed in a very heavy accent.

At this a second head popped over the side and gazed at me. He was similarly dressed and grubby but his features were pinched with a rather long nose. Neither of them looked like reputable characters, but they were my means of escape so I held up my arms for assistance.

"Och aye, she is a bonny lassie," head number two said with an evil grin. "Mibbie she wull be worth mair than th' usual £7. 10 shillings."

Head number one shrugged his shoulders and said, "Hulp me hurl her oot."

They grasped my wrists and I felt myself being lifted out of a coffin. The relief of being free was overwhelming but equally I was very wary of the pair. I saw I was in a graveyard and instinctively I yanked my wrists trying to free myself.

"Na, na, wull ye stoap struggling," said the first as he took a firmer painful grip of my wrist.

"Shuid we kill her?" asked the second as he twisted my other wrist behind my back and then produced a cudgel from his belt. I screamed in pain.

"Na, dinnae smash her skull, th' doctor wull mibbie wantae uise th' heid. Haun me th' sack we wull uise that."

I renewed my struggle to no avail.

"Och she is a wild yin, mibbie gie her a wee tap."

With that I felt the sack pulled over my head and wrapped tightly around my face.

*

I was terribly cold and my teeth chattered. I was on the windswept battlements of Wyvern gazing down at the tiny figures milling around beneath me. I clutched my clothes around me and pulled my hair out of my eyes. I saw a group of men on the practice field and tried to see a familiar face who might come to my assistance. There were others on the walkway that seemed oblivious of my presence; I hopped out of the way several times fearing someone would collide with me.

I saw a group approaching and after being momentarily surprised, realised it was Tom and Dylan from the craft course, with little Fiona tagging along behind them. I rushed forward to greet them but they looked straight through me and carried on. Running past them I turned and positioned myself directly in their path, there was no way they could ignore me now. They continued to chat amongst themselves and politely sidestepped to avoid me. I spun around and called out but they continued their walk, Tom indicating points of interest and probably giving a knowledgeable account of each. The other two were listening intently and totally unaware of my existence. More people were coming along the walkway so I stepped to the side to allow them past. I gazed over the parapet and saw the village below which was hustle and bustle and the traffic looking like little matchbox toys. How could this be? On the other side of the wall I had seen the soldiers in combat on the practice field.

Totally confused and more than a little anxious I put my head in my hands and rested my elbows on the rampart. It was then that I felt a hearty push in the middle of my back which was powerful enough to toss me over the wall. I screamed and clutched at the air, the fall being more horrific as I seemed to be descending in slow motion. Far from giving me hope that I might survive the fall it amplified my fears as I watched the once empty moat slowly fill with water. The closer I came to the bottom of the wall the higher the water level rose to meet me. Eventually I was engulfed in the cold black water.

I found myself sitting across the table from Helen in our favourite little tea shop. She was moving the crockery around to make space for our cream tea. She was chatting away happily and was giving the teapot a stir.

"Shall I be mother?" she asked, not really waiting for my reply.

I nodded dumbly, what on earth was happening? Had I transported back to my own time? If I had it was strangely different from my first trip, no headache, dizziness or sickness. I was hesitant to speak, afraid of giving myself away and having to explain my absence. I looked around me, everything was as normal, people chatting over a cup of tea or coffee and through the window I saw shoppers and traffic going about their business. Relaxing slightly I turned to take the cup and saucer which Helen was passing to me and right before my eyes she morphed into Hilda. I gaped stupidly but automatically raised my hand to accept the tea.

"There my dear," she smiled sweetly, "a nice cuppa will do you the power of good."

Not exactly Hilda's phraseology, something was amiss here. No one seemed to notice a twelfth-century lady in a long gown with a full wimple and veil sitting with me. Helen and Hilda were my dearest friends but from different timelines; everything was mixed up. I would go to either of them if I was in trouble or had a problem. Perhaps this was symbolic; if I hadn't time hopped perhaps I was dreaming.

Hilda had taken out her sewing and was humming softly as she worked; it was comforting but I knew this was not possible. I leaned forward over the table to speak but something passing the window caught my eye which stopped me in my tracks. Sir William was walking in full armour down the street; he paused to allow a car to pass and then crossed to the other side. I scrambled out of my chair and out of the tea shop. I tried to hail him but my throat closed and not a sound came out. I attempted to clear my throat but still I was totally mute. There was nothing for it, I must chase him before he got away. I swayed forward and almost landed on my nose. My legs were like lead, it was impossible to move. Tears started to stream down my face, my legs felt as if they were embedded in the concrete pavement. Perhaps I could crawl. I was at the point of trying anything but as hard as I tried I was unable to move forward and all the time William was getting further away.

I felt desolate and cried silent tears. This was all wrong. I had no hope, I must be dreaming and if I was I needed to wake and wake up pretty fast.

Regaining consciousness was far more of an effort this time. My lashes were stuck together, my throat parched and my mouth felt as if I had been sucking cotton wool. My head was pounding and I tried to keep it still as the slightest movement caused the pounding to increase. I lay still listening, hoping for some clue as to my whereabouts. As far as I could discover I was laying on something hard totally restricted by straps at my wrists and ankles. The ever present darkness was pressing in on me. I was cold and I kept getting a whiff of that unpleasant smell which kept me company in the tiny antechamber Brother Anselm had locked me in. This situation seemed very real unlike my previous experiences which unfolded quite quickly. Closing my eyes, I waited. I couldn't say the room was spinning because I couldn't see the room, but I felt very unsteady and I feared I had been drugged.

I was frozen and my limbs were stiff and becoming numb due to the restraints. I was miserable, this was no dream. I had no idea how long I had laid on the incredibly hard surface before I heard a muffled noise on the other side of the door. I held my breath hoping for rescue rather than the alternative. Slowly the door creaked open and the glow of a torch entered the room followed by a robed figure. It was Brother Anselm and my breath came out in a relieved sob.

"Oh Brother Anselm, thank God, come and untie these ropes and free me."

He seemed unfazed to see me and calmly turned and placed the torch in a sconce by the door.

"No, no my dear, we have much work to do."

"Work, what sort of work? You knew I was here?"

He had started to walk toward me but changed his mind and went back for the torch. Crossing the room he lit a second torch and then returned the first to its position by the door. The extra light illuminated my surroundings a little better and even though my head still hurt I slowly turned my neck to get a better view.

The room was arranged rather like a lab with me positioned in the middle tied to a large metal table. To one side was a bench running along the wall overloaded with parchments and a large bound book. There were candles and writing ink and a little stool pushed under the bench, presumably this was where he did his written work. I still had no comprehension what his work was or how he thought I could help. He saw me frowning and with a flourish of his arm he pointed to the shelf above the bench which was filled with large glass jars.

"My work," he proclaimed proudly.

I squinted trying to focus on the contents and then realising what I was looking at began to retch. I broke out in a sickening cold sweat and stared at him in horror. Each jar contained a piece of human anatomy. Some of the fluid was murky and I had difficulty in identifying the contents but I clearly saw a heart in one and the jar nearest to me contained a tiny foetus. I closed my eyes and gulped down my distaste at what I saw. The unpleasant smell I had noticed was obviously the odour of blood and decaying flesh. Brother Anselm was the murderer!

He walked the length of the room gazing at each jar in turn and when he reached me he turned and his face shone with satisfaction and pride. I tried to regain my self-control; my bowels had clenched and I was relieved I had consumed almost nothing for however long it had been since he first came to my room proclaiming impending danger, or my discomfort would have been compounded. My stomach cramps caused me to grit my teeth making speech almost impossible but I managed to gasp haltingly, "I will be missed, Sir William will come looking for me, he knows I am here and so does Robin."

Brother Anselm was not at all concerned by my remark; in fact he raised his hands and laughed as if enjoying a joke. I was surprised and more than a little confused as to how he would explain my disappearance. He looked down at me and his expression was vicious.

"Sir William has already visited."

"Where is he? Did he not search for me?"

Anselm gave a mirthless chuckle. "I told him you had run away and he left." He turned as if the conversation was over, which angered me.

"He knows I would never run away, regardless of the situation, nothing you said could have made him believe that."

He turned to look at me once more and shook his shoulders a little, almost as a sign of triumph.

"Oh he believed me, I told him that when you found out he had a wife and had been away visiting her these past weeks you were heartbroken and gathered your belongings in the night and ran away."

"A wife?" I gasped.

Anselm looked into my eyes with a condescending smirk and continued. "Oh did he not tell you he was married?" he chuckled. "He seems to have overlooked that fact."

I was speechless and crushed by this revelation and lay limply on the table, all my strength having drained away. It was then that a soft voice called out Anselm's name. He spun to face the door and before I could gather my wits and call out, his hand clamped over my mouth and he grabbed a knife from the long bench. He waved it in my face and his intention was clear, one sound from me and he would slit my throat.

"Brother Anselm," the voice called again louder with a rap on the door, "it is Brother Benedict."

Anselm composed himself and calmly called back.

"What is it, Brother Benedict? I am rather busy right now."

"I am sorry to interrupt you but the Prior wishes to see you. He is unwell and wishes for you to make him a tincture."

Compressing his lips in annoyance at being interrupted he sighed heavily.

"Perhaps Brother Elric could be of assistance."

"Brother Elric is engaged elsewhere, the Prior needs you."

Anselm was very annoyed but could not ignore a call from the Prior so he assured Brother Benedict he would be there presently. He looked around and spotting a very grubby cloth, he pushed it into my mouth and hissed, "Not a sound until my return." He took one of the torches and left, locking the door behind him.

I lay motionless on the table too shocked to feel the cold penetrating my body. William was married and had not told me. I felt betrayed and tears sprang to my eyes. I snivelled for some time and with my hands restrained was unable to wipe away the tears or blow my nose. What a ghastly sight and I wallowed in self-pity. Eventually the tears dried up and my mind was capable of stringing a few logical thoughts together.

William had never held me or kissed me or made any declaration or inappropriate promises to me. He had always been a complete gentleman and I had foolishly misinterpreted his actions. He had always been an attentive friend and it was my attraction to him and wishful thinking that had made it out to be more. I was heartbroken, but heartbroken because I had been a fool and acted like a schoolgirl with a crush. If I ever escaped from this predicament I would be too embarrassed to face him again; even if he had been unaware of my feelings, Anselm's comments would have certainly drawn attention to them.

The cloth in my mouth was almost gagging me and it didn't taste very nice either. Each time I had gulped in air whilst sobbing the cloth moved further back in my mouth until now it was almost tickling my tonsils. With a snivelling snotty nose I realised I was having more trouble breathing. Self-control had never been my strong point but now I had to summon every ounce I had and try to calm down. This in itself proved difficult as I wasn't able to breathe deeply, but eventually I was still and calm enough to try and push the cloth out of my mouth with my tongue.

Eventually with the cloth dislodged I tried to spit to remove the awful taste but my mouth was completely dry. Should I shout? But if Anselm was the only one to hear me he would be angry and my demise would be sooner rather than later. Lifting my head I gazed down the table and saw that my only covering was my slip, no wonder I was freezing. I relaxed my head and glanced to the side and saw my shredded clothes lying in a heap on the floor. I refused to look the other side as I could not bear to see the jars filled with the victims that had come before me.

I wasn't sure how much time passed; I was numb, not just my body but my mind too. I was on mental overload and all I was capable off was lying in a stupor. Anselm did eventually return, his annoyance clearly visible as he huffed and puffed whilst fixing the torch to the wall. He moved about as if he had forgotten my existence, which was a foolish hope. Finally he stood beside the table gazing down at me. I expected some reaction when he saw the dislodged gag but there was none, he seemed deep in thought. For some reason I thought if I could get him talking it might help my situation, I knew I wouldn't be able to talk him out of it but delay tactics could provide time for someone else to appear. He was crazy and crazy people don't always act as you expect them to.

"Brother Anselm, I can see you have been so busy here," I started shakily, "will you tell me about your work?"

At first he seemed surprised but his eyes stayed calm. He frowned as he considered my request. I hardly dared breathe. I had no idea in which direction this would proceed. Finally he nodded enthusiastically and perhaps pushing my luck I asked him to start from the very beginning of how it all came about.

"I was a soldier, you understand." He had a faraway look in his eyes as if reliving his past. "I fought in many bloody battles, so many."

He paused and I was worried he would not go on but he gave himself a little shake and continued.

"The battles were many and all around me was death and injury and illness, it made me sick. I had not wanted to be a soldier but it was expected of me by my family, if I refused my father would have disowned me, left me destitute but eventually I could stomach it no more so I escaped to a monastery and begged to be allowed to stay. When I came to this order I was placed in charge of the infirmary."

There was a faint smile on his lips and I had the impression he had finally found his purpose in life. He had started with such good intentions. Why had he changed into such a monster? He walked to the bench and started shuffling the parchments haphazardly.

"I sought all the knowledge I could find on herbs and remedies but it was not enough to save all my patients. I needed to know how the body worked, how it was constructed."

He looked at me, concerned that I understood his frustrations, his need to know and strangely I did understand and I found myself nodding. Wasn't this the way the physicians and surgeons of the nineteenth century began? Their desire to further modern medicine had started with human dissection, even in my time people would leave their body to science for experimentation. Hundreds of autopsies were carried out worldwide because of the 'need to know' and no one protested, it was common place.

"I used bodies from the graveyard but it was not satisfactory, some had begun to decay."

He started to inspect his array of glass jars, removing some from the shelf and then tenderly replacing them after peering through the murky liquid examining the contents. I sensed a change in his demeanour and when he turned to me once more there was a crazed look in his eye definitely giving the impression of one who was totally unbalanced.

"I needed fresh bodies for my work," he continued.

"So you killed." My statement was a whisper.

"Yes I had to, you understand, it was necessary. My work is important, important for all mankind."

"But you murdered innocent people, how can you justify your action?"

There was a flash of anger and I was afraid I had pushed him too far with my question; I held my breath and tensed my body fearing he would strike out, but he paused and I could see he was considering my question like a teacher would just before imparting an important scrap of knowledge to a pupil.

"Yes, yes that is a valid point," his enthusiasm had returned and I exhaled gently, "and I prayed to God for guidance. I prayed long and hard for many days for some sign that it was his will. I walked the Priory and the grounds in constant prayer and then one evening, there you were, you were my sign."

"You were the one who discovered me in the wood?"

"Yes, God had sent you to me."

He was getting very excited now and paced the small room, gesturing with his arms and looking heavenward with a fiery look in his eyes.

"You were drowsy and not wanting you to see me I hit you on the head with a stone. Unfortunately before I was able to complete the attack Brother Elric appeared, so I told him you had been injured and we needed to get you to the Priory. Once again the Lord showed his hand to guide me, for you recovered and it was then that I saw you had lost your mind and the Lord wanted me to investigate your madness."

Anselm grasped his hands and closed his eyes as if in prayer.

"Madness?" I uttered, my voice still no more than a whisper.

"Why yes of course, my dear. You thought yourself to be many years hence and convinced we were all under the rule of Elizabeth."

"I was confused from a head injury, that was not madness."

He shook his head refusing to listen.

"You left here yet Robin returned you, that was proof you were destined to help me with my work, God's work."

I gaped at him in disbelief; he surely was insane. He rummaged on the bench and moving the large book I saw a selection of instruments, one of which was an ugly butcher's knife. I felt the blood drain from my face and I felt nauseous. He leaned forward and reached for a large axe which was against the wall. I knew my time had come and I started to scream. He pushed his left hand into my hair and wound the strands around his fingers securing my head on the table. I screamed louder and louder in terror trying to arch my body away from him but I was totally incapacitated. He tugged at my hair drawing my head further away from my shoulders, leaving my neck exposed. His right hand gripping the axe slowly rose above his head and I shut my eyes as tightly as I could and let out one last scream.

"Brother Anselm."

We both heard the call. It came again this time with a rap on the door. I halted mid scream and bit my lip trying to prevent any further sound escaping for fear of Anselm's reaction. He too had paused and looked from me to the door. He was hesitant and started to lower the axe.

"Brother Anselm you need to open the door so that we can speak."

It was a calm voice, one I didn't recognise, but Anselm obviously did for he kept looking from the door to me and back again, his composure deserted him.

"Father, I am very busy, may I come to you when my task is complete?"

He managed to keep his voice steady but the look in his eye betrayed him. It was the look of a crazed man, a crazed man who would do anything if cornered.

"No, Brother, I need to speak with you now," was the reply.

Anselm's hand was still entwined in my hair which he twisted in agitation causing me to gasp. With no warning there came heavy thudding at the door as if a battering ram was causing it to shudder under the force and then the wood splintered as axes crashed through the panels. It swung open revealing a small elderly man with white hair. He looked unfazed by the site that greeted him and he smiled as he tucked his hands in the sleeves of his long robe. He cautiously entered and edged his way along the side of the table opposite Anselm. Anselm immediately raised the axe and tugged my hair making quite obvious his intention. His eyes never left the old monk who bravely kept edging along the wall drawing my captor's gaze away from the shattered door. I sensed several figures slip into the room, unfortunately so did Anselm.

"Stand back," he yelled. "You are not allowed in here. You have no right to interrupt my work."

The old man gently removed one hand from his sleeve and gave a slight signal for them to halt. I tried to look to see who it was but it was difficult as my hair was tugged to emphasise every word Anselm spoke. Sir Godfrey stood with his sword drawn, William stood at his shoulder equally prepared. Other figures hovered outside the door but the lighting was dim and they just appeared as shadows.

"Brother Anselm, if your work is so important why did you not come to me to inform me? I could have released you from your other duties so that you could dedicate your time to it."

The old monk was trying to humour Anselm and he was doing very well, but a bead of sweat trickled down his forehead showing the strain he was under. He gestured to the shelf at the jars.

"I can see you have spent considerable time at your study."

Anselm glanced quickly over his shoulder and then returned the old man's stare with a look of pride.

"I am studying the human form to better understand its functions so that I can be a great healer. It is the vision God has bestowed upon me."

The old monk nodded as if understanding his explanation and then placed his hand on mine where it was bound to the table.

"And what part is Mistress Evelyn to play in this work?"

He gently squeezed my hand to give me courage. Anselm looked down at me as if he had forgotten my presence. He nodded enthusiastically and was eager to explain.

"We have discussed her role," he began and slowly he raised the hand hold the axe. "She understands the importance of my work and is in agreement."

His eyes flashed and he extended his arm over his head ready to strike. I let out a sob and screwed up my eyes. The whooshing noise I heard was not the descent of the axe but an arrow flying across the room from the doorway. It embedded itself in Anselm's arm causing him so scream in pain. He tried to grab his arm with the hand that was still gripping my hair; he struggled in frustration with the tangle almost tearing my hair out. The force of the arrow had thrown back his arm causing the axe to crash into the shelf, smashing several jars which showered their contents over him.

Men rushed forward to capture him; there was lots of noise and commotion and I turned my head away. The old monk bent and retrieved my cloak from the floor and gently placed it over me, covering my near nakedness.

"You are safe now, my child," he said and I just smiled and cried in gratitude.

I felt hands at my limbs cutting the ropes that had bound me; I could hear Anselm screaming at his captors that they had no right to touch him for he was doing God's bidding and I felt the monk place his hand on my brow and offer up silent prayers.

"Evelyn." William was looking down at me with a concerned look. "I will take you back to the castle."

He pulled me to the edge of the table, making sure the cloak was around me, and then lifted me into his arms. He climbed the steps to the corridor and then proceeded to the entrance. He was solid and warm and I was too exhausted to feel awkward or embarrassed. I would deal with that at a later date, for now I allowed my head to fall on his shoulder and closed my eyes. I rode back to the castle on his horse still cradled in his arms; he didn't speak but allowed me to try and process what had taken place and for that I was thankful. Many horsemen rode beside us and soon we entered the keep. It was night but many people were about and as the horse neared the castle steps I saw Hilda waiting with Maggie and Avis. I was helped down and immediately Hilda held me close; she was shaking but soon recovered herself and ordered everyone to stand clear and let us pass.

She whisked me to her room where I was placed on the bed still wrapped in the cloak. Extra covers were piled on me for I shivered and my teeth were chattering. Now all the commotion was over I seemed to have no control over my body. I felt light headed and as hard as I tried I could not stop shaking.

I heard a tap at the door and someone entered and came and stood beside the bed. I was startled to see Master Hook who bowed in greeting.

"Mistress Evelyn, may I be of assistance?"

He was polite and his face was calm, he showed no malice. I peered out from my mound of covers to see if he was carrying anything. He must have realised I was looking to see if he carried a bleeding bowl and a slight smile passed over his face for a mere second. He felt my brow and held my wrist, he noticed the rope burns and the chafing and upon inspecting my other wrist and both ankles he applied some soothing balm. He asked if I had other pain or injuries and I shook my head. Lowering his voice he asked if I had suffered any personal attack which confused me momentarily and then realising he was referring to rape or sexual assault, I assured him I had not.

He turned to Lady Hilda and explained that I was in shock and required plenty of liquids and rest. He paused as if waiting for me to challenge his diagnosis, when I did not he handed her a powder and instructed her to add it to my drink. He bowed courteously and left. I protested about the mixture having been drugged constantly over the past few days but Hilda reassured me it was just chamomile to relax me, which it did and soon I was asleep.

I woke late this morning, my physical ailments no longer causing me problems but my head was all over the place. After consuming a light breakfast Maggie and Avis gently sat me on the stool and started to wash me from head to toe. They were cautious not to hurt me but it felt so good to be clean once more. No one spoke and I started to feel uncomfortable. Several taps were heard at the door but Hilda told them in no uncertain terms I could not be disturbed. Eventually I could stand it no more.

"Hilda, we need to speak about what happened."

"We feared it would upset you and were waiting till you were stronger."

"I am not that fragile," I replied. "There are large spaces in my memory I need to fill."

She was not forthcoming so I looked to Maggie and Avis; Avis especially was always aware of anything happening in the castle. They looked sheepishly at Hilda who finally relented.

"I do not know all the details," she began, "but I know a little. When William went to find you and was informed you had run away. He was surprised even when told the reason for your departure."

Hilda did not look at me when she said this, whether to avoid my embarrassment or her own discomfort I wasn't really sure but soon continued the story as the girls washed and revived my body.

"William came to me and told me he was uncomfortable with Brother Anselm's explanation and intended to go back to the Priory unannounced and see what he could discover. On his return visit he stumbled upon Brother Elric and remembering the high regard he held for you, spoke of his concerns. Since Brother Elric cannot speak, it was a rather one-sided conversation, but William formed the opinion that he too was surprised by your sudden departure. William asked him by any means he was able to inform him if he found out anything. That was all until last night when a message arrived from Father Jerome the Prior."

Maggie and Avis were absorbed with the storytelling and had stopped to listen when Hilda clapped her hands to draw their attention to the fact I was sitting half naked and she was concerned I would take a chill. Avis busied herself trying to find clean undergarments as mine had been shredded while Maggie tried to dry and untangle my hair.

"What did the message say?"

"I do not know accept Father Jerome was trying to keep Anselm busy allowing time for the garrison to arrive to help him."

"He acted very bravely," I said, remembering what a major part he had played in my rescue. "He definitely saved my life."

There had been more tapping on the door which was dispensed with by Hilda but a message had arrived to say that our presence was required at the trial of Anselm. I was astonished at the speed at which things had progressed and was overcome with a sudden attack of nerves.

"Now, now, Evelyn. I will be beside you." And to the girls she ordered, "Find some apparel from the trunk, quickly."

"I do not want a formal gown. I desire to wear simple dress, please."

So I wore a plain grey skirt similar to those worn by the serving girls, with a faded blue short tunic gathered at the waist by my belt on which hung my purse. I took a plain linen scarf and put it on my head, passing one end across my throat and over my shoulder. I pushed my feet into soft leather slippers and within half an hour was ready to enter the Great Hall for the trial.

We had to wait at the sturdy wooden doors to the hall, two guards making sure we did not enter until summoned. Eventually our turn came and we stepped into the hall. The trestle tables had been removed leaving just the head table on the dais. It was crowded but there was a free space down the centre of the hall. Given the number of people present it was eerily quiet and as Hilda and I stepped forward all heads turned toward us. I wasn't expecting this and hesitated but Hilda was at my elbow coaxing me on. I swallowed hard and moved forward keeping my eyes fixed on the Duke who sat in the middle of the long table. On his right was the old monk who I realised must be the Prior, Father Jerome. Also seated were Sir Godfrey, William and several other knights. All had solemn faces and watched every step I took. To the side surrounded by guards was Brother Anselm, his wrists in shackles. He seemed oblivious to his surroundings and swayed gently as if keeping time to a rhythm in his head. I dare not look around, my throat was tight and I knew tears were not far away.

Hilda and I curtsied to the Duke and then she took a step back and I felt alone. The Duke spoke very calmly and smiled occasionally to help put me at ease. I felt under everyone's scrutiny and had to keep reminding myself I was not the one on trial. The interrogation lasted a long time with questions firing from all directions. I had to recount events since my arrival at Wyvern and finally retell Brother Ansell's confession to me and the reasoning for his actions. I felt very exposed and nervous and at one point I felt Hilda step forward and place her hand on my shoulder. Finally it was over and the gathered crowd ceased to 'oh' and 'ah'.

I moved to the side and watched as the members of the top table put their heads together in discussion. Finally the Duke signalled to the guards and Anselm was hoisted to his feet and stood before him.

No one was surprised when he was found guilty of all the gory murders, but Anselm stood silently with a faraway look in his eyes; he was obviously a very mentally sick man.

As Duke Richard gave the verdict there was a flash across my eyes and I put my hand out and grabbed Hilda's arm. I was so giddy I thought I might fall down. It passed as soon as it had arrived and I reassured her I was alright. Richard went on to announce the punishment; tomorrow Anselm would be burnt at the stake for his crimes, I was sickened. Finding my voice I rushed forward and pleaded for mercy.

"My lord, I am aware of this man's terrible crimes, crimes where his victims suffered barbaric treatment, but if he is made to suffer so cruelly are we any better than him?"

Once again the hall was silent mainly due to my outburst of challenging the court. Richard's eyebrows shot up and he looked startled, whereas Godfrey was outraged and banged the table with his fist.

"My lord he is obviously a very sick man, he has lost his mind, he does not even realise he has committed wrong, he has lost all understanding."

There were a few shouts and boos from the assembled crowd who disagreed with me wholeheartedly; only Father Jerome gave me an understanding look.

"This man must pay for his crimes," said Richard, standing. The assembly gave a cheer. "However," everyone fell silent, "if one of his victims can show mercy for his lost soul, then who am I to be merciless? Brother Anselm will be executed tomorrow by the hangman's rope."

With that, Richard marched out the hall followed by his knights. I felt sick and dizzy again and clutched at Hilda who practically dragged me from the hall into the fresh air outside. She sat me on a bench and started to fan me; the fresh air felt good but the buzzing in my ears continued and the nausea came in waves. Hilda pushed my head down to my knees in a most unladylike position; if people were staring I didn't care.

Breathing deeply I started to recover and attempted to raise my head only for Hilda to force it down again, telling me to take my time. I closed my eyes and carried on with the deep breaths and suddenly remembered another time I had sat in the keep doing exactly the same. I had been on the battlements with the crafting group when I had felt this way; in fact I was sitting on the same bench where either Tom or Dylan had used the identical remedy. When my colour returned we strolled a little so that I could enjoy the fresh air, linking arms with Hilda as I was still a little unsteady.

I was quiet for the rest of the day, refusing visits from William and Robin who came to the door. Hilda assumed it was the trauma of the past and sweetly didn't press me for conversation but allowed me time with my thoughts. Little did she know I had a different worry with which to contend. My headaches, dizziness and nausea were all symptoms I had suffered before when I had travelled back in time. Did this mean I was about to travel again? I was drowning in my emotions, excitement I would be going home, fear of the actual travelling and sadness at leaving my friends.

Through the night the uncomfortable bouts continued, so by morning I looked and felt a wreck. I had difficulty keeping upright when Avis tried to dress me; we were expected to attend the execution, but eventually Hilda told me to retire back to bed and she would explain my absence. The headache was becoming unbearable so I asked for my canvas bag and under its cover took two paracetamol out of the box.

Hilda was heading for the door and suddenly I realised I might not be here when she returned.

"Hilda," I called, "you do know how much I love you and appreciate everything you have done for me?"

She turned and came back to me, picking up a cloak and gently laying it over me.

"Evelyn, I am so fond of you and I am sure our friendship will continue. Now rest, my dear."

I could hear noise coming from below in the grounds; people were assembling for the execution. Each time I thought of it the buzzing in my ears increased. I pulled the strap of my canvas bag over my head and pulled the cloak up to my chin. Outside the noise stopped; Anselm must have arrived. Suddenly I remembered that if I was leaving I would need my keys and other belongings hidden in the headboard. With much effort I slipped my legs over the side of the bed intending to retrieve them. There was a collective gasp from below followed by cheering. *Anselm must have met his fate,* I thought, as I slid from the bed and hit the floor.

CHAPTER TEN

The sun was beating down, burning my flesh. I needed to find shade but I had taken such a beating, movement caused me pain. The sky was clear and blue but the sunlight hurt my eyes, or rather hurt my eye, for my left was swollen completely shut. I tasted blood in my mouth. All was quiet now, the screaming and shouting, the gun shots and sobbing, all had stopped. Dare I move? Could I move?

Raising my hand to try and shield my vision I took a deep breath and immediately regretted it. The pain in my chest was sharp and intense and as I tried to roll onto my side it increased in intensity and I cried out. A broken rib or ribs seemed likely. Now with my head turned to the side I panted shallowly not wanting to experience the pain again. I broke out into a sweat which made me nauseous as I was already burning up.

Eventually I opened my eye and gazed at the carnage before me, the wreckage and the bodies, and it was then that I saw him. He sat astride a beautiful horse, his back straight and head held high. He was a Native American Indian and he and his horse were motionless. Perhaps the heat and injuries were causing me to hallucinate so I closed my eye and counted to ten. When I opened my eye he was still there but now he was surveying the scene before him. He dropped the reins of his horse and swung his right leg over its head and nimbly slid to the ground pausing a second and then started striding toward me.

My travel from Wyvern was not as I had hoped; I expected to wake in the car park or at least in the vicinity of my car but instead I was in a cart of sorts squashed amongst what appeared to be someone's entire possessions. My head was not painful this time, probably due to the absence of Brother Anselm and his handy rock, but I was disorientated and a bit dizzy. The ride was rough with endless bumps and although I was under cover from the sun's rays it was rather stuffy. The only ill effect of the time travel this time was an overwhelming tiredness, so it was no surprise that with the swaying back and forth of the cart I was soon lulled back to sleep.

The next time I awoke the motion had stopped and two small faces were peering at me over the end of the cart. I smiled and said 'Hello' which caused them to run off shouting for their 'Mutter'. I managed to sit up and waited to see what would happen. A woman appeared who was pleasant looking and beaming in welcome.

"Guud, guud you are avake. Kommen sie, you are hungry?"

And so began my friendship with the Gunsche family.

As I sat at their camp fire that first evening sharing their food, I was apprehensive and a little nervous but I realised I wasn't panicking. Normally my anxiety at anything new would cause me to flee to the nearest loo and lock myself in to avoid the situation. Of course there was no loo but I didn't feel the need to escape, in fact I was curious. I didn't know where I was or why I had come here but my time at Wyvern had taught me to just accept what turned up and deal with it as best I could.

Communication between us was rather haphazard as they were German with very little English and of course I was English with no German at all. It did work in my favour as it meant they didn't question me too much regarding my past. Apparently they had found me unconscious on the trail and assumed I had wandered away from a wagon train and found myself in difficulties. I told them my name and that I was from England and widowed and then said I could remember nothing of what happened. They accepted my explanation and said I must travel with them until my memory returned or we encountered the wagon train from which I had been separated. They seemed quite happy with the situation because after all what other explanation could there possibly be?!

Over the following days and weeks I tried to ascertain when and where I was. The Gunsches comprised of two brothers and their families who wanted to 'Go west' and claim some land. They were farmers, the oldest brother was Wilhelm and his wife Mila was the one who gave me the hearty welcome. They had two children, Willie and Anna, who were about ten or twelve years old. The younger brother Otto had just become a father for the first time to little Anneliese who was named after her mother Annelie.

I soon realised from the fragmented conversations that I was in North America and tried to convey my concern that they were travelling alone. Pioneers suffered many hardships and dangers and I thought there was safety in numbers. It appeared they had been part of a much larger group but Wilhelm's wagon had been damaged and almost washed away crossing the big river and he had to make repairs only to have Annelie go into premature labour and become poorly. The main wagon train could not wait indefinitely so it was decided that the Gunsches would follow on or return to the nearest town and wait for another train. Unfortunately the trains were not that frequent and the brothers were impatient to forge on. Some journeys took up to six months and took enormous preparation so for another one to happen along seemed doubtful but I kept quiet.

The journey was hard. Mules pulled the two wagons but they were for the belongings and food and water barrels so mainly we walked.

At first I could not keep up or last the whole day but soon it became a way of life. I helped the women with the cooking and chores and often tended to the baby to give Annelie a little respite; she still didn't seem fully recovered from giving birth. They were good people and so generous in taking me in, I felt I needed to make a contribution and in my position all I could offer was physical work.

I discovered that the 'big river' they referred to was the Missouri so I assumed we were on the Great Plains; however, the plains covered many states so we could have been anywhere. I was cautious in my questioning as any blunder could give me away. Some states hadn't even joined the union and my ignorance of US history and geography really didn't help.

The land was mainly flat grassland that stretched for miles but as we progressed there were a few forested valleys and intermittent streams. We started to see low hills so I assumed we were heading to the Rockies. It wasn't a dust bowl so I didn't think it was the more southern states but quite honestly I hadn't a clue. I walked and just followed where they led. At first I was afraid of snakes and wild animals but I was so exhausted by the end of the day that soon after the evening meal I would curl up by the camp fire and sleep soundly, usually cuddled up to Anna and Willie.

We rose with the dawn which was about four o'clock, ate a meal and made ready for the day's journey setting out at seven, this way we covered quite a distance before the heat became too much. For me it was always too much. I shed my underskirts but kept my long skirt and long-sleeve tunic to protect my skin from the sun. Everyone wore hats so I used my scarf to drape around my head to try and prevent heat stroke. There was often a breeze which was warm and would blow up the soil and dust, but sometimes it became much stronger.

Wilhelm tried to explain to me that we were in the tornado season which was a little unnerving. He said that he had been told that just before one hit, it would become very still and then there would be a rotating column of air which would roar and if it hit the ground it could do untold damage and often be fatal for anyone in its path. It was a sobering thought because we were totally exposed to the elements as we trudged along, there was nowhere to take cover.

We were fortunate for many weeks and faced no dangers and only had the heat and harsh terrain to contend with. My feet hurt all the time as my soft leather shoes gave little support or protection. If we ever encountered civilization again sturdy boots were my main priority. Little Anneliese was asleep in the back of the wagon and Annelie and I walked along together. We didn't talk very much but it was just nice to have companionship. I was gazing around in my usual manner taking in my surroundings looking forward to a change in scenery as in the distance small hills had started to appear.

In the distance I saw four horses but I couldn't see who was riding them. I nudged Annelie and nodded in their direction. She shielded her eyes but couldn't see any better than I could. She shrugged and I thought that was the end of the matter but later over our meal she started telling Wilhelm and Otto. Their English was improving since I had started teaching them a little every day; everyone seemed to enjoy the lessons but although I tried to make it fun I realised, to them it was a serious matter as English would be the language used when they settled in their new home and they could not afford to be ignorant to what was happening and being said in their new environment.

The next day I could see that the men were taking extra care to be vigilant and they told us to keep our eyes open. Both had their loaded shotguns at hand at the front of the wagons and some other firearms were loaded and ready if the need arose. I had never fired a gun and was apprehensive I would need to, but if it meant protecting our little group I'm sure I would find the courage somewhere. Otto gave me a very quick lesson and my hands shook, what on earth would I be like in an emergency?

We set off in our usual way the only difference being we women and children walked in touching distance of the wagons. Without staring openly at the band of men we kept them in our peripheral vision to be prepared for whatever they might be planning, but for most of the day they just kept pace with us. Eventually they closed the gap and came to walk alongside Wilhelm in the lead wagon.

The four men were what I would have referred to as cowboys, rather shabbily dressed, shaggy greasy hair and covered with dust from the trail. I don't suppose I should have held that against them as none of us were exactly fresh and tidy, but I felt uncomfortable especially when I saw they all carried rifles on their saddles and wore gun belts.

The one who looked the oldest casually drew alongside Wilhelm and hailed him in a friendly enough manner, tipping his hat and smiling. He introduced himself as Mr Wyatt and then pointed to the others and named each in turn, his son Clay, Mr Jones and Mr Pickett, who also tipped their hats. It was all very polite but it didn't quite sit right with me, but then I had never met a cowboy before so what did I know? They spoke for a while but I couldn't quite hear everything as I was on the far side of Otto's wagon at the back. I noticed Wilhelm did not slow the wagon and he used broken English when I knew he was capable of much better.

Later over our meal he told us that Mr Wyatt said we were in dangerous country and perhaps he and his men should ride with us in case we came across Indians. He kept his voice low as the men had set their camp just a small distance from ours and he didn't want them to know he had misgivings about their presence. We all agreed we might benefit from their protection but then we also thought they may be just as dangerous. Wilhelm impressed upon us not to engage in conversation with them hoping hearing the family speak German would discourage them approaching us. I was told not to speak within their earshot and the children were instructed to curb their natural curiosity and stay away from them. We had been a happy bunch but now the cowboys had caused a whole different atmosphere to our journey.

We rose as usual, ate and then prepared to leave. The cowboys were up too and called across to us a good morning greeting and sure enough as we pulled away in the wagons they were ready to leave also. I could not relax as we walked; I was trying not to let my agitation show. They walked abreast of the lead wagon and chatted amongst themselves from time to time, not bothering us at all, but still I felt uncomfortable.

The terrain was beginning to show new features, slight inclines and in the distance a rarity, trees. With high evaporation and low rainfall trees were not common but sometimes a few grew along riverbeds. I assumed some rain came off the hills and formed a river or more likely a stream, and trees took root and even in the summer drought were hardy enough to survive. I would have enjoyed discovering them but I was constantly aware of our travel companions and could think of little else.

Anneliese had been a bit grizzly for a good part of the journey; perhaps she sensed her mother's anxiety, so Annelie had joined Otto on the wagon so she could cuddle her and try to soothe her. I noticed one of the men, the one called Jones, kept turning his head to stare at her. She had noticed too and looked very uncomfortable. Normally she would feed the baby as she sat up front but wanting more privacy she climbed into the back of the wagon. Soon Anneliese became quiet so she obviously appreciated her feed.

The men huddled together and talked amongst themselves; when they had finished they started to reposition their horses. My heart started to pound, something was about to happen. Under the guise of being friendly Mr Wyatt drew alongside Wilhelm and started up a conversation, while his son dropped back parallel to Otto and Mr Jones joined the group positioning himself more to the rear of the wagon. Meanwhile Mr Pickett slowed his horse letting the wagons pass and then started to walk on my side. I called to Anna and held out my hand which she took, and I positioned her between me and the wagon so I sheltered her from him.

I was so nervous my hand shook so I squeezed Anna's hand and she looked up at me with the biggest eyes and most frightened look imaginable, a look which would later return to haunt me. My heart was pounding so loud I was sure the cowboy could hear it; however, I took a deep breath and strode on as he drew alongside of me.

And then it just happened with no warning.

Wyatt and his son drew their pistols and shot Wilhelm and Otto where they sat before either could reach a rifle to defend us. We stood transfixed in horror. Willie was the first to respond and scrambled up the wagon to reach his father's rifle but Wyatt just aimed his gun at him and blasted him in the chest. The force catapulted him backward into Mila's arms who collapsed to the ground, gathering him up into her arms, sobbing. Then she screamed, "Renne, Anna renne."

Anna took off like a rocket running as fast as she could ,not stopping to think, just obeying her mum. Pickett reached for his rifle and started to grin. I didn't know what to do so I moved forward and slapped his horse hoping to spook it and give Anna a little more chance to escape. He turned around and gave me a back hander across the face, splitting my lip and causing me to stumble backward. He then took aim and shot the poor little girl in the back and she dropped like a stone. I was horrified and started screaming at him that he was a bastard and then I started to run towards Anna. I half expected to get a bullet in my back too but a different fate awaited me.

Pickett slid off his horse and gave chase laughing as if it was a game. He tackled me from behind and I landed on my face all the air leaving my lungs with a whoosh. He flipped me over and straddled me, he smelt of body odour and urine and when he brought his face near to mine there was a strong smell of chewing tobacco. He disgusted me and I tried to struggle and get him off me. At first he thought it was fun and he was getting excited but after a couple of my blows landed he got angry and balled up his fist and punched me. It hurt so much I saw stars and was dazed, completely disabled I went limp. I felt him ripping my clothes and his whiskers were rough on my breasts, he bit me several times. The rape was brutal and demeaning but there was no fight left in me. I looked away trying to avoid the horror but the vision that greeted me was even worse.

Wyatt had just risen from presumably raping Mila who lay motionless in the dirt. He took out his gun and shot her. Anneliese had been screaming but was now silent and Jones was hauling Annelie out the back of the wagon. She was sobbing and trying to push him away but he dragged her to the ground and brutally assaulted her. He was grunting like an animal and as he groaned with lust his hands closed around her neck and she too was silent.

Pickett rested on his knees after he was finished and wiped himself on my skirt. He rose, adjusted his clothes and reached for his gun. He was just about to shoot me when the younger Wyatt ran up saying he wanted his turn. Pickett laughed and told him to go ahead but reminded him what his daddy had said about leaving no witnesses and to take a scalp so the Indians would be blamed.

I think I had just accepted my fate and lay quite still while Clay Wyatt crawled on top of me. I soon realised he was very inexperienced and was all over the place and then things had finished before they had even begun. He looked flustered and a bit embarrassed and screamed at me not to look at him. I really couldn't move and was semi-conscious from Pickett's punch so when I didn't turn away he thought I was mocking him. He started too kick me and somehow I managed to curl up against the blows. I don't know if he was too embarrassed or thought I was dead but he ran off to join the others who had ransacked the wagons looking for coin or other valuables and were ready to ride out.

I don't know how long I lay there on the ground but now the Indian was making straight for me. Before he reached me I had to cough and it caused me to cry out in pain. I gripped my side and moaned; I had clapped my other hand over my mouth hoping to stifle the noise but the pain was too intense. There was blood on my hand, I wiped it on my skirt and then tried to pull my tunic to cover my naked breasts.

He stood beside me, I couldn't really make out his features because of my swollen eye, but he didn't seem to be showing any emotion. Squatting beside me he reached out and touched my side where the pain was; he pressed, I screamed.

"If you are going to kill me just get it over with, don't torment me," I screeched between sobs.

He stood and walked to the wagons and around the camp area and presently returned with two sticks and my cloak. He drove the sticks into the ground either side of me and then draped my cloak over them, making a very crude shelter. He weighted the ends of the cloak with a couple of stones so it would stay in place. I was surprised but so pleased to get the burning sun off me. I stammered my thanks and then closed my eyes.

CHAPTER ELEVEN

The Indian did not act as I expected and I was ashamed. I was guilty of stereotyping him, my only knowledge being based on cowboy and Indian programmes I watched in my youth. After he had provided me with shelter and water he looked about the area and then made for the wagons. The cowboys had taken two of the mules to carry the plunder they had helped themselves to, but now the Indian unhitched the other two and led them to the tiny patch of shade the wagon provided. He fetched his own horse which had stood patiently not offering to run away, it was a white and brown pinto with a long mane which it tossed leisurely from time to time. Willie's hat lay on the ground where he had fallen so he picked it up and dipped it in the water barrel, giving each animal a drink.

He looked at each body in turn, rolling them over if they were face down, then he went inside the wagons. He started throwing things out of the back making an untidy pile. I kept closing my eyes and dozing due to the heat and the pain and the next time I looked he was approaching me with a tiny bundle. Squatting, he held it close to my face so I could see. It was Anneliese, her little body blue and stiff. He had wrapped her so that any injury was not visible but I still found it difficult to look at her little face. He gestured to her and I thought in his fashion he was asking if she was mine. I shook my head and closed my eyes as the tears ran down my face.

For a long time I lay with my eyes closed trying to blot out the horrific scene. They had been good people, people who willingly took me in and gave me their friendship. People I had a fondness for, people I watched being butchered by greedy evil men. I think it was at that moment I wanted to revenge their death, that moment I visualised each evil face and committed them to memory for all time.

When next I opened my eyes I saw that the Indian had been very busy. All the bodies had disappeared; I later realised he had placed them together in Otto's wagon. The items he had salvaged were packed in bundles and loaded on the two mules and he had contrived some sort of stretcher which hung from the pinto and would drag along the ground as it walked. I realised that was meant for me and when he brought the horse close to me I raised my hands and shook my head. Lying still was painful enough but to be dragged along rough terrain would be excruciating. I started to get a little hysterical but he paid me no notice. He took my cloak and draped it around my body to preserve my modesty since my garments were ripped and falling off. I pushed at his chest as he stooped over me and it was like pushing on a piece of iron. He must have seen the terror in my eyes for he placed his hand over my face so that I had to close my eyes and he remained that way until I calmed down. I was terrified that if he scooped me up in his alms my ribs would puncture my lung or worse still my heart, apart from causing awful pain. Somehow he seemed to have realised that and with a swift movement drew me up to an almost standing position without bending my body. It hurt and suddenly becoming vertical my head swirled and I fell against him in a faint.

Fainting was an advantage as it turned out; for by the time I revived I was on the stretcher and bumping down the trail. The proximity to the pinto's rear was a little too close for comfort, but I was in no condition to complain, I just sent up a silent prayer that it didn't need to relieve itself. The two mules plodded along to my left and to my right a plume of black smoke rose into the sky. The Indian had set fire to the wagon containing my friends to prevent them falling prey to the wild animals and to set their spirits free to join one another and their ancestors in peace.

I don't know how far the journey was, it felt like a million miles, I had never experienced such pain and by the time we finally stopped I had coughed up a substantial amount of blood and was semiconscious. It was strange, for the first time in my life I wasn't anxious or afraid. If the Indian killed me then so be it, I really believed I was going to die anyway. He had only showed me kindness so far and acted in my best interest, so presumably he would carry on doing so and in a strange way even in such a short time I was beginning to trust him.

In my dreams I felt pain and found it difficult to breathe. When I was hot and delirious I felt cool water on my body and a water bottle pressed to my lips so that water dribbled into my mouth and on reflex I would swallow it. However for the most part I was unconscious and knew little of what was happening. Other dreams were more vivid as my mind replayed the slaughter I had witnessed and I would wake momentarily with a start and cry out.

Eventually one day I awoke and had no fever or severe pain as before; my mind was clear and I looked around curiously. We must have reached the foot hills because I was surrounded by rock and stone, not a cave exactly, more a large overhanging rock to a natural inlet of the hillside. It shielded from the sun and wind and the elements and afforded a cosy nook for me, the bundles from the mules and the Indian. Between us were stones arranged in a ring and ashes where he must have made a fire.

I just lay there watching him as he worked on some sort of animal skin. I remembered from when he had stood me up he was tall, his frame slender and muscular and he had held himself erect. His complexion was reddish brown shining copper in sunlight, his features regular with an aquiline nose and small eyes I had seen full of fire but were now black. His hair was long and coarse, black as a raven and he wore it loose with a section from the front held back by two feathers. He wore a breechcloth and leggings which looked like buckskin. His fringed tunic lay beside him on the ground and he was bare from the waist upward although a very intricate and elaborate necklace covered most of his chest.

At close inspection he wasn't a young brave, I could see old scars on his chest and he wore a grave and dignified expression, more like a seasoned warrior. There was a streak of grey hair which was very noticeable since it was part of the hair that was secured by the feathers. I had no idea how to age an Indian, probably not as old as they looked, weathered by a hard life, so maybe forty or forty-five. I was concentrating and frowning as I tried to make a decision when he looked up and I jumped at being caught starring at him.

I nervously said hello but he didn't reply, just looked at me. I wasn't sure what to do perhaps he didn't either. Then he stood and brought a canteen over to me and raised my head so that I could drink. He pulled one of the bundles behind me to prop me up and then resumed his seat opposite. He made no effort to communicate so I started to fidget, rolling and unrolling my cloak around my finger. It wasn't a comfortable silence so I thought I should make an effort.

"Do you speak English, err, white man's tongue?"

Oh God, that wasn't an appropriate start, I really should forget those westerns I used to watch. I tried again.

"Can you understand me?"

No response, he didn't even blink. I pressed my hand to my chest and said, "Evelyn, my name is Evelyn." I then gestured to him and nodded and smiled encouraging him to tell me his name, still no response. Then he touched his side and pointed to my injured side. I nodded enthusiastically and said it was much better. Then he covered his eye with his hand and pointed to my eye. I closed my good eye and peered around with my once very swollen one, I could see and so I nodded and smiled assuring him it was better. It seemed that this was to be our way of communicating. He then swept his hand over the lower part of his body and once again pointed. I was a little embarrassed and gazed down at my hands which were once again fiddling with my cloak, he obviously knew I had been raped and beaten. I nodded slightly but didn't raise my eyes to meet his.

"Thank you for saving my life and caring for me," I said, not knowing if he understood how grateful I really was.

The silence resumed and I tried to move to get more comfortable. My body was still sore and I winced. I lifted the cloak and saw that I still had my filthy clothes wrapped around me and I wrinkled my nose in distaste. The lower part of my body was lying on wads of grasses which were damp and not too fragrant. I suddenly realised he had placed the grasses under me to absorb, shall I say, bodily fluids for the time I was unconscious. I gasped and my eyes flew open in shock as I quickly put down my cover. He was still looking at me and I felt my colour rise with my embarrassment.

I rubbed my hands together and then mimed washing my face and then my body. I lifted part of my ripped tunic and once again mimed throwing it away. I prayed he understood me for now I was fully conscious I realised what a smelly mess I was. He pulled over another of the bundles and used his knife to cut the cord holding it together, inside where various pieces of clothing that belonged to the Gunsches. It really saddened me to see them and for quite a while I just sat staring at them. Eventually I sifted through them and found a skirt of Mila's and a check shirt that had been Wilhelm's. I selected a few other items and saw my old canvas bag at the bottom of the pile which I grabbed and held to my chest. The Indian watched me hugging it and even though he didn't understand a word I said, "I brought this with me from my home, it holds many memories."

Gripping all the items I tried to stand and grimaced at the aches and pains. I wobbled a bit and he stepped forward and held my arm to steady me. I took my arm away and turned slightly, I wasn't ready to be touched again by any male and I also stank. We descended the hill very slowly it was rocky and I was very weak. He didn't try to hurry me but walked in front and pointed to the best place for me to step. At the bottom was a riverbed with a trickle of water and some hardy trees growing from the bank. A short way away I could see his horse and the mules. He took me to the water and then turned and left. It wasn't deep enough to immerse myself but it was glorious to strip off and wash thoroughly. There were still bruises and bite marks but with the blood and grime removed my appearance was much improved.

It felt glorious to be clean and wearing fresh garments even if they weren't my own. I found some moisturiser at the bottom of my canvas bag and applied it liberally to my sunburnt face. I sat on a boulder with my head wrapped in a cloth rubbing vigorously to try and dry my hair. I looked up and the Indian was standing a short distance from me, I hadn't heard his approach. As I opened my mouth to speak he lifted his rifle took aim and fired. I clapped my hands over my ears and screamed, then hesitated, I felt no pain, I looked down and there was no blood. When I looked behind me there was a rattlesnake practically blown in half. I shot up and started retreating as fast as I could; it had easily been in striking distance. Snakes were my biggest fear. In England it was a manageable fear, I could avoid reptile houses at the zoo, scrunch my eyes closed at films or the television when one appeared and we had few native species to worry about. Here it was a totally different problem and I stood shaking; just the sight of it filled me with terror. The Indian went over and picked it up and then started to head for out little camp. I wasn't about to wait around and see if the rattler had a vengeful friend in the rocks so I grabbed all my belongings and charged after the Indian, all aches and pains forgotten. I called for him to slow down but he just kept going so I hurried and grabbed his arm to get his attention. As he turned his body toward me the hand holding the snake also turned and the thing hung too close for comfort. I jumped back and screamed. He didn't laugh, nor did he crack a smile but his dark eyes sparkled and I knew he saw the funny side of my pathetic behaviour.

We had snake for supper and it tasted surprisingly good, similar to chicken. I had tried again to find out his name but with no luck, I was sure now he didn't understand me. He watched as I struggled with my hair and I had pointed to his grey streak and said grey repeatedly but there was no response. The only communication between us we acted out. Actually, the fact he didn't understand my language was quite cathartic. I found myself talking to him about big things, little things, anything at all. He never gestured for me to stop and being able to speak what was on my mind was very therapeutic. I gave him the name Grey Feather. He stayed with me, feeding and protecting me until I was back to full strength.

At first I did chores at our camp to keep busy while I mended. I sorted through the bundles to see what could be salvaged. There were a couple of blankets, always useful, another shirt I could use whilst washing the one I was wearing, a pot, plate and spoons. The cowboys took everything having a worth or a use, however they missed a small amount of coffee beans that were in the grinder ready to use, some salt and some flour. There were other items of clothing that I cut into drying clothes or strips for bandages; I tried not to waste anything. I washed and mended my cloak. I repacked the bundles apart from the things we used regularly and sorted and repacked my canvas bag with my personal things.

I cut some brush from the hillside and used it to sweep the camp, I also used the name Grey Feather whenever I addressed the Indian, smiling as I did so and after a while he would look in my direction, and this was a huge achievement I thought. He still did not speak but was a very patient listener. I still had nightmares and would wake every night crying out and with my chores done in the day I did not like to stay at camp alone when Grey Feather left so I took to going with him. At first he tended his horse and the mules and I watched and learned. Then he would hunt and I begged to go too. That wasn't a success at first because I was noisy and impatient and my flimsy footwear still caused problems because it was not fit for purpose. One evening over the camp fire he took my shoes which were ripped and worn thin and covered them with an animal skin. He put them back on my feet and used stripes of hide to tie around my ankles and legs. The shoes were now supple and soft and comfortable and my ability to track animals with him improved.

I was physically healed now but my dreams and thoughts were troubled. I spoke to Grey Feather, hoping it would help. He was my friend, my protector, my psychologist and confidant. I could tell him anything and not be judged, or belittled or laughed at because he didn't understand me. I realised that during my nightly chats I told him about my home, my time travelling, the people I left at Wyvern, my hopes and fears, my heartbreaks. I didn't mention age because I wasn't aware of how old I was, I suppose vanity was rearing its head. I didn't look or feel the age I was when I left home, but I certainly wasn't still nearing thirty as I was at Wyvern. I think perhaps I was somewhere in the middle, maybe forty. Time travel was hard enough to get my head around let alone sliding up and down the age range.

It occurred to me that now I was healed he would leave me or take me to a town, but there was one more thing I needed his help with. The next time he left the camp I ran after him and planted myself directly in his path. He stopped and looked down at me. I carried his bow and arrows and held them out to him and said, "Please teach me to use these." I shook the bow and then hit my chest and repeated, "Please teach me." He stood for a while and then reached out and pushed my hand holding the bow down and held out his rifle to me. I stepped back holding up my hands and shaking my head. I disliked firearms and having seen what they could achieve I really didn't think I could handle one. He held out his rifle again and I stepped back once more and said, "Grey Feather no, I'm afraid of guns." He finally seemed to understand and shrugged his shoulders and nodded his head. I danced around him beaming like a silly child, thanking him; I was so relieved and excited. He tolerated it for a moment and then gave a stern look and I knew he meant business.

Training was hard and exhausting. I could not hold the bow steady at first and had difficulty drawing back the string. When I knocked the arrow it just kept falling off the rest I made with my bow hand so I was having real problems even before I managed to shoot the arrow. My arms and chest ached to the point I had difficulty lifting my arms. On the few occasions I did manage to shoot an arrow my technique was so poor the bow string ran down my inner wrist, taking off some skin and bruising it badly. Grey Feather made me a leather wrist guard which helped stop further injury. It was much harder than I imagined and I felt like giving up.

My nightmares continued and increased in intensity. I saw Anna's big round terrified eyes looking up at me, the sound of the bullets tearing through flesh and bone, Annalie's sobbing for her baby and the pools of blood on the ground where my friends had been scalped. I could feel and smell Pickett's body weighing on mine and I was fighting all over again to beat him off. I wrestled and screamed till I was breathless, I clawed at his skin, I swore at him and sobbed. He shook me by the shoulders until I was senseless and still he continued until I open my eyes. Through the tears it was not Pickett's face I saw but Grey Feather holding my shoulders and trying to help me escape from my bad dream. I fell into his chest and wrapped my arms around him and he held me and let me cry.

Finally I pulled away from him and looked him in the eye, for that one moment I wished above anything else that he understood me.

"I'm going to kill those bastards," I hissed through gritted teeth. "I am going to track them down and kill them one by one."

Saying it out loud strengthened my resolve and I lay down to wait for the morning when I could train with renewed determination. All I needed was four shots, each arrow flying strong and true.

My new resolve in training began to show results and it also strengthened the bond between Grey Feather and me. We began to know each other much better and interpretation of our body language and signs became our second language. It also made us much closer physically. Since the first time I had removed my arm from Grey Feather's helping hand he had not touched me in any way except when I suffered nightmares and he would shake my shoulders to waken me. Now he needed to physically show me how to use the bow. He would stand behind me and move my leading leg into a shoulder width position with his foot and pull my shoulders back against his chest to give me the necessary upright stance. His left arm would lie under mine to steady my bow and his right arm would encircle me as he showed me how to pull back the string so that my index finger was under my chin and the string would touch my nose.

I had always found this part difficult so he would press my back muscles till I felt them strain against his hand and finally understand that I needed to use my back muscles to draw the string not my biceps. His face would be next to mine as he demonstrated how to look down the arrow and align it with the target and after I slowly released the arrow he held me still so that I maintained my body position until the arrow hit its mark.

Strangely I felt comfortable with the proximity of his body and when my technique improved I rather missed his closeness. I was totally at ease with him now; my only concern was how he felt about me, if he would just smile occasionally it would at least give me a hint but he maintained his solemn look. Sometimes he seemed on the verge of cracking a smile and I would tease him, telling him I knew he liked something because his eyes were dancing. My shooting was by no means perfect but I could hit a target so now I had to try and explain my plan to him and then hope he would go along with it.

I walked with him down to the stream and asked him to be seated. The ground was sandy so I took the bowl I had brought along and fetched water and wet it thoroughly. I carefully smoothed it and patted it flat so that I had a large drawing surface. Grey Feather watched me curiously as I drew wavy lines on the right and said Missouri River, then jagged peaks on the left and said Rocky Mountains. I began my explanation and illustrated it by little drawings. First two wagons heading west to the Rockies and the Gunsches each represented by stick figures, the females had a triangular skirt and the males a cowboy hat. I had his attention for he watched and listened with interest.

Next came four men in cowboy hats, I wanted to emphasise they were not Indians even though the party had been scalped. I pointed to each in turn and repeated their names, Wyatt, Clay Wyatt, Jones and Pickett. I then acted as if I was shooting a rifle and put a cross through the men and Willie and Anna. I looked at Grey Feather and he nodded gravely. I then pointed to one of the cowboys and said Wyatt and then I pointed to Mila, not really knowing how to explain rape I just swept my hand over the lower part of my body and then I pretended to shoot a pistol and put a cross through her stick figure. Pointing to Jones I said his name and then put a cross though little Anneliese, sweeping my hand across my lap I pointed to Annelie and then acted out choking her. I pointed to Pickett, just saying his name made me feel nauseous, and then to my stick figure. First holding my face and then sweeping my hand across my lap. Grey Feather looked at me and I had to swallow hard before I could continue, saying Clay Wyatt I acted out that he too had raped me and then kicked me repeatedly.

I sat back on my heels and waited to see if Grey Feather would react. He sat quietly digesting what I had conveyed to him and then brushed the sand smooth once again, knowing there was more to come. I drew two figures him and me, his stick man had two feathers and I smiled to show how happy I was that he had found me. I acted out looking in the distance, my hand to my forehead shading my eyes, and then I drew Wyatt, Clay Wyatt, Jones and Pickett repeating their names again hoping that he would somehow remember how important they were. Drawing a bow in my hand and an arrow flying through the air I crossed out each man in turn. He stood and brushed his foot over my illustration, pointing to his chest then his eyes as if they were crying, pointing to me and then acted out shooting the bow. He was sad I wanted to kill. He tapped his chest and then shot the bow; he would do it for me. Overwhelmed, my eyes filled with tears and I shook my head; how could I explain I needed to do it to stop the nightmares? Stepping forward he gently held my shoulders and lowered his head so that his forehead rested on mine. We stood like this quietly feeling the intimate connection between us. It had developed slowly as the understanding between us had grown into a friendship built on trust and respect.

CHAPTER TWELVE

We rose at daybreak and readied ourselves for the journey. It was my turn to watch and understand our picture language now as Grey Feather smoothed the ground and began to draw; he had obviously given our trip a great deal of thought. He drew different symbols which I didn't understand and so a game of charades ensued until I finally understood or thought I understood the plan.

Rejoining the pioneer trail we would travel to the Rockies, crossing them at a specific pass. Once through the pass we would travel a given distance; I had no clue to how far it was, it could have been ten miles or a hundred miles but I nodded in agreement. At this point we would need to make a decision as to which route we took as there were three branches; the first went south a short distance and stopped, the next went southwest right to the coast and the last went north west and finished at the coast. I thought the ones ending at the western seaboard were the California trail and the Oregon Trail, but my poor United States geography let me down as to where the third ended.

Grey Feather rode the pinto who seemed very happy to be on the move after such a long time hobbled. Our belongings were packed on the first mule and I had the second. I had never ridden before and was quite intimidated by the whole thing but I tried to approach the mule like it was no big deal, as Grey Feather watched with a bemused look. I thought the friendly approach was best so I rubbed the mule's nose and then whispered in his ear.

"Come on now, Muffin. I'm new at this, be kind."

I landed on his back after a swift leg up from Grey Feather and grabbed the reins when he passed them to me. There was no saddle and I found it very difficult to keep my balance and even more difficult to grip with my knees as I had been instructed. I had slit the side seam to my skirt so that I could sit astride the animal and maintain a little dignity and I wore a cowboy hat to keep off the sun. I felt ridiculous and probably looked it to but tried to give a confident nod when Grey Feather indicated we should go.

Our pace was slow at first as I tried to master Muffin, as I had christened him. The pinto walked beside me with Grey Feather leading the other mule. Sweat was pouring off my brow, partly from the heat but mainly because I was concentrating so hard on staying mounted and gripping the reins till my knuckles were white. Muffin for his part gave no trouble but plodded on steadily, he obviously sensed he had an idiot on his back.

The days merged together as they were all the same. We rode, we ate and we rested. My rear was so sore and my inner thighs were chafed but each day I became more proficient at riding. Our pace increased and the Rockies came into sight. So far we had encountered no one, apart from once we saw a small band of Indians which I pointed to but Grey Feather shook his head emphatically and we increased our speed. They didn't attempt to follow us; there was a large Indian nation but apparently all the tribes didn't mix.

The environment was changing, there were still large open plains but now I could see more greenery which clung to riverbeds and of course the Rockies were a breath-taking backdrop. We were almost at the pass when I saw Grey Feather turn on his horse and watch something behind us. I was sufficiently proficient now to shift my position on Muffin and also turned to see a single rider following us at speed. In no time at all he was parallel but with still a respectable width from us and he slowed his horse to our pace.

Tipping his hat he said, "Ma'am," in greeting.

I nodded back and then I saw him look past me and inspect Grey Feather. He edged his horse closer and then cleared his throat and hesitated before he asked, "Is all well with you today, ma'am?" as he pointedly returned his gaze to Grey Feather. I nodded again, assuring him I was fine. He kept pace with us and again attempted to start a conversation.

"This is mighty rough country for a lady to be travelling alone."

"I wasn't alone at the beginning of my journey, unfortunately my travel companions met with an unforeseen demise. I have Grey Feather now; he is my guide and protector."

I emphasised 'protector' and I think the stranger realised I wasn't such an easy target as I looked. He didn't offer to travel on and presently commented that I didn't sound like I was from this part of the country. Grey Feather had positioned the pinto closer to my mule, which the stranger was aware of, but still he tried to start a conversation and I thought he was being neighbourly and might have some useful information.

Walking on together I told him I was from England and jokingly said I wasn't actually sure where I was now and he smiled and said perhaps he could help me out there. He introduced himself as Thaddeus Brown and he travelled this trail regularly, the Oregon Trail, from Independence Missouri as far as Bridger in Wyoming. Apparently since the Great Migration in '43 more pioneers travelled this way and a few outposts had been established along the way, Bridger being one of the first in '42. He was charged with bringing messages, mail, papers, and small items which he could fit in his saddle bag. Apparently Bridger was some 120 miles from the pass which he referred to as the South Pass. He had been very helpful and it was refreshing to speak to someone who could speak back to me. Immediately I felt guilty as I looked at Grey Feather who sat very proud on the pinto with eyes straight ahead. I would be lost without him but I missed the sound of someone's voice.

Mr Brown made his apologies and said that he needed to move on as he had a timetable to keep to, but as he made to leave I asked if by any chance he knew anyone named Wyatt. As soon as I mentioned the name he narrowed his eyes and shook his head.

"Ma'am, you be sure to steer clear of him and his band of thieving cutthroats. They are notorious for travelling the trail ambushing travellers."

I thanked him and he took his leave. Grey Feather and I exchanged looks and pushed on hoping to clear the pass by tomorrow.

The pass was nothing like I expected. It was in fact miles wide and provided a semi-flat terrain suitable for wagons, very similar to the trail we had been on. The Rockies stretched to my left and right and as we travelled through I smiled to myself and thought I was finally 'out west'.

We forged on using the daylight until we were ready to make camp. Grey Feather built a fire and had hunted down something for dinner, I didn't ask what, I was too tired and just thankful we had something to eat as our provisions were exhausted and my stomach was growling. I sat on a boulder and watched as he worked at the fire, with his back to me.

"Grey Feather I think we should go to Bridger, we can get some supplies and that's where the trail divides."

As I was thinking I would need to draw some pictures to demonstrate my idea, he nodded. He nodded! I was shocked, surprised, not really sure what I was. He had paused what he was doing and remained motionless, squatting by the fire, back very straight.

"Grey Feather, would you turn around please?"

My voice quivered slightly and I gave a small gasp as he stood and slowly turned to face me. My mouth gapped open as I stood and faced him.

"You understand my words?"

He nodded.

"Have you always understood my words?"

He nodded once more. I was speechless until I felt anger shoot through my body.

"I told you everything, my thoughts, my past, my feelings, my secrets. Everything!" I repeated.

I could feel my cheeks burning as I took a step towards him.

"You deceived me, I trusted you."

He reached out his hand toward me but I slapped it away.

"How could you?"

I really wanted to hit him, let him know how much he had hurt me. I ranted and paced back and forth screaming at him. He stood there and took it all and that angered me more, so in frustration I pushed him in the chest and stomped off away from camp. I struggled and tripped several times but my rage propelled me on. My rage turned to hurt and the tears streamed down my face, but then the hurt dissolved into fear.

I was in the middle of nowhere and it was pitch black; the stars were twinkling but there was no moon to light my way. There was rustling and chirruping and my mind ran wild thinking of coyotes and snakes, especially snakes. He had not chased after me which was another blow to my ego so I realised I would have to swallow my pride and return to camp, but where the devil was it? I wiped my face on my skirt, took a deep breath and turned to face the direction from which I thought I had come. In the distance was a light, a warm glow in the black expanse. I made for it, dancing about nervously hoping I wasn't disturbing any snakes, finally getting close enough to see Grey Feather standing in the centre of our camp holding a burning stick above his head to guide me back to him.

I ate my supper and then bedded down by the camp fire. It grew cold at night so I wrapped myself in my cloak and a blanket, but still could not sleep. I kept remembering all the things I had told him, even travelling through time, I was horrified. I must have dozed because the next thing it was day break and Grey Feather had packed up our things ready to leave. He had left a small amount of food by my side which I ate and then washed it down with water, leaving a drop to wash over my face. I felt pretty wretched and avoided looking at him as I made ready. I let loose my hair and tried to comb it. It had grown quite a bit and I was able to pull it to one side and plait it so that it didn't stick to my face and neck and so I could get my hat on. As I walked to Muffin, Grey Feather stood in my way and gestured that I should return to camp. I gave an exaggerated sigh and did as he bade, sitting on the boulder while he started to smooth the ground. He acted out that he wanted to make a picture story and that I was to say out loud what he drew.

I watched expectantly as he started. He drew tepees and lots of stick people and I asked if this was his village and he nodded. He continued to draw and as I spoke his story out loud my heart sank. White men had attacked his village taking the young and strong Indians as prisoners and slaughtering the rest. The village was burnt to the ground and nothing was left. The prisoners were taken far from their home and then used as slaves to work on the land.

He paused and seemed hesitant to continue; for the first time we looked at each other, but then he smoothed the ground and drew two Indians. The Indians held hands and Grey Feather indicated one was him. He pointed to the other and put his hand over his heart. I wasn't sure what he meant so I asked if the other was his brother but he shook his head. Was it his good friend, I suggested? But he shook his head and placed his hand on his heart again. He obviously loved the other brave and then I realised and blurted out, "You are gay."

Of course 'gay' was a modern term which he didn't understand so I asked if the other brave was his lover and he nodded. He had never shown any inclination he was gay so I was a bit taken aback; I had never heard of any prejudice among Native Americans during this era, in fact I remembered reading an article once that gay people were accepted and revered by their tribe who thought of them as spiritual with a wisdom of seeing things from two sides. I frowned slightly and was going to ask what the problem was but he pointed to the ground, there was more.

He drew a white man and then took out his knife and pointed to his partner. He demonstrated with his own knife how the cowboys had tortured him, not sticking the knife into him but inflicting long cuts over his entire body. It was cruel and must have caused immense pain, I was horrified. Grey Feather finally put a cross through the stick man and then pointed to the one that represented him and started the process again. He lifted his tunic and when he moved aside his ornate necklace his body was covered in long scars. I had glimpsed some scars on him before but now that he was voluntarily showing me, the view was sickening and I covered my mouth. He smoothed the ground and sat patiently waiting for my reaction.

It took some time before I could speak, his story had upset me.

"You learnt my language when you were a slave?"

He nodded. I put my hand on his arm.

"I am so sorry for what happened to the one you loved, it was wicked."

He nodded and stood ready to leave but a thought had struck me, a thought which upset me even more. I looked into his eyes.

"Did you think because I was white I would think the same way those men did? You thought I would be disgusted and treat you badly, so you pretended not to understand me so we could never talk about it?"

He didn't answer, just gazed at the ground. I felt ashamed, hadn't I only been forthcoming about myself because I thought he didn't understand me? I put my arms around him.

"You are my friend and you will always be my friend."

He lowered his forehead onto mine and circled his arms around me. We finally understood each other and we continued on toward Bridger.

As we journeyed on I rode in my own little world. Since we had crossed the Rockies the reason for my mission was at the forefront of my mind. I felt a little sick every time I visualised shooting a man and became more anxious, worrying if I could shoot straight, if I could actually release the arrow and kill someone, four someones. I would never have dreamed of killing someone at home, yet here I wanted to kill; just because it was a different century didn't make me any less of a murderer. It weighed heavy on my conscience but then I would remember the sickening carnage I had witnessed and in the absence of the law, decided I needed to stop those evil men.

"Do you think we should try and get another horse?" I asked. "Given the circumstances if we needed a swift get away I don't think Muffin would be up to it."

Communication with Grey Feather was greatly improved since his revelation and the conversation flowed, he still didn't speak of course but his gestures and facial expressions were immediate responses. He looked at Muffin and gave a half smile, something else he was willing to share now, and nodded. I tweaked Muffin's ear; I had become very fond of him, he had never been stubborn and showed extreme patience with my first attempts at riding.

"We will see what is available at Bridger," I concluded.

We saw other travellers from time to time but on the whole kept ourselves to ourselves, never knowing the reaction to a lone woman travelling with an Indian. At one point we saw a rider approaching at speed who slowed as he got closer. I shielded my eyes and squinted and saw it was Thaddeus Brown so I raised my hand in greeting. We stopped and he tipped his hat and said 'Ma'am' to me and nodded to Grey Feather.

"Are all your deliveries completed at Bridger?" I inquired.

"Sure thing," he said, pushing his hat back on his head and taking a brief rest.

"You don't have far to go now, you should reach Bridger by dusk."

"Oh that's good, we need supplies and are hoping to get a horse," I said.

"Well there are supplies and horses but take care, you may pay over the odds." He shrugged and continued, "No competition for miles. If you aren't too late you may get supper too."

That was encouraging and we made to ride off when he said, "Ma'am, Wyatt and his gang passed through there a while back, it's said they went on to a place called Respite where they planned to join up with some cousins. They are causing all sorts of trouble, best if you steered clear of them."

I smiled and thanked him for his concern but said I needed to find them. Mr Brown sucked his teeth and pulled his hat back over his eyes.

"You take care then, ma'am," and with that he was off at pace.

Bridger proved to be a great disappointment. It consisted of two log cabins about forty feet in length connected by a fence to hold horses. There was a blacksmith but very limited supplies and as Mr Brown had warned, overpriced. We had no money so we traded by barter, our host being very proficient and basically had the attitude 'take it or leave it' knowing we had little choice. Eventually we came to an agreement, for a horse and saddle and a dish of stew, we exchanged both mules, one of Grey Feather's furs and a blanket. Our host definitely had the better deal but said we could have a cup of coffee and bacon for breakfast on the house.

We decided to camp away from the buildings and any other travellers, but I slept poorly even wrapped in my cloak and blanket snuggled up to Grey Feather. It was all becoming very real and my stomach was churning. We ate our breakfast and filled our water canteens and then headed out to collect the horses. The pinto was alert and ready to go; my mount seemed enormous after riding Muffin. Grey Feather checked it over and nodded but before I would mount I went over to Muffin and gave him a cuddle. Our host shook his head and gave a sigh as much as to say, 'Women!!' but I wouldn't leave until he assured me that if the mule was still here when we passed again he would trade it back for the horse.

When I mounted I had the luxury of a saddle and stirrups this time but I still felt extremely high off the ground and I could feel the power of the horse beneath me, now my stomach was really churning and I felt nauseous. I waited until Grey Feather was positioned next to me so that when I asked for directions to Respite he could hear the reply because I couldn't guarantee it wouldn't go in my ear and straight out the other. This was definitely grown-up stuff and I was worried I wasn't up to the task.

We travelled light. I had added a kerchief to my clothes to provide a mask against the dust which we kicked up now that we moved faster and to obscure my face if necessary. I had my canvas bag slung across my body under my cloak and my hat jammed down on my head. I carried my blanket and canteen on my saddle; I also had my little eating knife from Wyvern slipped in my belt. Grey Feather carried the bow and arrows and his rifle on his horse.

We spoke little on the journey; we had made our plans the night before. We would approach Respite on foot in the dark and get the layout of the place, where the men were and what routines they had if any. It was necessary to strike quickly at all of them pretty much at the same time because if we missed one he could alert others and we would have no escape. The landscape afforded more cover to hide us than before but we would still be exposed.

Respite, when we saw it from a distance offered practically as little as Bridger. It lay in a slight valley which was beneficial to us because we could see the layout while we were still at a distance. There was one street with a few log buildings either side. There was one building further back from the street with a corral, presumably the stabling facility.

Our horses were cobbled near some scrub bushes which gave a little cover and Grey Feather and I sat and waited for nightfall. Finally when the time came we crept to the town and settled down to watch. There was one long building which was very noisy and men would go in and out throughout the night and we both guessed this was where the drinking and gambling took place. Near to morning a few stumbled across the street to some sort of lodging but the number coming out didn't match the number that went in so I guessed they had fallen asleep in there. Behind the saloon was an outhouse that was visited a few times but mainly the men came out and peed in the scrub. When all was quiet we sneaked back to the horses. We moved to the top of the valley and settled down to rest.

We continued this routine for several nights, we also watched during the day to see who rode into town and who rode out. It was very tiring and uncomfortable but the amount of adrenaline pumping through my veins allowed me very little rest or sleep. I really wasn't sure when we should make our move until one day the decision was taken out of my hands.

Even having watched the occupants of the town I still wasn't one hundred percent sure the Wyatt gang were there. Then one morning we both saw a lone rider leave town on the track that climbed the slope and passed us. He had his hat pushed back on his head and was smoking; the horse was walking casually, obviously not in a hurry. As he drew closer my heart started to pound and my mouth went dry, it was Pickett. I gripped Grey Feather's sleeve and nodded in Pickett's direction. I said I was sure it was him; I had had an up-close experience and Grey Feather knew what I meant. I was afraid and froze but Grey Feather took control and guided me through the motions. We sneaked to the edge of the road concealed by the shrub and coarse grasses until Pickett was a yard or so away and then Grey Feather stepped out in front of him pointing his rifle. Pickett was taken by surprise; dropping his cigar and raising his hands he started to stutter and ask what was going on. I felt sick and was shaking and didn't know if I could do this but took a deep breath and moved into the road holding the bow with the arrow nocked.

"Take off your hat," I ordered, I needed to be sure it was him.

"What?" he stuttered. He definitely wasn't so bold when he was on his own.

"Take off your hat, Mr Pickett."

"You know me?"

"Yes I do, Mr Pickett, don't you remember me?"

He pushed his hat back and I knew it was him, he was looking confused.

"Don't you remember the German family on the trail, the family you and your friends slaughtered? Don't you remember the little girl who was running for her life who you shot in the back? Don't you remember slapping and punching me in the face before you raped me?"

Even under his weathered and tanned skin I saw the colour drain from his face; he remembered all right. His hands very slowly started to drop but Grey Feather saw it and stepped closer with his rifle pointed at his chest.

"Do you have anything to say?" I said.

He shook his head; he knew he was outnumbered. I took aim, held my breath and released the arrow. I had aimed for the heart but it was an upward shot and I was in a daze and the arrow went through his neck. He fell backward onto the horse's haunches, startling it, but Grey Feather sprang forward and caught the reins. He motioned for me to help him but I was frozen to the spot. Finally he grabbed my arm and pulled me to the horse. With some difficulty we pulled Pickett forward so he was draped over the horse's neck. Grey Feather checked he was dead, nodded to me and then broke the end of the arrow and pulled it out of his neck. Using the reins Grey Feather secured the body to the horse and then gave it a hearty smack on the rump and it galloped off in the opposite direction from town.

I rushed to the side of the road and started throwing up the contents of my stomach. I was dizzy and clammy and had no control over my body. Grey Feather pulled me back under cover of the scrub and laid me down in the merest spot of shade, wetting his hand and placing it on my forehead and then forcing the canteen to my lips so that I would drink. He resumed watching the town while I rested. After the shock passed I cried for a considerable time and then lay motionless, revolted by what I had done.

It was coming up for dusk and by pictures and gestures Grey

Feather made it clear we had a decision to make. Either we could pack up and leave before Pickett's body was found or we must finish our mission before we lost our element of surprise and got caught. He would go along with whatever I wanted to do but it was for me to decide. I wanted to run away but I could visualise the murdered bodies of my friends, still hear their screams in my dreams and knew I must go on. Today had taught me a very important lesson, it wasn't easy to kill and there might be a good chance we would be killed ourselves. Grey Feather shrugged and held my hand, so be it but we would be together. I was so humbled by this man's friendship and devotion.

We took up our position behind the saloon, having agreed that if none of our intended victims showed up during the night we would wait till the early hours of the morning when there was a chance of them sleeping or being passed out drunk, and seek them out. The night was long; we saw figures going to the outhouse or relieving themselves behind the saloon. At one point a man pulled a woman up against the wall and we had to endure an episode of giggles, grunts and groans, fortunately it didn't last very long and they disappeared back inside. I had just about given up and was trembling thinking we would have to seek them out in a more public place, when two figures emerged from around the corner. They leaned on each other, staggering slightly obviously worse for drink. They stopped with their backs to us fumbling with their trousers and complaining about some game of cards where they had lost their money, unfairly so they thought.

One voice was complaining very loudly and I recognised it as the younger Wyatt, Clay; the other answered, it was Jones. I nodded to Grey Feather and held up two fingers meaning both of them were the target. I stood and nocked my arrow, taking careful aim. Clay Wyatt turned and had to lean on the wall to keep upright, I released the arrow and it struck him in his chest. Jones was so surprised he spun around with his trousers undone; he staggered slightly but my next arrow hit home. He fell immediately but Clay was still propped against the wall. Grey signalled for me to lose a second arrow at him, which I did and he fell forwards onto his face.

Grey Feather was about to sneak forward to remove the evidence and pull the bodies into the bush to give us extra time to track down the older Wyatt when another figure appeared. He almost tripped over Clay Wyatt and let out a shout when he saw the two bodies. We knew we had to get away before all hell let loose so we merged back into the darkness and headed for our horses. Grey Feather took the bow and arrow and then bumped me up onto my horse. My bag strap was wound around the pommel on the saddle so I quickly unwound it and threw it around my body, then pulled my cloak around me and pulled up the hood. It afforded me little disguise as the sun was rising on a new day.

We took off at speed, I had no idea of the direction, I just followed Grey Feather. In the distance I could hear shouts and hollering but dare not look back for fear of falling off my horse. My mind was blank, I just focused on the pinto's tail and tried to keep up with it. It felt like we galloped endlessly. There was a slight incline in the ground and ahead I saw trees, we must be heading for the river we had seen on our journey to Respite. I prayed my mind was playing tricks on me and the thunder of galloping hooves was just my imagination, still I didn't turn to look. Grey Feather was an expert horseman and I could not maintain the speed he was capable of or manoeuvre the horse and as I began to tire, without warning I was thrown to the ground. All the air left my lungs with a whoosh and I lay in a crumpled heap on the ground. My horse kept going and started to race the pinto now that it was rid of its burden. Grey Feather saw the riderless horse and spun to come back to me. I screamed at him to keep going but he ignored me.

He halted in front of me and held out his hand to pull me up next to him but it was too late, our pursuers were upon us and there were six guns trained on us.

"Grab that murdering Injun!" shouted Wyatt. "You killed ma boy and you're gonna pay for it."

Grey Feather was dragged from his horse and his hands secured behind his back. Someone dragged me up from where I laid and pinned my arms against my sides. Wyatt looked around and seeing a tree steered his horse toward it.

"Over here, boys, get the rope."

We were both dragged along and I realised they were intending to hang Grey Feather.

"I mean to see justice done," said Wyatt.

He was so pompous that I started to rant at him.

"Justice, justice, what do you know of justice? What justice was there for my friends you and your cronies raped, murdered and scalped back on the trail?"

Two of the men had thrown a hangman's noose over a branch and were grinning and laughing thinking it was great entertainment. The pinto was placed below the rope and Grey Feather was being manhandled onto him. I was kicking and screaming.

"I did it, I killed them, leave him alone."

The men just laughed and jeered at me, saying a woman couldn't kill with a bow. As the noose was placed around his neck a sharp pain flashed in my head and there was buzzing in my ears. I was wrestling to free myself but Gray Feather sat calmly astride the pinto. My head was spinning, I felt so dizzy but still I tried to get to him. He looked at me, his eyes were dancing and he said, "Eev-ee-leen."

With that one of the evil men slapped the horse's rump and it took off, leaving Grey Feather dangling from the branch. The pain in my head was incredible and I was nauseous. I knew what was happening. I screamed and fell to the ground; the one who had been holding me stooped to lift me up and with both his hands busy I used it to my advantage and grabbed his gun which was tucked in his belt. He sprang back fearing I would shoot him but that was not my intention. I spun around and through my blurred vision, aimed in the direction of Wyatt. I pulled the trigger.

CHAPTER THIRTEEN

B efore I opened my eyes I said a silent prayer that I had returned home. I had not. I was disappointed. I had always planned everything down to the last detail but my travels had impressed upon me that planning wasn't always possible and I needed to stay calm and deal with whatever came along. The little voice in my ear said, *Don't worry. You've got this, girl.* The light was failing and there were not many people about but I could hear a noise, so straining my ears I held my breath to listen.

"Oh for Christ's sake," I said under my breath. "They are speaking bloody French!"

I just closed my eyes and went back to sleep.

When I woke I felt marvellous; no headache, no nausea and no buzzing in my ears. It seems that the unpleasant symptoms of hopping about in time were now restricted to before the jump and as long as I had a good sleep on arrival there were no ill effects. I had slept well and was now refreshed and full of energy, in fact I had more energy now than I had experienced in years. I was younger too, I could tell and quickly checked my scars; it seemed crazy to work out how old I was by looking at old scars but it had worked before. The scar on my wrist was there, the one on my leg was not so by my reckoning I was between twenty-six and thirty.

It seemed totally unjust that the one time I felt physically well I was at the lowest point emotionally. Grey Feather was no longer with me, my friend, and my protector who had died because of me. I could still see his dancing eyes and hear him trying to say my name. He had taught me a wealth of knowledge, not only how to use a bow and survive on the prairie, but human nature. I resolved not to let him down now that I had a new self-confidence, but could feel my throat close and my bottom lip tremble as I thought of him.

For a time I sat where I was, lost in thought, then one thought struck me. If I had travelled further back in time, which I was convinced I had, he wasn't born yet; his time was yet to come. So, as long as I didn't return to his time and place he would be safe, well, safe from me anyway. I clung to this thought as I knew it was the only reasoning which would get me through the sadness of losing him.

I think it was just after daybreak since people were beginning to bustle about. I had spent the night on some sacking beside a building so it was best to rouse myself. It looked as if a market was being set up so I wandered over to watch the people going about their business. My stomach was growling too so I was looking for food. There was a small monument in the centre of the square and a water trough for the animals to drink from. I wet my face and then sat at the base of the monument to organise myself; luckily everyone was busy and took little notice of me. I tidied myself up; fortunately my garb wasn't too out of place but I wore my cloak so it was mostly covered. I foraged in my canvas bag which I had secured across my body, and found my belt with my little hand-sewn purse. I put it on and then examined the contents. I found some coins from home which would be of no use here but I still had those from Wyvern. I kept some in my hand and patiently waited until the stall holders started selling their wares, hoping someone would take pity and accept the English coin.

Most of the people were speaking French, I recognised it from my school days but they spoke so quickly I couldn't understand them. I learnt it for two years and was pathetically poor and my repertoire now was limited to asking someone to open a window or close the door and a few other odd words. The smell of fresh bread was too much to ignore so I took a deep breath and approached a stall. I pointed to a small loaf and the stall holder asked for money so I just held out my hand with a few small coins in it. He heaved a loud sigh and shrugged his shoulders. I put on a pathetic face and said it was all I had and he took pity on me and helped himself to a couple of coins from my outstretched palm. By the time I had visited several stalls I had bread, cheese, a couple of apples and a drink, I felt pretty pleased with myself and took no time in consuming a satisfying breakfast. I wrapped what was left and put it in my canvas bag for later.

The streets were beginning to fill so I thought I could mingle without drawing too much attention to myself. Some of the buildings were quite substantial, constructed of stone and quite impressive. I stood gazing at one such building when an old man stood next to me and started chatting. I understood the odd word and nodded and smiled where I thought it appropriate; he said 'cathedral' and 'fire' and by the state of the structure I could tell it had been severely damaged and was undergoing reconstruction. We bid each other 'au revoir' and went our separate ways.

The day was fresh but pleasant and I was enjoying my stroll. The buildings changed a little and it became noisier as I came across a river on which was considerable traffic with many people on the bank, working, talking, coming and going. I found a comfortable spot to bide my time and observe and listen to what was going on. It was fascinating but I heard no English so eventually I asked a woman standing near me, "Excusez-moi, quelle riviere est-ce?"

She looked a little startled, probably due to my poor accent but eventually smiled and said, "C'est la Seine." OK, so I was in a city on the Seine, could it be Paris? I examined names on boats, unloaded cargos and names on nearby buildings but didn't see Paris, but I did see Rouen. I knew there was such a city because as a schoolgirl I had a pen pal from there in an attempt to improve my French, which it didn't and the communication ceased. Did she tell me Rouen was on the Seine? People started to drift away and the day was becoming a little cooler so I decided to consume the remainder of my food and head back to the market square and find somewhere to stay for the night. I wasn't sure what era I was in but I thought my best plan was to try and get back to England, to Wyvern where all this had begun.

Stall holders selling food to me for English coins was one thing but would a tavern or inn accept them for a room? By the time I reached the market square all the stalls were packed away and several dogs and scruffy children were fighting over any scraps left behind. But the square was by no means empty; people were walking around and going into taverns, some of which were very noisy. I walked over to the trough for a sip of water and to refresh my face. I was rather dubious which inn to approach and stood looking around trying to summon the courage to enter one thinking perhaps I would have to spend the night where I had slept the night before. Of course I wasn't as tired as I had been then and doubted I would sleep so easily.

Several women sauntered past me openly staring as they did so, and then hung around at the edge of the square until a man approached them and they disappeared around the corner. After it had happened several times I realised what was going on, they were prostitutes plying their trade and me hanging around here was no longer a good idea. Nervously I looked around; there were three men rather worse for drink practically falling out of a tavern door and on the opposite side of the square stood a tall hooded figure leaning against the wall. I had to make my mind up quickly and started for an inn halfway between the two.

Unfortunately I wasn't quick enough and the drunken trio surrounded me, jabbering away and making lewd gestures. I couldn't understand them but it was pretty clear from the expressions on their faces I was intended to be the entertainment for the evening. I stood up straight and tried to push past them only to be gripped by the arm and swung around. One of them had me in a vice-like grip and was trying to push his face into mine.

"Get off me, you drunken bastard!" I shouted as I brought up my knee and connected with his crotch. He crumpled to the ground and the other two made a dive for me; it was surprising how quickly they sobered up and they were angry now. I was being pushed and pulled about, the third one having recovered enough to slap me so hard I landed on the ground. I am not really sure what happened; then it all happened so fast.

The hooded stranger appeared and took them all on. He knocked one out completely and was pummelling the other two who were either falling to the ground or just trying to get up. Seeing his chance he reached down, pulled me up and yelled, "Run!" He had my hand so I had little choice so I scurried after him.

"You're English," I said between ragged breaths and just kept running.

I was having difficulty breathing after so much exertion so he turned between two buildings but we found it was a dead end. I was bent double gasping as he looked around for an escape. There wasn't one so he grabbed me and pushed me against the wall covering me with his body. I started to protest but he shook me and told me to shush! My face was buried in his tunic so he bent his head so his mouth was right next to my ear and I could just about see over his shoulder.

"Can you see them?" he whispered.

I shook my head, he was pressing so close to my body I could feel his chest rising and falling and I'm sure he could feel my heart hammering away. It was extremely up close and personal but I couldn't move and all I could think at the time was, *Thank God, he is English*. There was a commotion at the end of the alley; the three not so drunk men appeared cursing loudly.

"They are here," I whispered nervously.

"Are they coming up the alley?"

I gave a slight nod.

"Put your arms around me," he hissed in my ear.

I just did as he said without even thinking, at which he buried his head in my neck and pushed me hard against the wall again. I gave a loud gasp, I couldn't help it but instead of him telling me to shut up he said, "Good, do it again."

And so we continued. The three men came to a standstill and watched the little spectacle we were putting on. They began to laugh and then one of them nudged the others and they turned and walked back the way they had come.

"They have gone," I said as I tried to push the stranger away but he held on breathing deeply. I smacked him on the arm and tried to knee him but he dodged away nimbly so I hit him on the arm again and pushed.

"Ouch, Evie will you stop hitting me? I was trying to protect you."

I stopped mid swing and stood motionless, eyes wide and mouth gaping. I had told my nickname to only one person since I had left home. The stranger tossed back his hood so that I could see his face.

"Robin!" I squealed.

I launched myself at him, he rocked back on his heels and threw his arms out to the side to try and keep his balance. He didn't put his arms around me; he probably thought I would hit him again. I pulled away from him to look him in the face with tears streaming down my cheeks. Yes, it was Robin. So I hugged him again and this time he held me gently and chuckled.

"It really is you," he said. "Many times I have thought I saw you, only to find I was mistaken."

His face turned serious momentarily and I was touched he still thought of me. Then he grinned and continued.

"I caught a glimpse of you as you entered the square so I waited and watched. Of course as soon as you started cursing at your attackers I knew there was no doubt."

"And you came to my rescue once again, you are still my champion."

He gave a mock bow and we both laughed.

"Why are you in France, Robin?"

"I am trying to get Sir William back to England."

"Trying?" I asked. "Is something wrong?"

Robin sighed and nodded his head; he looked very concerned so I knew it was not a trifling matter.

"William was taken hostage and by the time I returned with the ransom his leg was festering from a wound. That is why I was in the square; I had been trying to buy bandaging. I must get back to him, will you come with me?"

"Of course I will, Robin," I replied with no hesitation.

We crossed the road and turned several times; my heart was racing and I was a little breathless, not because Robin was stepping out and I had to hurry to keep pace, but because I was just so excited at seeing him again.

We finally reached an inn which was comparatively quiet with just the low hum of people eating and drinking. Climbing the stairs we reached a room at the rear of the building. Robin opened the door quietly and stood back to allow me to enter. It was dark and gloomy and I had to wait for my eyes to adjust. The room held very little and it was stuffy with an underlying odour. As I approached the bed the occupant stirred a little and I was shocked to see the condition of William. He was painfully thin with no colour, his face covered with a shaggy beard, his hair unkempt and he wore the expression of a man in pain with very little reason to go on. I tried not to let my dismay show and smiled and scotched on the edge of the bed. He studied me through squinting eyes which flew open when he realised who I was. He reached out a trembling hand and touched my arm.

"Evelyn." His voice was hoarse and weak. "Evelyn, it is you?"

He closed his eyes and sighed; when he opened them they were moist as were mine.

"Why are you here?"

"To look after you of course, to make you well so we can all go back to England."

He smiled and said, "You have not changed in all these years, still vivacious and determined."

I gave his hand a squeeze and smiled. I wasn't sure what he meant by 'all these years', surely I had only been away twelve months at the most. I stood with my hands on my hips and surveyed the room.

"Right, let us get started. Robin I will need your help."

I think he looked a little relieved that I had taken over the role of carer and followed my instructions to the letter. He rekindled the brazier to keep the room warm because the first thing I did was throw open the window. It was evening now and a little cool but fresh air was a priority. The inn keeper kindly brought a pail of hot water and two bowls as requested, one for dressing the wound and the other for washing William. I decided the latter was first on the list so went about bathing him; he was a little embarrassed but didn't have the strength to stop me. He lay meekly on the bed and it took a great deal of self-control not to show how saddened I was seeing his emaciated body. I brushed his matted hair and kept apologising when he winced, then tied it back off his face. He was beginning to look better and I hoped feel better. Robin looked startled when I told him to shave William whilst I got things ready to dress his wound.

When I took off the old dressing I gasped; there was an open wound around his ankle, and it resembled raw meat. The skin above it was red and hot with inflammation and the skin on his foot was pale and discoloured.

"My goodness, William how did this happen? Surely not in battle, that was months ago."

"No, not in battle, I tried to escape on numerous occasions so I was shackled to the wall inside my cell."

I shook my head and then went about trying to clean and dress his leg. I knew it was causing him pain; the old dressing was stuck to the dried blood and the sweat was forming on his brow, but he said nothing. I needed to distract myself while I worked or I would retch.

"Robin is this how ransom victims are usually treated?"

"Not usually," he replied.

"The men on the losing side are killed; it costs more to feed them so it is not worth keeping them alive. Knights and gentry are taken hostage because their families will pay to get them back, they are stripped of their armour and horse and with the ransom money it is the method of accruing wealth."

Robin had managed to get clean linen cloths for bandages and a pot of salve, but I thought it would be of little use. The wound had gone too far, he needed penicillin and even that would not guarantee recovery. However, he looked better and said he felt a little better after my ministrations and agreed, after some coaxing, to drink some soup Robin had fetched from downstairs. I sat on the bed and spoon fed him and his eyes never left my face for a moment.

"Why did you leave us, Evelyn?"

His eyes looked sad and I had great difficulty meeting his gaze. I didn't want to lie but now was not the time for long explanations.

"I did not leave of my own free will; you know how much I care for you and Robin and Hilda."

A thought struck me. If according to them I had been gone years, was Hilda still alive?

"She lives," said William. "Perhaps one day you will tell us what happened to keep you from us."

I could see he was exhausted and promising I would reveal the reason for my disappearance sometime in the future he settled on the pillow and soon closed his eyes in sleep. We left him to benefit from sleep while he could and went to the main room downstairs. It was still crowded but Robin found a little table at the rear and we sat and asked for some food. I'm not sure what it was but it was palatable and I was hungry so we both sat in silence whilst we devoured the meal.

Robin was the first to speak. "We must get William back to England."

"I do not think he would survive the journey. His wound is very serious, he needs medical help."

He looked concerned, he had only known William to be strong and a survivor and the thought that he might not live was something he couldn't contemplate. He opened his mouth to say something but I held his arm across the table and quietly told him of my fears.

"Tomorrow you must try and find a physician, Robin; my care will not be enough."

He slowly nodded and placed his hand over mine.

"Why were you fighting here in France?"

"We were further south in Aquitaine, the lands that belong to the Queen Mother Eleanor. Since John rose to the throne he has lost control of much of Normandy to the king, Phillip of France, and looks to lose even more. Eleanor was always a strong queen but at her eighty years has decided to enter the convent at Fontevraud. King John is not popular and there is much disquiet back in England, surely you are aware of this?"

I shook my head; I wasn't sure how to field this question.

"I have been abroad and lost touch with things that have been happening, I wasn't aware I had been away so long."

"I was in my sixteenth year when Brother Anselm was executed and you disappeared, I have just entered my twenty-third year."

"Seven years, surely not!"

"Indeed it is but you seem not to have aged at all."

As I looked at him I could see he had matured. His wiry frame had filled out and he had stubble on his chin. The hair was still a muddy blond, perhaps a little better groomed, but his eyes were still the sparkling green of his youth. He was rather handsome and his easy caring nature made him more so.

"Have I changed, Evelyn?" he asked.

I playfully looked him up and down and nodded.

"How?"

"You grew up," I teased.

He rolled his eyes and then joined in when I started to laugh.

I was given a tiny room, little more than the size of a cupboard which only contained a bed. It was better than sleeping in the street but I had a troubled night. William would have great difficulty recovering from his wound in this day and age; he may even lose his leg. I heard movement from his room several times during the night; I was not the only one having difficulty sleeping.

Just after daybreak I tapped on their door; Robin answered looking rather dishevelled. I saw a blanket on the floor; he must have slept next to William close at hand if he was needed. William's brow was burning with fever; he was obviously worse. Robin asked if he should fetch water and more linens but I shook my head and told him to go and search the city for a physician and bring him back as soon as possible. The morning passed swiftly as I tended to William. The inn keeper was very helpful considering the language barrier, and slowly I managed to wash and tend to William's needs. Today he refused to eat and at times was a little delirious so I delved into my bag and retrieved the paracetamol and managed to get him to swallow two.

It was noon when Robin returned so I motioned we should go downstairs and not disturb the patient who was just benefiting from the medicine. It wouldn't last long but it was all I had to offer. Robin looked weary so I ordered a drink and some bread and cheese, the last thing I wanted was for him to become weak and fall ill.

He had no physician with him and none was coming; he was angry and worried. He said he had found several physicians all of whom refused to come for one reason or another and he was blaming himself.

"I should have escorted one on the end of my sword!"

"What good would that have done? Stop blaming yourself, we will think of something else."

For the life of me I had no idea what and it would have to be someone of great skill to pull William back from the brink. The inn keeper came over and started to talk to Robin and I was astonished as he replied in fluent French. They spoke for a while then our host nodded and left the table.

"Robin, you speak very good French, where did you learn that?"

"You forget that William is of noble Norman stock, I grew up using both languages. Then when we fought here over the years it improved."

"A man of many talents," I teased and he smiled briefly.

"The inn keeper says there is a monastery to the north where the monks are known for their healing, perhaps we should go there, but it is a full day's ride perhaps further."

We sat and discussed the pros and cons; this was our only chance but could William survive the journey? Neither of us wanted to make the decision so we crept upstairs to see if William was awake. He stirred as we entered the room; he still had the fever but thanks to the sleep he was lucid.

It was decided we would leave at daybreak to take advantage of as much daylight as possible. Robin was dispensed to procure a cart on which we could transport William; I told him to try and get more dressings and speak to the inn keeper to see if we could buy provisions from him rather than wait for the market. He seemed to function better when he had a mission and left confidently reassuring me all would be ready for morning. I remained bedside, sponging William's face trying to give him some relief from his high temperature. I had sent for a jug of boiled water and when it cooled coaxed him to drink as much as he could. He would doze then wake sometimes holding my hand and asking me to talk to him. I did willingly but had to take care not to divulge anything that even hinted of the twenty-first century. I think during the afternoon we really got to know one another well, we appreciated our time together. I told him how Robin had rescued me yet again and he chuckled and asked for a detailed account. He thought it was ingenious that we had been brave enough to stand our ground even though we were pursued. When he muttered something about a swyve saving the day I didn't understand but he closed his eyes to take a rest again and I wasn't about to disturb him.

We repeated the previous evening's regime tending to William's needs and then taking time to feed ourselves. The cart was in the inn's stable with Robin's mount and the provisions were packed in a basket. Everything was ready. We were just leaving the table when I asked Robin what swyving was. He sat back down with a jolt and asked if I had to speak quite so loudly. Several heads had turned and were regarding us with interest. He seemed surprised I didn't know especially since I had once been married. He hummed and hawed for a while and then said it was when two people mated. I felt a bit daft and said in my part of the country we called it something different.

"You do? What?"

"Well," I began, I had never really had to give the 'birds and the bees' talk before and I thought he was more than likely passed that stage, "we call the actual physical act 'having sex', but if it is with someone you really care about it is called 'making love'."

He nodded his approval and said he would remember. Although the room was filled with French-speaking customers it felt as if every eye was on us as we climbed the stairs together.

I told Robin he must use my room tonight and I would stay with William. He didn't want to, saying a lady shouldn't have to sleep on the hard floor, that's if I managed to sleep at all. I told him in no uncertain terms that I had slept on many a hard ground especially in my recent travels. He tried to protest but I ushered him into the room and closed the door. The floor was very uncomfortable but William became worse during the night and most of my time was spent tending to him. I administered more paracetamol, the main reason I wanted to share his room, but my supply was rapidly becoming depleted so I was aware I must be more frugal.

CHAPTER FOURTEEN

L'abbaye de Saint Luc was an awesome sight silhouetted against the setting sun. It raised heavenward looking more like a castle or mighty fortress; even in the dusk the light creamy stone emitted a warm welcoming glow.

The journey took much longer than expected and all three of us were weary. Robin had lined the cart with fresh straw to make William as comfortable as possible but every stone or rut in the road caused him to wince in pain. Although he never complained it was necessary to take far more regular stops. The weather was cool but dry and the inn keeper had packed a generous basket for us, but we were eager to reach our destination because it was obvious William was deteriorating. The first night we made an unscheduled stop in a barn and on inspection his leg was shiny and hard with a very unpleasant smell, some of the skin was peeling off and I was helpless to do anything except try to keep it clean.

The next day I had stood by the cart while Robin approached the abbey and rang the bell by the huge gates. A monk appeared at a little gate within one of these gates and listened to Robin's plea for help; he was dressed in a black robe, common to the Benedictine order I later found out. When he disappeared back through the door I started forward thinking he was refusing us entry. However there was the sound of sliding bolts and much to my relief one of the gates creaked open allowing us entry.

Things happened very quickly from then on, even though we had arrived at vespers, which was one of the many prayer times for the monks. William was taken straight to the infirmary while Robin and I were asked to wait on a bench in the cloisters. After prayers, we had been approached and taken to a small hall containing a long table where a small basic meal was offered to us. After explaining about William's wounds we were escorted to individual cells for the night. My cell was sparse, very similar to the ones I occupied at Wyvern. It was all I needed; I was exhausted and slept soundly until woken very early by the prime bell calling the monks to prayer. I stumbled around, lost, the place was immense, but eventually I found Robin.

The abbey was built around a square cloister. One side was the actual abbey and voices in prayer and song could be heard emanating from it at regular times during the day and night. Another side was the infirmary which housed the many sick and injured brought to the monks hoping for a cure. The third side was the accommodation for the monks and finally the last side was sort of the utility block which also provided modest cells for travellers such as us. The architecture was impressive but it was difficult to appreciate as the only thing on my mind was William.

Brother Tomas came to inform us of William's progress; he conversed in French so I needed to wait for Robin to translate. The monk spoke in a gentle voice but I could sense Robin was becoming upset, he nodded several times and at one point raised his hand and rubbed his brow. The monk touched his arm and gave a sympathetic smile then looked at me and nodded before returning in the direction of the infirmary. Robin looked pale so I led him to a bench and sat him down and tried to be patient and wait for him to tell me what was said.

"They have put maggots on his wound," he blurted out, his lip curled in disgust.

"But Robin that is very good," I said, trying to sound positive.

"It is?" he replied, not sounding convinced.

"Why yes, the maggots feed on the dead tissue so his wound will be very clean in a few days."

"Brother Tomas said he was sipping willow bark to help with the fever and inflammation and if the pain becomes too great they use some kind of sponge soaked in herbs, it is put under his nose and when he breathes it in he sleeps."

"It sounds as if they are doing all they can to make him comfortable," I said.

I was thinking to myself it wouldn't be enough, he needed proper antibiotics, but I had heard of these 'soporific sponges'. They were used as early anaesthetics and contained opium, hemlock and other herbs which could pack a punch, equally they could be dangerous if too much was administered. It was some comfort to see that the monks understood illness was attributed to natural causes and not punishment or the result of sinful behaviour. They were using herbs and various other means as well as prayer; formerly the latter had been the only remedy offered for recovery. I noticed Robin had more to say but was finding it very difficult. He sat with his arms resting on his knees and his head was bowed staring at the ground. I slid a little closer on the bench and rested my hand on his forearm, our knees were touching, and I wanted to support him. He slowly turned his head toward me and looking into my eyes he said almost in a whisper, "They want to cut his leg off!"

The revelation did not come as a shock to me; I had suspected gangrene before we had left Rouen. However, confirmation of my fears was very upsetting and I could find no words of comfort for Robin. He clasped my hand and rubbed his thumb across my knuckles.

"Brother Tomas wishes me to speak with William, to obtain his permission to proceed."

"Oh dear," I murmured and rested my forehead on his shoulder.

Robin in turn pressed his face to my hair and I felt him shudder. Even if he lost his leg the chances of William surviving were extremely slim.

"Does Brother Tomas wish for us to go to William now?" I asked.

Robin nodded and my stomach did somersaults. We stood and with our hands still clasped for moral support we walked to the infirmary.

Imagine my disappointment when I was barred from entering. I started protesting, looking at Robin and willing him to state my case, which he did, but the young monk shook his head and said something to me I could not understand. I was so frustrated I moved forward trying to enter but was gently pulled back to Robin's side. He held my shoulders and looked into my eyes as he explained that it was not the monk who didn't want me to enter but William. I was crushed. Tears sprang to my eyes but then realising the odious task facing Robin I swallowed hard, nodded and stood aside to let him pass through the door.

I wandered around the cloister endlessly. I pulled my cloak around me and was hugging myself, not because I was cold but because the hurt was so intense I was afraid my emotions would overflow. I lost track of time and direction until the young monk from the infirmary materialised in front of me. He smiled sympathetically and beckoned for me to follow him. My hopes were raised thinking he was taking me to William but instead we approached the abbey. He didn't try to speak, knowing I didn't understand, but opened the door to allow me to enter. The interior was beautiful, the sun shining through the windows throwing shafts of light across its breadth and reflecting off the many candlesticks. I could visualise the brothers gathered here for prayers and their chants ascending to the lofty ceiling. We walked toward the altar which had two single lit candles, their flickering light reflecting on a huge simple cross which hung above it.

He motioned for me to kneel and he joined me, hands clasped and head bowed and we prayed.

At first I begged God to save William, I even tried to bargain for his life but the prayers gave me no comfort, so I stopped. The quiet was bliss and the sunlight lit all the nooks and crannies in the abbey, nothing was hidden. I likened the sunbeams to God; he was everywhere, seeing all. I found myself opening my mind and just praying that His will be done and that He gave me the strength to cope with whatever that was. I thought the monk must have sensed the calmness which engulfed me then, because he crossed himself and rose, offering me his hand to help me up.

Robin was walking slowly in the square when I left the abbey; he was distracted deep in thought and didn't notice me until I was by his side.

"Shall we walk?" he asked quietly. I nodded and we walked toward the huge gates. The little gate was open so we passed through without having to seek out a monk. It was approaching autumn and some trees were showing signs of changing colour. There were still a few wild flowers amongst the grass and hedgerow and the grass was green after scattered showers. I still felt the calmness from the prayer time so I didn't press Robin for information, but waited patiently for him to gather his thoughts.

"There is no improvement in William despite the effort from the monks, especially Brother Tomas who stays by his side practically all the time. He says the poison from his leg is spreading causing high fevers where he shakes repeatedly and becomes delirious. The herbs he is given affect his mind also, but that is the only way they can try and control his pain."

I had seen rigor before and it could look very dramatic, the patient shaking violently and complaining of cold when in fact their temperature was extremely high.

"He refuses to have his leg... removed. He joked and said a one-legged knight was of little use and there was no guarantee he would live even if he survived the actual..."

Robin trailed off and turned to look over the valley, I think he was trying to regain his composure or at least not allow me to see how he was being affected by all this.

"Sometimes he is delirious and then has a period of being quite lucid, he knew who I was when I was beside him and wanted to give me instructions and arrangements for when he..."

Once again the words stuck in his throat and he couldn't finish the sentence. I stood beside him and gently rubbed his arm; none of my words would make it easier for him but I was there.

He turned and gave a brief smile.

"He asked me to give you a message."

"He did?"

I was relieved he had remembered me.

"He would not let you see him because he wants you to remember him as he was. He finds comfort in thinking of your time at Wyvern when he first saw you and was intrigued by your very independent manner."

Robin gave a slight chuckle and relaxed for a fleeting moment.

"He declared he had never met anyone like you." He shook his head and sucked his teeth. "I do not think any of us had, oh, Evelyn why did you leave us?"

That remark caught me quite off guard, even more so the beseeching look he gave me.

"I told you I did not leave by choice."

He took a swipe at a tall grass beside him.

"If you had stayed he would have been happy and not hell bent on fighting in every battle that came along."

His tone was accusing, almost angry.

"Are you blaming me for all this?"

I was indignant and let it show in my voice. He immediately regretted his comment and apologised, saying he was upset but that was no reason to lash out at me. I forgave him instantly of course. It was perhaps suitable to keep quiet as neither wanted to hurt the other, we were just privately battling with our own emotions.

We passed the day together mainly in the cloister, so that if a monk came out of the infirmary we could go to William immediately if we were needed. Evening came and in the dining hall both of us mainly pushed the food around our plates. The young monk appeared just as we were about to retire to our cells. He spoke rapidly to Robin and beckoned him to follow him. Robin turned and opened his mouth to speak but I raised my hand to stop him.

"This time I am coming."

We sat with William through the night; he was a pitiful sight and I understood why he had not wanted me to see him. Now it did not matter for he was oblivious of his surroundings. Brother Tomas had indicated that his passing was imminent and Robin and I wanted to be with him right to the very end.

I woke with a start. My head had sunk onto my arms which were on the bed and I must have dozed. Now I was wide awake, I looked to Robin thinking he had woken me but he sat calmly, resigned to the impending loss of his lord and mentor. He was gazing at me and then we looked to William who lay calmly on the bed. He was so calm I feared the worst and placed my hand on his chest, but I could detect the shallow rise and fall. I held his hand and hoped he knew we were there. Brother Tomas came and stood with us; he prayed and then whispered to Robin.

"He needs to know we will release him, allow him to pass over," Robin said.

I was confused and looked to Brother Tomas who nodded to assure me what Robin had said was correct. I thought it a little strange but indicated to Robin to go ahead, but he shook his head it was too much for him. He held Williams hand and I lifted the other to my lips.

"William," I began softly, "I am here as is Robin and we will stay with you, the three of us together, bonded in love. You have fought hard and suffered much." I hesitated, the words beginning to catch in my throat. "But now you deserve to rest, we give you leave to find that peace with your maker believing we will meet again."

I really couldn't say more. I bit the inside of my mouth to prevent me from crying. He gave my hand a gentle squeeze. Startled, I looked at Robin who looked equally surprised; he must have felt it too. William knew we were there; he gave a sigh and left us. The pain was gone from his face and he looked at peace.

William was buried at the abbey the following morning; it was a simple grave, no sword and shield to mark his resting place since his captor had stripped him of all his possessions. He had not wished for his body to be returned to England but was content to remain in the land of his ancestors. I placed some wild flowers on his grave and Robin left funds for the monks to erect a stone bearing his name. We prayed in the abbey and then bade farewell to the monks. Having no possessions we left the cart with them and I rode the horse that was larger and stronger than Muffin had been but plodded at a gentle rate having been used to pulling a cart.

We spoke little as we set out on our journey heading for the coast and a passage to England. In Normandy we were relatively safe as the land was ruled by King John but as we ventured north we would need to pass in to that ruled by King Philip II of France. Who knew what we would have to face there but for now we could plod along with our thoughts, mourning the loss of our friend William.

CHAPTER FIFTEEN

Trooper was not built for speed. Having spent most of his life pulling a cart he didn't see the point of dashing about the countryside. He had great stamina, a sturdy build and a lovely temperament, so when Robin commented on his steady pace, I had patted the horse's neck affectionately and said I thought he was a trooper. Robin shrugged his shoulders; he saw no harm in it at the moment but said he wasn't sure what would happen if a hasty getaway was required. I asked if it would come to that and he said he had no idea but we needed to be prepared.

The mornings and evenings were getting colder and I usually sat huddled in my cloak. My clothes had been intended for the hot dry prairie climate so offered little warmth and to add to which they were worn and ripped. I hoped we would come across a market but Robin seemed intent on avoiding towns and villages. Nonetheless I enjoyed our journey. As our emotions moved on from the raw painful stage we started to chat and often laughed. Sometimes we came across an inn but often we made do with a shed to spend the night. The farmers were very friendly on the whole and agreed to us spending the night and for a few coins would offer us milk, bread and cheese. I wasn't sure how much money Robin had so one evening as we prepared to bed down for the night I pulled out my purse and started rummaging for coins. I also had some in my canvas bag but I didn't know if it would cover our sea passage. Robin watched me with an amused look on his face.

"Evelyn, I have enough for our journey."

"Perhaps, but I should make a contribution, after all you did not know you would have me with you."

"I have sufficient for two."

I realised he had prepared for two on the return journey, but it should have been William and not me. Nevertheless I insisted that if necessary I had a little to help out our finances. He just chuckled and said, "Very well."

"When we reach England, how long will it take to ride to William's manor?" I asked.

Robin frowned and looked puzzled.

"William's manor?" he queried.

"Yes, surely breaking the news to Lady DeLacey must be out first priority."

"Evelyn, the Lady DeLacey is dead. She died some seven years past."

"Oh!"

I was quietly counting on my fingers.

"She died whist I was at Wyvern?"

"Yes, surely you remember William's absence whilst you were hiding at the Priory?"

I nodded; he had said nothing, but then he had not told me he was married either. I had come to believe he was a very private person.

"Truth be told she was dead to him long before then," murmured Robin.

We were in a shed with the horses so we couldn't light a fire and seeing me shiver, Robin patted the straw next to him. I made myself comfortable, near enough to appreciate his body warmth but not too close to invade his personal space and asked him to tell me about the Lady DeLacey.

"I was a small boy when he brought her to the manor, she was beautiful and all the household and villagers took to her straight away. Her name was Cecelia and she and William were very much in love. She became with child soon after their marriage and they were overjoyed, but she suffered great sickness. My father was a thatcher and although he was William's serf he would be allowed to travel to nearby villages to work, so while he was gone my mother worked at the manor and tended to m'lady. I would be with her and William always took time to speak to me and helped me with my first bow and arrow.

"When time came for her confinement Lady Cecelia had a terrible time and William feared he would lose her, however, she finally gave birth to a son. He was a sickly child so my mother said, and did not live beyond a day. They were heartbroken. As if that was not enough sorrow, m'lady had a strange seizure and when she finally woke from it her face was contorted and she wasn't able to move her arm and leg on her left side. She did not improve over time; she could do nothing, speak, walk or feed herself.

"My mother became her carer and William gave her whatever she needed to make his wife comfortable. It was terribly sad and for a long time William shut himself away praying his wife would return to him but she never did. He took me as his page and then his squire and I was with him always."

It was such a sad tale, no wonder William always wore a sober expression. Robin lowered his head and I shuffled closer and linked my arm in his and gave it a squeeze. Losing William must have been like losing a father for him.

"He was a good man, Robin, and he raised you to be a good man too."

He smiled briefly and nodded his head.

"When you arrived it was as if he woke up, he took an interest in things he usually ignored. He was intrigued by your actions and unusual way of speaking."

I frowned. "Unusual way of speaking? What do you mean?"

"You are very open; speak your mind as if you were a man."

"Are you saying I am unladylike?" I teased.

"No, no! I mean you seem to know things that other women have no idea of or no interest in."

"Oh, you mean women are empty-headed ninnies?"

"No, Evie, you are twisting my words," he said, looking a bit flustered.

I was giggling and when he saw me trying to keep a straight face he realised I was teasing and gave me a playful shove, which of course I returned only a little harder.

"I think if you had not disappeared he would have asked for your hand," Robin continued, suddenly becoming serious.

"I don't know about that."

"I'm sure he would have."

"Perhaps he might have but I meant I don't know I would have accepted."

Robin was shocked and turned so that he could look at me full in the face to see if I was still teasing.

"Robin, I didn't really know William that well if you think about it. I was definitely attracted to him. He was tall and handsome and carried himself well and I was beginning to see he was caring and understanding, but every time I started to get to know him something happened to keep us apart. Most people can be nice when they are dressed in their best clothes and on their best behaviour, but you need to get to know them, experience life with them; marriage is a long time with the wrong choice."

He gave a slight shrug. "I suppose that makes sense, but most women just want to make a good match for security."

"I am not most women, Robin. I will only marry for love and that love will depend on respect and trust as well. Half the men at Wyvern have little respect for women, they treat them as possessions."

"They are possessions, are they not?"

I rolled my eyes and tossed my head to let him know what I thought of that. He sat quietly, deep in thought, perhaps I had come across a little too twenty-first century.

"Do you not think you can lose your heart on the first meeting?"

"You mean love at first sight? Well I don't think I could, why, have you lost your heart in such a way?"

I had said this quite light-heartedly but he seemed very serious and after a pause he nodded.

"From the moment I saw her I was in awe, my heart raced and I was breathless."

"That sounds like lust to me," I joked but he remained serious.

"No," he was quite definite, "each time I saw her I loved her more."

I realised I needed to take him seriously.

"Did you tell her how you felt?"

Slowly shaking his head, he said, "No, it was not the time and what did I have to offer her?"

"Yourself, Robin, what more could she wish for? She may be just as in love with you as you are with her."

He lifted my hand to his lips. I put my arm around his neck and hugged him; unrequited love was the most painful love of all.

As we set out this morning I looked at Robin afresh. Our conversation last night had buzzed around in my head and it was as if my eyes were seeing him for the first time. Gone was the teenager I knew and was so fond of. He was a man now and I should show him the respect he deserved and not be so outspoken and playful in my twenty-first-century way, but he was so easy to get along with.

He rode slightly in front of me for the track was narrow, so it gave me the opportunity to study him. He was tall, strong and muscular but he moved with great agility. He would swing up into his saddle with one graceful movement and then sit with a straight back controlling the horse with his knees, hardly needing the reigns, unlike me who still needed practically throwing onto Trooper and then gripped the reigns and saddle as if my life depended on it.

His jaw was strong and covered with stubble at the moment and his hair was still a little unruly but this was due to us travelling, usually he made an effort with his turnout. His eyes were brighter now; they had lost their sparkle when we first met in Rouen and the worry over William had given him dark smudges beneath them. His face glowed and his smile came easily when I looked at him. He didn't have land but he had served William well and Duke Richard so surely that offered some security.

He had taken great care of me on more than one occasion and I had complete trust in him. His loyalty was beyond doubt. It was sad to think he had never followed his heart. I had encouraged him to but I realised if he did I would lose him forever and I didn't like that idea at all.

Mid-morning we passed into King Phillip's territory. Robin had told me we would act as husband and wife journeying to Flanders and I was not to speak English in hearing distance of anyone. The journey was uneventful, we kept to ourselves and Robin guided us to the coast with little trouble. We arrived at the port at midday on the second day when it was at its busiest so we easily mingled with the crowds. Our first task was to sell the horses. I was sorry to leave Trooper behind but Robin explained he would be extra fare, the journey would upset him and horses were always plentiful at ports. With the extra coin we went to the harbour to find passage to England. The wharf was chaotic with many boats and cargo stacked ready for loading or waiting to be taken to warehouses. I kept out of the way while Robin spoke to various captains. The boats seemed rather small, all powered by sail and I was rather worried of how they would fare on a rough sea. He finally returned looking quite pleased with himself. Our passage was booked on a cog taking cargo to Dover; he pointed it out to me and I tried not to let my apprehension show. It was a small boat with a single mast, steep sides and a flat bottom, currently being loaded by its crew. It was called the Mermaid and had been delayed by fierce winds so now the Captain was eager to leave on the next high tide which was in the early hours of the morning. That suited us fine and I asked how long it would take to reach England. He shrugged and told me it depended on the wind. Coming from England to France was always faster, but the reverse journey often took longer due to a head wind.

Robin wanted us to keep on the move so we wandered around the town. It was very busy with lots to see and I was really enjoying myself after so many days in the saddle. At one point Robin bought two pies from a street vendor so we found somewhere to sit and ate them. I wasn't too certain what they contained but it was the first hot meal we had consumed for a while so we appreciated it. There were lots of stalls with people peddling their wares and Robin indulged me and let me browse; I did notice that he was constantly looking around alert for any surprises. I found it exceedingly difficult to keep quiet; I wanted to draw his attention to so many things and he had to squeeze my arm constantly to remind me. I did let out a squeak of joy when I saw a stall selling garments. I scurried over and started to rummage and found a woollen dress, very plain and rather shapeless but I thought it would fit. The stall holder was chatting away and not having a clue what he said I just kept smiling and nodding my head. I was searching my purse for coins when Robin's hand closed over mine so tightly it made me wince. He wouldn't let go and started chatting to the stall holder and looking at me and smiling. He passed over his money and then steered me away and into a quiet corner.

"You hurt me," I said indignantly; it was difficult to be angry whispering. "I have money you know, I could have paid myself."

He sucked his teeth and replied, "Yes, with English coins."

"Oh, sorry, I didn't think," I apologised, realising paying in English coin would have drawn attention.

I found a little secluded spot and with Robin standing guard I changed into the dress. It was a bit loose but after tying my belt around my hips it didn't look too bad and it was a joy to feel warm again.

In the evening we found a seafront tavern which was loud and busy but we found a bench under the stairs out of the way. We ate a meal and then settled to wait till it was time to board.

It was still dark as we walked up the gangway. The cog was full of cargo and the few passengers found somewhere to sit amongst it. We were not undercover so it was cold and the breeze was fresh to say the least. We set off and almost immediately the vessel began to rock. I prayed it would be a speedy crossing and started breathing deeply, trying to relax and quell my churning stomach. I clamped my lips shut fearing I would be sick but eventually I could not control it any longer. I struggled to the side of the boat and promptly vomited over the side. Vomiting brought little relief, the motion sickness continued and I gripped the rail to try and steady myself. Robin appeared at my side and leaned over to look at my face. He grimaced and then tried to offer advice.

"Look to the horizon, Evie, it will help steady your stomach."

He obviously had his sea legs and showed no sign of sickness, in fact he was in rude health. Just before I vomited again I looked daggers at him and declared, "I can't see the horizon, it's too bloody dark."

He didn't offer any more advice after that but hung on to me to prevent me going over the side and pulled my hood and hair back to prevent them getting splattered. The journey was relentless and so was the sickness. I vaguely was aware it was getting lighter and Robin leaned closer and spoke in my ear.

"Look Evie, the sunrise, it is beautiful."

My forehead was resting on my hands which gripped the side of the boat; I wasn't in the mood to appreciate the dawn but was too tired to protest. I slowly lifted my head and looked. The sea was calmer now and the sun was peeping over the horizon casting its golden glow over the waves causing them to sparkle in the distance. The sky was clear and in the distance I caught the glint of white chalk cliffs.

"It is beautiful," I acknowledged, "and look," I nodded to the cliffs, "home."

I was exhausted and after drinking in the view Robin lowered me down to the deck where I collapsed onto his chest and had a fitful nap until we reached England. I was weak but tottered down the gangway eager to reach dry land. How I could travel through time with little discomfort but not be able to cross the English Channel I could not fathom, but I stepped onto the quay and almost immediately relief flooded my body.

"Our first priority," Robin began, "is to find—"

"Food." I interrupted. "We need to find food, I'm starving."

He looked at me in disbelief but we set off to look for some nourishment. Breakfast was not considered an important meal during these times. Meals were eaten at midday, dinner, and then again in the evening, supper, but simple food could be provided for children, the sick, the rich and travellers. Since we were included in the last group I was hoping for something.

After consuming some rye bread with a very fatty slice of bacon perched on the top, washed down with a mug of ale we set off for Wyvern. Robin had been correct about the availability of horses and had selected two more suited to speed than Trooper had been. Home was in sight and he had no intension of plodding along at walking speed. My horse was a handful. or perhaps I was just not a good horsewoman, probably the latter. He had a habit of tossing his head and catching me unawares, either he would rear up and practically smack me on the nose or nod, almost pulling me over his shoulder. At one point Robin had jokingly asked if I had named him yet. I had replied that I had but was too much of a lady to repeat it. He frowned and then shook his head, chuckling. We rode on and gripping the reigns and spurring my mount on I muttered 'Evil Bastard' under my breath.

We made good time and thankfully found shelter for the night. It was late in the year and the day had been very grey and of course the days were growing shorter. Robin helped me dismount 'EB'; my rear and inner thighs were sore and I ached all over from the tension I had maintained to keep from falling off. As I landed on the ground I pulled a face and groaned. Robin didn't offer to release me and we stood staring at one another.

"You did very well today, you must be tired."

"And then some!!"

He laughed at my phraseology; he was becoming accustomed to the way I spoke. I no longer tried to fit in with his way of speaking, I felt comfortable with him, although at this moment I felt a tingling from his touch and my heart missed several beats, I'm sure. His eyes were vivid green and were drawing me in, I was transfixed. I felt him sway forward a little and was so surprised I tensed. He must have felt it, as he drew back and smiled.

"You go into the warm while I tend the horses."

I nodded and watched him walk away. What an idiot! I'm sure he was going to kiss me and like a shy schoolgirl my reaction caused him to stop. The dynamics of our relationship had gradually been changing on our journey. I realised I had feelings far more than friendship for him and perhaps he did too.

We had shared the same sleeping space since our reunion in Rouen but tonight felt different; his closeness to me was exciting but at the same time I was nervous. I tried to act naturally but I was finding it difficult. He stoked the wood fire to encourage it to give off more heat – it was a cold night. He sat next to me on the bed stretching out his long legs to the heat and leaned back on his elbows.

"Robin, what are your plans when we return to Wyvern?"

I tried to sound casual, just have a normal conversation before we slept.

"I am not sure," he said, rummaging in his tunic, "it depends on the content of this."

He produced a rather squashed scroll.

"William dictated this to one of the monks when he knew he was... when he knew he would not return to England."

"What does it say?"

He flipped it over and I saw William's seal, it was unbroken so obviously he hadn't taken a peek.

"I am to give it to Duke Richard; I would imagine it is instruction regarding his manor house and possessions as sadly he had no heir. There was trouble at the manor when I was last there. It was the first place I went when I needed a ransom for him. In his absence his brother-in-law Hugo had taken possession, saying he was protecting the land in the name of his sister Cecelia. I knew he wanted the house and land for himself and was hoping William would not return from battle. He refused to give me Williams's ransom so I had no other choice but go to Richard for help. All this took extra time and I feel if I had managed to return to France sooner William may have survived."

"It wasn't your fault, Robin, you did your very best and I am sure William knew this. You were devoted to him and if you had returned sooner our paths would not have crossed."

He sat up straight and looked into my face and gave a brief smile.

"What of you, Evie? What are your plans on arrival at Wyvern?"

I shrugged; plans were not something I could make.

"Will you stay?"

He took my hand gently and looked at me hopefully.

"I don't know if I will be able to."

He looked disappointed and placed my hand back on the cover. He moved awkwardly and made as if to rise but I grabbed his sleeve.

"Please wait, I need to explain."

I took a deep breath, my heart was in my mouth, I wasn't sure it was the right thing to do but I cared so much for him I needed to tell him the truth.

"The first time I visited Wyvern," I began, "was in the year 2020."

He sat dumbstruck as I recounted my tale; he didn't interrupt once, it was almost as if he had lost the power of speech. I omitted nothing, it was the hardest thing I had ever done, nothing compared to when I told Grey Feather. Then it had been easy because I didn't think he understood a single word. Now I felt I might lose the one person who made me happy. He hardly blinked but listened intently and his expression began to change, to disbelief, to anger, sadness, whatever it was I sensed I was losing him.

"And so you see, I have no power if I stay or go," I concluded.

He looked at the floor and swallowed hard; he rose and reached for his cloak. I jumped up, preparing to stop him leaving but deep down I knew I needed to let him digest what I had said and form his own opinion, make his own decision.

I sat on the bed, I felt as if my heart had been ripped out and I wept and wept until no more tears would come. I stared at the dying fire. Perhaps it was right he had left; if we had explored our feelings and embarked on a romance, how would it be if I left again? Or, should we just make the best of the time we had? Worse still, was he still in love with the girl who stole his heart and I was a distraction? I cried again at the thought of him loving another. My head ached, my eyes were swollen and I was in despair, then I noticed the scroll lying on the floor. He may leave me but he would come back for that.

Someone touched my shoulder and I woke with a start.

"Evelyn we must leave now, we still have a long journey ahead of us. There is a mug of ale for you. I will wait with the horses while you make ready."

I peered up at him through swollen eyes and nodded. He bent and retrieved the scroll from the floor and left. I felt wretched; I drank the ale, splashed water on my face and tidied myself up as I followed him, afraid he might leave without me. He helped me to mount EB and when he saw I was ready led the way down the road.

It was a sharp morning and the cold air on my face helped me to focus. It was evident he did not wish to discuss what I had told him so I decided to refrain from mentioning it again. He made no conversation as we journeyed on but being the gentleman that he was would enquire if I needed to stop, wanted to drink or eat, and basically still looked after my welfare. We rode hard and I found it very tiring especially since I had hardly slept the night before. We could only find lodging in an outbuilding and it was very cold since we kept a distance between us. Before he bade me goodnight he said we should be arriving at Wyvern the next day. I told him that would be good even though I dreaded it because I was sure our paths would then go in different directions. It hurt, everything hurt but the worst thing of all was that he no longer called me Evie.

The next day it rained, the sky was grey and totally suited my mood. When Wyvern castle came into view it still filled me with awe. We steadily climbed the hill allowing the horses to go at their own pace. As we reached the moat I looked to my right and glimpsed the Priory through the trees; they had lost most of their leaves and didn't provide much of a barrier now. I had wondered if I would spy my car waiting for me in the gravelled car park but instead the land was occupied by several cottages. Our horses clattered through the large gates into the Keep and a couple of young stable lads ran out to take charge of them.

Robin helped me down but immediately released me as soon as I touched the ground. Together we mounted the steps and walked into the hall. Little had changed and people were bustling about or sitting talking out of the cold. He sent a message to Duke Richard announcing our return and the page returned very quickly and said Robin was to follow him to his private apartment. After a few steps Robin turned and looked at me where I stood waiting and suggested perhaps I wished to seek out Lady Hilda, that was all he said, no goodbye or farewell or see you later. He was gone.

I fled up the steps thankful that the rain was dripping off my soaked hood and hair and mingled with my tears. I rapped at the familiar door which was presently opened by a very pregnant Maggie.

CHAPTER SIXTEEN

"Arise, Sir Robin."

He rose from where he knelt before Duke Richard and had recited the knights' code of chivalry. He had spoken clearly and calmly vowing, to fear God and his church, serve his liege Lord with valour and faith, protect the weak and defenceless, live by honour and for glory and to respect the honour of women. He bowed and then turned to face the assembled crowd in the Great Hall. I had stood with my hands clasped and raised to my lips as I had felt my throat tighten and tears spring to my eyes. I was so terribly proud of him and when there was a spontaneous cheer I joined in. I looked to Hilda who was cheering too; we were both happy for him, he had finally fulfilled his ambition.

I hadn't seen Robin since we went our separate ways on arrival. I was welcomed with open arms by Hilda, literally. She hugged me so much the front of her gown became wet from my soaked clothing. After one more hug she held me away from her and inspected my dismal appearance. Ever practical, she told Maggie to go and find Avis and bring hot water before I caught my death of cold. She tried to remove my clothes but I begged her to wait because I needed the garderobe. Compared to modern toilets it was sadly lacking but after months of squatting behind bushes it seemed luxurious.

On my return I was greeted by Avis who was carrying a pail of hot water, followed my Maggie who had drying linens. I think Hilda was aware that my sorry state was not entirely due to the weather and I suspected she had warned the girls or women as they were now, not to ask questions.

What followed was a medieval pamper session. The brazier had been stoked so the room was fairly warm, thankfully, for I was stripped and scrubbed from head to toe. After a clean nightdress was slipped over my head, my wet hair was wrapped in a fresh linen, I was tucked up in the large bed with pillows behind me so that I could sit comfortably and drink the hot mead Hilda had prepared for me. Maggie and Avis disposed of the water and dirty clothes and then we all sat around for what I would call a girls' night. We had supper in Hilda's chamber which I was a little disappointed about because I hoped I would have seen Robin in the Hall, however, their company and chatter was balm on my troubled soul.

We caught up on events since my last stay at Wyvern, which for them was seven years. Maggie had married one of Duke Richard's soldiers and was expecting their first baby imminently. Most of her duties had passed to Avis who was as blunt and inquisitive as ever. On several occasions I noticed Hilda raise her eyebrows at her in a warning look. The Duke and Lady Alice now had two sturdy sons and she was with child again, secretly hoping it was a girl this time to dress up and spoil now that she had produced an heir and a spare. Her younger sister Isabelle was on an extended stay with her and from the way Maggie and Avis pulled a face, I had the impression she wasn't particularly liked. Hilda commented that she was very young, insinuating she might improve with age.

I knew I must give them some news, I could tell they were eager to know how I found myself back at Wyvern. I would not lie to them so I was selective in my storytelling. I said that Robin and I had met in Rouen where he once again came to my rescue and how I was reunited with a very poorly William. I could be truthful about the events from then on. They were sad that William had died especially when I explained the circumstances. Hilda was very fond of him and shed a few tears.

Trying to lighten the atmosphere I told them about our adventure getting home and how brilliant Robin had been. I was sure I had seen them exchanging curious glances and was convinced they suspected I had omitted parts of the story. I moved on quickly, joking about my cantankerous horse EB and the rough sea crossing where I really wanted to die to get away from the dreadful seasickness.

I soon found my eyes were drooping and Hilda signalled for the girls to leave. The combination of little sleep and warm mead won over my sadness at losing Robin and I slid down under the covers and drifted off to sleep. I slept well and woke in the morning feeling a great deal better although my first thoughts were of Robin.

It was so comforting having Hilda by my side again, she said she only attended Lady Alice from time to time now as she was getting old and Alice had a selection of younger ladies in waiting to attend her and her active children, so we could take our time dressing and chatting. I looked around for my dress but Maggie who had just waddled in said it was still drying. She looked as if she might pop at any time and I had commented she ought to be resting. She scoffed and said she was perfectly fine, but I had noticed Avis did the majority of the chores particularly the fetching and carrying. I think Maggie found comfort being in the group; she had no mother and Hilda acted as matriarch to those she cared for.

I had suggested to Maggie that perhaps I could borrow something from the trunk whilst waiting for my dress to dry. When I asked if anything would fit she chuckled and leaned forward and whispered out of Hilda's hearing, that everything would fit. I look puzzled and Maggie said that when I left, Lady Hilda had taken to altering every garment to fit me. Maggie gave a sad smile and said she thought that by sewing the clothes Hilda filled her time and distracted her sorrow due to me disappearing. "She was sure that when she finished, you would return and she was right because here you were." It was a sad tale and I felt such love for this lovely lady.

I put on a simple dress and due to the awful weather, strolled around the castle with Hilda to pass the time. We ended up in the Great Hall which was busy; preparation was being made for a special meal and visitors arrived as we sat in one of the alcoves near a brazier. I saw a few familiar faces but there was no sign of Robin. We were finally ushered out of the way to make way for the trestle tables to be set up. Hilda had spoken of William and the journey through France but I noticed she had carefully avoided any mention of Robin. Since this evening was to be a celebration she suggested we really made an effort and dress for the occasion. With Avis and Maggie we prepared ourselves, we were in good humour and the time passed quickly. I wriggled into a cream dress with a gold belt and gold thread around the neck and cuff. I was to return to wearing a coif, unfortunately, so I wore a thin white veil held in place by the same gold twine I was using for the belt. I had leather slippers which were far daintier than my fur moccasins but not half as warm even with thick knitted stockings.

Avis and Maggie were to help serve so they disappeared. I went to my bag and retrieved some of my cream and cosmetics which I applied so sparingly it looked quite natural but covered the ruddiness of my cheeks exposed to all weathers for the past weeks. Hilda watched but made no comment and readily accepted a dab of cream and a spot of perfume. Inspecting each other and agreeing we looked very fine we made our way to the Great Hall.

The Hall was already teeming with people and with the arrival of extra guests we found ourselves even further down the hall, but at least we had seats. Hilda pointed out several occupants of the top table. Sir Godfrey I remembered although not quite as grey as he was now. Sir John I had not seen before. He looked pleasant, brown hair and about thirty-five. Hilda said his wife had died about six months previous and he had a small son and daughter. There was a young girl of about sixteen or seventeen who was identified as Lady Isabelle. She was quite pretty, not as much as her sister Alice the Duchess, and unfortunately what prettiness she did possess was slightly marred by a rather bored expression, obviously she was tired of waiting for things to begin. There were three vacant chairs for the Duke and Duchess and their guest. I scanned the hall but still no Robin, it was crowded but I would have spotted him as he would have been relegated to a seat on a par with us. I was just considering he may have taken ill when the Duke and Duchess appeared and we all stood.

Duke Richard was as I remembered him but his wife Alice had a new-found maturity and she moved gracefully with the first signs of pregnancy visible under her long gown. Next came Robin and I drew in breath rather noisily in surprise. He followed the Duke and Duchess down the hall to the raised platform where he stood to one side whilst Richard escorted Alice to her seat. He stood still and kept his eyes on Richard. I had never seen him so smart. He wore black leggings and black leather boots almost to his knee. His tunic was a rich wine colour; the only adornment on it was his sword belt. The stubble was now gone from his face and his hair was trimmed and swept back although one unruly lock threatened to fall forward onto his forehead.

"Evelyn dear, breathe," whispered Hilda.

I had no idea I had been holding my breath and exhaled as discreetly as I could.

"He cuts a very dashing figure, does he not?" said Hilda.

All I could do was dumbly nod my head in agreement. I listened as Richard began his speech but was totally distracted by Robin's appearance. He spoke of his friendship with William and the great loss to him and England and he was genuinely upset. He composed himself and then read word for word from the scroll Robin had carried home from France, which spoke of Robin's bravery and prowess in battle, his unswerving loyalty to William and the crown. He concluded that Robin was an honourable man who unselfishly protected and defended others, not seeking glory for himself and William's dying wish was that he be knighted and become heir to his lands and property.

Robin knelt before the Duke and recited his vows of chivalry and was then dubbed 'Sir Robin'. As he acknowledged the applause from the crowd his eyes swept the assembly, resting briefly on Hilda and myself. Both of us had tears running down our cheeks but we were practically bouncing for joy and a brief smile lit up his face.

The feast was marvellous but it was difficult to appreciate after such a surprise. My eyes kept wandering to the top table where Robin sat between Richard and the Lady Isabelle. When he was not in deep conversation with Richard, Isabelle used every trick she knew to gain his attention. I felt a stab of jealousy and I was disappointed he did not look in my direction at all, well, not that I knew of. I spoke with those around me and at one point a messenger came to invite Hilda and myself to attend Lady Alice the following day. I looked to the top table and she was looking directly at me so I smiled and nodded my thanks. She left the feast shortly after and sometime later Richard followed, signalling others may leave too.

I had no desire to stay and I was quick to agree with Hilda that we should retire. As we reached the stairs Robin materialised before us so we both curtsied to acknowledge his new status.

"Ladies, please," he smiled at us, lifting his hands and shrugged, "I am Robin to you."

Hilda moved forward and he took her hand and kissed it. She rose on her toes and kissed his cheek.

"Robin I am so happy for you. It is wonderful to have you home and you look so dashing."

He grinned rather self-consciously and still holding Hilda's hand reached forward and raised my hand to his lips. He didn't let go and I could feel my heart thudding wildly. With his usual easy manner he regarded us both.

"Yes, I am a fortunate fellow knowing such beautiful ladies as you."

Hilda gave her flustered little giggle and I could feel my colour rising. I wasn't sure how things stood between us but I wanted to return the gesture. If he was offering friendship I would grasp it with both hands even though I longed for more.

"Robin, I am so proud of you, I thought my heart would burst when the Duke read out William's words. You so deserve your reward, your dream has come true."

He held my eyes in a steady gaze.

"Not quite," he replied. "I need to speak with you, Evelyn, regarding William's last wishes. Will you meet with me tomorrow?"

I managed to say I would, before we were interrupted by the Lady Isabelle. She took one look at us all holding hands and pushed in so that Robin needed to relinquish my hand, and then she turned her back on me so that I needed to take a step backwards.

"Ah, there you are, Sir Robin," she whined. "Now you know you promised to escort me to my chamber."

Robin inclined his head and gave a half smile while trying to turn her around.

"You know Lady Hilda but may I introduce Mistress Evelyn."

As soon as she took her gaze from his face the smile left hers and she actually looked down her nose at me, which was quite an accomplishment as I was much taller than her. I resented her attitude but out of politeness I gave a slight bob.

"Pleased to meet you, Lady Isabelle," I said.

She gave a half smile which resembled a sneer and returned her attention to Robin. She linked his arm and positively gushed over him, trying to guide him away from us. Robin bowed to us.

"Goodnight ladies."

We climbed the stairs and I said to Hilda, "No amount of time will improve that little madam."

The visit with the Duchess started quite pleasantly. She was in good health and much calmer with this pregnancy. She proudly introduced her two sons, Edward who was six and Henry who was three. They bowed and greeted us which was very sweet, chatting lively, describing how they both hoped their father would present them with their very own horses when the weather improved. Once the conversation veered away from subjects in which they could participate they became restless so Alice called for their nanny to take charge.

Alice was full of questions. Where had I been, what were my plans, did I still sew, and did I still use my medical remedies? I simply said I had been abroad which she readily accepted since she knew I had travelled from France with Robin and then continued discussing all manner of subjects. Unfortunately Lady Isabelle made an appearance and she quickly dominated the conversation and her main topic was Robin. She gushed over his good looks, his riding ability, his new manor, and his charm, his everything. As the one sided conversation continued, for we barely had a chance to nod in agreement, she made it quite clear she had set her sights upon him.

Lady Alice did manage to interrupt at one point and asked if the two of us had been introduced to which I replied we had last evening. When she informed her sister that I had travelled with Robin from France Isabelle gave me an icy stare and then commented that he was so caring he would help any stranger in distress. The hairs on the back of my neck were bristling and good manners or not I wanted to put her in her place.

"Actually, Robin and I knew each other many years ago," I began. "We have quite a history together."

As quick as a flash she retorted, "Things have developed and moved on in your absence."

For a fleeting moment I wondered if this cocky little miss was the one Robin had lost his heart to. Surely not, anyone could see she was shallow, and vain and conniving, or was it just me viewing her through a green mist of jealousy? I opened my mouth to speak but Hilda touched my arm.

"My dear I fear I have rather a headache," she smiled weakly, "obviously too much excitement."

She then asked Alice if she be allowed to withdraw and rest a little. Alice was very sympathetic and readily gave her permission, suggesting I accompany her, which was Hilda's plan all along. She had sensed the tension and wanted to dissipate it immediately. Of course Isabelle had to have the last word and was cruel with her parting shot.

"Lady Hilda, have you made a decision on retiring to St Winifred's yet? I am sure the quieter lifestyle would suit you better at your time of life and of course the nuns would be on hand if you were unwell."

She gave a condescending smile and I could feel my hands curling into a fist; fortunately so did Hilda who curtsied to Alice and then practically pulled me out of the room.

"Slow down, Evelyn," said Hilda as she tried to keep up with me.

"I'm sorry," I replied, "but that young lady gets under my skin, she is so rude."

"Don't let her upset you, my dear."

"Doesn't she upset you? Whatever happened to 'respect your elders'?"

"Oh dear, another reference to my age, perhaps I am getting old."

"No, Hilda, I am sorry, she makes me so angry."

I took Hilda's arm and we ascended to her chamber at a more sedate pace.

"What was this reference to St Winifred's? What did she mean?"

"St Winifred's is a nunnery some distance from here." She gave an audible sigh. "Now that I have no usefulness here and no income it has been suggested that I retire to there to live out the rest of my life in peace."

I was shocked and stopped and looked at her, she was upset but was doing her best to conceal it.

"Richard would never send you there."

"No he would not, but that is all the more reason I should go. His family is growing, the castle is overflowing and I serve no purpose anymore. I will not live off his generosity any longer."

"Whose idea was it?" I asked but Hilda remained quiet. "I thought as much!!"

Hilda had no headache but she said she would like to rest. I changed my leather slippers for my moccasins and retrieved my thick cloak that William had loaned to me. Hilda and I had exchanged cloaks during my escape from the dungeon and she had carefully packed it away convinced I would return one day to reclaim it. Thus wrapped up against the cold I told her I wanted to take a walk to clear my head. Opening the door I almost bumped into Robin who was about to knock. I had forgotten we had planned to meet. How could I have forgotten? He was on my mind constantly, but Isabelle had annoyed me.

"Could we walk?" I asked. I could smell the freshness of the day on him, he must have just come in from outside.

"Of course," he replied. "It is cold outside but I think your temper will keep you warm for a while."

"Is it so obvious?"

He chuckled; he had softened since our return but we were not as we once were.

"I am afraid it is, won't you tell me what has upset you so?"

I shook my head and kept quiet; I couldn't really tell him what I thought if Isabelle was the one who had stolen his heart.

"Come now," he persisted. "Perhaps I can help."

Maybe I should tell him after all, he deserved to know what he was getting into. I was thinking with my heart and not my head which was not always a good thing.

"If that little shrew wants to belittle and insult me then she can give it her best shot, but when she picks on Hilda who is a gentle and loving soul I will not allow it."

At that moment we stepped outside and the cool air took my breath away, it also cooled my temper and I realised I had spoken out of turn and may have damaged the fragile link between us.

"The shrew being Isabelle, I presume?"

I just nodded, not wanting to look at him, but Hilda was my friend and I would defend her. He managed to prise the story out of me and listened gravely.

"What do you think of the Lady Isabelle?" he asked when I had finished.

"Not a lot," I replied.

We walked on and no more was said on the subject. It was winter and cold but fortunately it was dry. We passed the stables and turned right at the smithy and kept on until we reached a secluded area between the outbuildings and the castle wall. In the summer it was a sun trap and a long bench had been placed against the wall so people could take advantage of it. In winter it provided shelter from the wind so we sat down. Neither of us seemed eager to start the conversation. In our time of being acquainted I had never felt uncomfortable in Robin's presence so to feel it now was alien to me. Eventually he spoke.

"Even though Sir William was in great pain towards the end of his life he felt it necessary to note down his wishes. Not only did he bequeath me his property and possessions, he explained how he hoped I would use and develop them for my benefit and that of his serfs."

I nodded my head. "That sounds typical of William, he was thoughtful and caring."

"Yes, and I hope to continue in a manner that would make him proud."

"You will, Robin, I am confident of that."

"Consequently, I must leave tomorrow to confront his brother-in-law Hugo who believes he has a claim on DeLacey Manor."

"Do you think he will put up a fight?"

"Oh, definitely!"

This caused me concern. "You won't face him alone surely?"

"William took most of his retinue to France with him, unfortunately most were lost in battle. Those who managed to return would now be expected to fight under the new Lord."

"Surely they would come over to your side when they find out it was William's wish that you would inherit."

"I cannot take that chance. That is why I have had to wait for the arrival of more troops. Sir Godfrey has sided with me and we will go together."

I was surprised by this as he had thrown both of us in jail at some point and of course we had been aided and abetted by Hilda, who had spurned him years before. When I pointed this out Robin chuckled.

"He has always been a good man, over enthusiastic perhaps but basically just. He has mellowed and has become very supportive since William died. He respects Hilda and you too."

"Me?" I was surprised. "Whatever for?"

Robin gave a very accurate impression of Godfrey.

"The girl has pluck, pretty young thing too."

We both laughed, the atmosphere between us beginning to thaw. I was still worried about the upcoming confrontation though.

"That brings me to the reason I needed to speak with you. William requested that you became my ward so that you are under my care and protection."

Before he could continue I burst out laughing.

"I can't be your ward. I am older than you and I am quite capable of managing my own affairs."

He looked quite affronted by my reaction.

"Oh really? You have no husband, no dowry, no wealth or income. Do you expect to live off Richard's generosity forever?"

I thought of Hilda who was in exactly this position and the only solution it seemed was for her to enter a nunnery. He certainly had a valid point but the situation seemed ridiculous.

"What precisely do you intend to do with me?" I showed my annoyance but secretly I did want to know how he viewed the future. I don't know if he had thought it through because he hesitated.

"I will attend to your welfare until you make a good marriage or... leave."

"I think it most unsuitable that I live with you and your new wife."

"What new wife?" He was struggling now. "I do not have a wife, you know that."

"But it is expected that given your new circumstances you will marry in the near future." Under my breath I muttered, 'Even sooner if a certain person had her way.' "I relieve you of any obligation that has been imposed on you even though it was done with the best intent."

We were both getting frustrated and it was verging on an argument.

"You have no authority to relieve me of an oath I made to William."

I folded my arms after tugging my hood up over my head. Robin tried again, speaking with a calm voice.

"Evelyn, whilst I am away I have transferred your guardianship to Duke Richard. He was eager to do something in memory of his dearest friend. This means you can remain in the castle; you cannot be removed until my return when we can discuss this again if it is your desire. I could not venture on this mission to DeLacey Manor if I thought your need was not taken care of."

He was offering an olive branch and not wishing to distract him from his journey I agreed. He seemed relieved but I had the impression he wanted to say more. I looked at him expectantly.

"Will you be here when I return?" he asked quietly.

"I cannot lie, Robin, I do not know."

He looked disappointed. "Is there no way you can control this..." he waved his arms about as if trying to pluck the correct word from the air, "this travelling?"

"No, there is no way but I do have a warning it is about to take place. I feel very dizzy and the pain in my head makes me feel extremely sick. Finally there is an intense buzzing in my ears and then blackness."

I could see he was trying to understand.

"You told no one of this except me?"

When I had explained to him before I had skimmed over many details, deciding it would be too much for him to take in, now I would be more open. What more did I have to lose?

"I told Grey Feather."

"You trusted him more than you do me?"

"Not at all, he was mute and did not understand English, or so I thought. In America it was a time of pioneers venturing west across the land to make a better life for themselves, the land of opportunity. Unfortunately there were some men who did not work hard to make a living; they chose to prey on others. They would rob and rape and murder, some scalping their victims trying to make others think that the Indians, the native people, had caused the carnage."

"Did you come across such men?"

"Yes, my small band of travellers were some of their unfortunate victims."

I didn't realise how speaking of the Gunsches would upset me so; I could feel my eyes filling with tears.

"They were killed?"

I nodded.

"All the things you spoke of happened to them?"

I nodded. Suddenly his eyes flew open wide and he took my hand.

"My god, Evelyn, you were raped."

I could not look at him, the tears rolled down my face. He stood and paced up and down frustrated and angry. Finally he resumed his seat.

"I am so sorry, Evelyn."

He stared into the distance, not looking at me. It helped me to regain my composure. I wasn't crying for myself, it was over and I had survived, but the thought of that friendly family and goodness knows how many others was so sad, so wasteful.

"Grey Feather," I continued, "the so-called enemy, found me beaten and bleeding and even though he had suffered at the hands of the white man, took me and nursed me back to health. He then helped me to track down the perpetrators."

"Did he take revenge and kill them?"

"No…… I did."

The look of shock on his face made me think I should have withheld that fact. He recoiled away from me and just sat open-mouthed looking at me, but I had resolved I would keep nothing from him.

"You did?" he stuttered.

"Yes, three with a bow and the last one I shot after he hung Grey Feather."

Poor Robin looked flabbergasted.

"A gun?"

"It is a hand weapon that causes a piece of metal to shoot out the end after a small explosion. It is a very efficient killing device.

"Hung Grey Feather?"

He was having difficulty joining words together to make a sentence.

"When we were hunted down he was blamed for the murders. I screamed at them that I had done it but they just laughed and didn't believe me. Grey Feather didn't protest or struggle, he just took on my punishment."

"He was a special man," Robin said.

I had laid myself bare but it felt reassuring that he understood.

"Why did you not confide in me sooner, Evelyn? I could have tried to help."

"Robin, I gave Alice two headache pills and was imprisoned for witchcraft, what would have happened if I had admitted to being from the future? When I tried to tell you, you walked out and didn't return until morning. You hardly spoke to me for the rest of our journey. Have you any idea what it is like for me? At first I thought I was dreaming or I had a brain tumour."

His brow crinkled and I explained tumour.

"...A growth in the head sending me crazy. Everything was strange and terrifying. I was so afraid and an insane monk was trying to kill me. You and Hilda were my only friends I so wanted to confide in you but I was afraid."

"I let you down." He spoke so quietly and looked forlorn.

"Of course not, Robin, you were human, presented with a fantastic tale, hard to believe by any stretch of the imagination. You do believe me, don't you?"

He was sitting on the bench resting his arms on his legs, a habit of his. He hung his head but didn't answer me.

"Robin, you do believe me don't you?"

He still kept quiet and my heart sank. I rose and stood in front of him willing him to answer me. Slowly he spoke but would not raise his head.

"I believe you travelled across the sea and that you were attacked. I believe everything but..." he hesitated, "but to travel from another time," he shrugged his shoulders and lifted his head, "...I just do not comprehend it."

"You think I lied to you? You think I ran away?"

"Perhaps the bump on the head affected you in some way," he

suggested hopefully.

He stood and held out his hands as if begging me to say that was what happened. I was disappointed, I was hurt but most of all at that minute I was furious.

"Well, fear not, Robin, by the time you return I will have probably run away again," I spat out sarcastically. "In which case this is the last time you will see me, what a relief it must be to be rid of such a burden."

With that I turned on my heel and fled back to the castle. I heard him call my name but I kept going and did not stop until I was safely back in Hilda's chamber where I sobbed my heart out.

CHAPTER SEVENTEEN

It was no hardship to rise at dawn for I had slept little. I dressed quickly in my warmest clothes, careful not to wake Hilda. Regardless of the argument yesterday with Robin, I wanted to see him off because this really might be the last time I saw him. I knew he would leave very early to take advantage of the daylight because at this time of year the days were at their shortest. It was the worst time to go to battle; the weather conditions meant camping out would be freezing, there was little grass for the horses to feed on and of course fighting in mud or even worse snow, would give poor footing leading to all sorts of disadvantages. But the longer Robin waited would give Hugo the advantage of making his occupation of Delacey secure.

Waiting at the entrance of the Keep was not an option, Isabelle might appear to bid her own farewell or coming face to face with Robin might cause a continuation of yesterday's confrontation. I could not bear that and it was not fair to allow his departure to be any less than prepared for, so I headed for the battlements. The steps were steep and slippery and the darkness made it treacherous. I was a bit breathless and I gasped in surprise when I heard a whispered voice.

"What are you doing up here? It is not safe for you."

I clutched my cloak to my chest and just starred at the guard. My hood was blown back from my face and he smiled when he saw who I was.

"Mistress Evelyn," he said, giving a slight nod.

"You know me?" I managed to ask.

"Well not personally but my Maggie talks about you."

"You are Maggie's husband?"

He gave a broad grin. "Jon Archer, mistress, at your service."

He had a pleasant face and I relaxed.

"Please to meet you, Jon, may I stay here for just a little while? Only I want to see Sir Robin's party depart."

"Aye, Maggie said you were great friends, would you not be more comfortable at the Keep?"

"I would prefer to stay here if you would let me. It is very cold, how do you manage to survive all night on duty?"

He chuckled. "I have a brazier over there in the bastion and you are welcome to share it."

I could see why Maggie had chosen him for her partner; he was friendly and good natured, but still looked quite menacing in his helmet. I was relieved he was a friend and not a foe. I was just declining his offer when noise rose up from the bailey. I could see perhaps eight horses.

"Goodness, that's not many."

A few more joined but that still only numbered about a dozen.

"Don't worry, mistress," Jon reassured me, "Sir Godfrey's castle is en route, they will gather the foot soldiers there."

I nodded, not completely convinced. Jon returned to his brazier after telling me to call out if I needed him. I pressed myself against the wall shielding against the wind and also trying to feel a little more secure perched on top of the walkway.

The men mounted and I could make out Sir Godfrey but I couldn't spot Robin. Finally I saw him lingering on the steps of the Keep, perhaps waiting for Isabelle to wish him God speed. She did not appear, presumably preferring the warmth of her bed. Finally he mounted and went to the front of the troop alongside Godfrey. My chest was tight and my throat closed, this really could be the last time I would see him. The wind whipped my face causing tears to roll down my cheeks which mingled with my tears of heartbreak. The group moved off and I edged along the wall so that I could watch them for as long as possible. Just as they were about to pass through the gate Sir Godfrey looked up and spotted me even though I leaned back trying to conceal myself. He raised his hand slightly to acknowledge me, but Robin kept his eyes forward. I watched them descend the hill as the sun came up; it reminded me of watching the dawn together whilst on board ship, perhaps he was reminded of that too.

I felt a gentle tap on my shoulder; I could hardly turn I was so cold.

"Mistress," Jon spoke quietly as if not wanting to interrupt my thoughts, "he is long gone out of sight, will you not let me escort you down the steps? You must be frozen."

I couldn't speak so I nodded and he led me down carefully. He took me to the Great Hall where the fires were being lit and sat me in one of the alcoves he thought might be the warmest. I did manage to thank him before he hurried back to his post.

Time crawled by. Christmas came and went. It was a pleasant distraction much different from what I was used to. We attended midnight mass in the little chapel and then attended a short service of thanksgiving on Christmas Day itself. There was a Yule log in the grate and we ate goose. I wasn't partial to its taste but there were lots of special pastries and sweets which were delicious. Greenery had been collected to decorate the castle including a large bunch of mistletoe which produced much of the entertainment for that day. I graciously accepted kisses on my cheek but as the ale and wine flowed demands became higher and I spent a large amount of time dodging eager suitors. Every time I turned around I found myself face to face with Sir John whom Hilda had pointed out to me on my return. He was pleasant enough but was becoming increasingly annoying. I asked after his children and he assured me they were well and at home with their nurses. I was not impressed, the poor things alone at Christmas with neither mother nor father.

January brought snow which covered everything like a huge fluffy white blanket. It was pretty at first but more and more came, isolating us indoors. No messenger from Robin would be able to make the journey. The drifts were high and roads impassable. I accompanied Hilda to visit Lady Alice as little as possible because I physically could not tolerate being anywhere near Isabelle. She took great pleasure in trying to humiliate people, Hilda and me particularly, or whining forlornly about the absence of Robin. She insinuated incessantly that he would propose on his return and would gloat in my direction every time. I kept my head down and concentrated on my sewing, turning to Hilda and asking her which colour swatch I should use for my patchwork, as if I had not a care in the world. It was a hard pretext to maintain and we would leave with any excuse we could fabricate at the time.

Maggie, who had grown so large she could perform none of her duties or even stand, finally gave birth. The village women were correct, she had been carrying two babies and safely delivered a boy and a girl. The snow drifts were still high so I could not get to the village to see her, but together with Hilda we started putting little things we had sewn and other treats into a basket ready for our first visit. Jon was still on duty, no paternity leave available here, and he brought us news as often as he could.

If I had been left alone I would have managed much better, but having to cope with Isabelle and the constantly hovering Sir John I began getting stir-crazy, so as soon as there was the merest improvement in the weather I set off to the village to see Maggie. Hilda wasn't quite so brave but sent her best wishes. By the time I arrived at the little cottage my feet and legs were wet and frozen, my skirt was wet through too but I was joyous at seeing Maggie and the babies. Various neighbours visited every day to help her and she looked well and the babies were thriving. I sat in front of her little fire wrapped in a blanket rocking one of the babies; my skirt was draped nearby drying. We chatted for a long time exchanging bundles so that I could have equal cuddles with each infant. She sent a message via Jon of my intention to stay overnight and attempt the return journey the next day, so that Hilda would not worry. The distance was short but I didn't need asking twice to stay in the little cottage all bundled up together to keep warm.

The next day the thaw had begun and I started watching out daily for a messenger from Robin. One finally arrived drenched, frozen and exhausted, but he headed straight to the Duke. I paced about impatient for news, but it wasn't until the next day that we were summoned, not by the Duke but Alice his wife. It became obvious that relaying any message to me was not deemed that important, as there was the usual gathering of ladies chatting and sewing, including Isabelle.

"Lady Hilda, Mistress Evelyn we have received good news," she began. "All is well with Sir Robin at DeLacey Manor."

I sighed with relief but refrained from comment in front of the gathering, or more to the point, Isabelle. I did not want to betray my feelings, opening myself to more ridicule from her. Instead Hilda stepped forward and asked how things had fared. After Alice bade us to sit she started to relay the news. Apparently Hugo resisted when Robin and his men arrived but they were too strong for him. When Sir William's men saw that it was Robin they laid down their arms and asked to join him. Robin agreed as he knew and had fought alongside most of them. With Hugo's force greatly depleted, rather than surrender he stole away in the night.

The snow had hit the manor as it had us and they were snowed in. With the first signs of the thaw he had been able at last to send word that much had to be put right after Hugo's occupation and he needed to stay, so he would not return until spring. Clearly Isabelle was not happy about this but Alice tried to raise her spirits, saying that the manor needed making ready so that all was prepared for Robin and his bride if he chose to take one. Isabelle pouted to show her annoyance but then agreed with her sister that making ready the manor must be a priority. She gave me a very smug look which I tried to ignore thinking that the preparation Robin referred to was more likely concerned with his serfs and the crops, not making the house pretty.

A short time after Robin's news, I received a message from the Duke requesting my presence. I had never had an official audience with him so I was a bit apprehensive when one of his servants showed me into his private quarters. It was a small area partitioned from a larger chamber containing a large carved chair and a table covered in all manner of items and papers. There was a log fire and the air smelt of smoke. This was where he discussed his plots and plans, at the moment however, I thought it more likely this was his 'man cave' where he could escape the Duchess who was close to confinement and rather grumpy.

There were some stools in the room but he didn't ask me to sit, instead he rose and walked to the front of the table, so I curtseyed. His manner and greeting were pleasant enough but I had the impression this meeting was of a serious nature.

"Mistress Evelyn," he began. "How fare you?"

"Quite well, sir, thank you."

"As you are aware, in the absence of Sir Robin I am responsible for your welfare."

"I am, sir, and I am very grateful for your protection and generosity."

He half smiled and waved away my gratitude.

"It is nothing, my dear. I have been approached for your hand in marriage and after considerable thought, I see it as a good match and a very beneficial union."

I gaped in surprise, I was speechless. He looked at me as if I should be overjoyed at the prospect.

"Who?" was the only word I could form.

He chuckled, finding his omission of the party involved quite funny. I, however, could find no humour in the proposal whatsoever. I had become very hot and I had to clasp my hands in front of me to stop them shaking.

"Why, Sir John, has he not been most attentive?"

Annoying was the word that came to mind. Richard looked at me encouragingly and then he frowned when I made no response.

"Come now, my dear, this is a very generous offer. You have no dowry or title and for a knight of the realm willing to put all these shortcomings aside and ask for your hand, is most charitable if not astonishing."

All I could do was shake my head and he did not seem at all pleased.

"This rebuff is quite insulting, how do you intend to live if you refuse this proposal? I think Sir Robin will not be happy with your response. Why do you feel it necessary to refuse?"

"I do not love Sir John," I stammered.

"What rubbish, what has love to do with this? To be sure love is always preferable but not essential when you are offered a title and wealth and all the security it brings."

"I will not marry him." I had finally found my voice.

Richard raised his hands in frustration and paced in front of me, the colour coming to his cheeks. He turned to face me and was obviously going to make a second attempt.

"Mistress Evelyn," he began once more, taking great care to keep his voice calm. "Evelyn, Sir John is a good man. What would you have him do to prove his devotion and love?"

"I am not questioning his goodness, my lord, I am saying I do not love or wish to marry him. If he wishes to prove his love and devotion perhaps it would have been better to show it to his children who he has deserted and left alone since the death of their mother. They would really benefit his outpouring of love, rather than I who am quite happy to look on him as a friend."

I was rather breathless after delivering this speech to the Duke but I was determined to stand my ground. I didn't particularly want John as a friend but I didn't really want to insult him. His proposal had been made in good faith or perhaps he just wanted a substitute mother for his children, either way I did not want any friction between us. Richard exhaled noisily down his nose presumably in frustration.

"I will not pass on this refusal at this time. We will wait for Sir Robin's return and perhaps he can talk some sense into you. This offer may be the best you receive; it may be the only one you receive."

I gave a small bob and left the room. I felt it wrong that Richard would not pass on my refusal; it wasn't really fair to play with Sir John's emotions. I didn't believe Robin would make me marry him, but it gave me a little time to devise a plan for my future. The next day Sir John set off for his home hopefully to concentrate on rebuilding a relationship with his children, unfortunately one month later he returned.

I did not mention the proposal to anyone and I spent much of my time trying to devise a plan and worrying about my future. Hilda noticed I was quiet and becoming withdrawn and one night as we prepared for bed she approached me. She used her gentle manner but there was an underlying firmness, which usually meant she would not take no for an answer. I began to speak and immediately could feel the emotion rising to the surface and my voice quivered a little. She made herself comfortable in her usual chair and folded her hands in her lap.

"Come now, Evelyn," she said, "there is obviously something causing you great stress. I thought the news of Robin's imminent return would cheer you but it seems to have had the opposite effect."

"I am very pleased about his return, but I worry about my future."

She looked a little puzzled and I could see her selecting her words carefully.

"I thought you would enjoy a happy reunion, you have always been friends and I believe there is a little more than that blooming now."

She looked at me expectantly but allowed me time to respond to her leading question.

"I hoped there was something too, but I confided something to him which he has found difficult to accept."

"My dear, I cannot believe it is anything so terrible, he would forgive you anything. Will you not confide in me? Perhaps I can offer you advice or speak to him. It saddens me to see you like this."

I wanted to tell her everything but was so afraid she would take the revelation in the same manner as he had. I could not bear to lose Hilda as well. We sat quietly and I wiped my nose on my sleeve in a very unladylike fashion. She handed me a handkerchief.

"Dry your eyes, take your time, there is no hurry," she encouraged.

I blew my nose, wiped my eyes and took a deep breath. I couldn't look at her but focused on the floor.

"Robin could not come to terms with where I am from."

"What is so objectionable about the shire of Northampton?"

"Not where, Hilda," I said. "but when."

The tears started to flow again and my story began to tumble out. She listened intently with no look of shock or disbelief registering on her face. I told her absolutely everything, including my recent marriage proposal. I confessed that I felt my friendship with Robin had blossomed into love. My tale lasted long into the night and when I had finally concluded I waited nervously for her reaction. She eventually leant forward and took my hand.

"This must have been a great strain for you to bear alone. I can hardly begin to comprehend your fear and confusion and of course your heart aches. I do understand, Evelyn."

I was surprised at the calm way she had taken on board every word.

"You do?" I exclaimed, a rush of relief enveloping me.

She stood and went to her private trunk by the bed, lifting the lid and feeling beneath her garments. Returning to her seat, she unwrapped the bundle she had retrieved. My eyes flew open wide when I saw my wrinkled 'Next' bag containing my belongings which I had hidden in the bed head. She passed me the bag and I removed my items one by one and held them to me.

"How long have you had these?" I asked.

"Soon after you left and Isabelle arrived. She wanted this chamber and the bed was going to be moved but proved too heavy. She was quite put out at not getting my room. With all the pushing and heaving the parcel was dislodged. I kept it safe until your return."

"What on earth did you think when you looked inside?"

"Well," she gave a little laugh, "I could see they belonged to you and that one day you might explain them to me, if it was your wish."

I was so overcome by her trust and love for me. I threw my arms around her and hugged her for all she was worth. We both slept well for what was left of the night and I felt a great weight had been lifted from my shoulders. When we were alone I would explain what my belongings were and she listened full of wonder. It was our secret and the bundle was returned to its hiding place in the bed head for safe keeping.

One morning I told her I had made a decision. I had already explained what happened to me just prior to travelling and that I had no control over it, but if she was agreeable I would go with her to St Winifred's and stay with her. She was very reluctant at first because she thought a young woman like me had a long life ahead of her. I explained that marriage to the one I loved was impossible and although Robin had taken an oath to protect and keep me I could not be near him if he was married to another, especially Isabelle. I found a marriage of convenience for security was unacceptable to me so I preferred to stay with her. She seemed very touched by the sentiment and finally agreed although I had to explain I had no idea for how long it would be.

CHAPTER EIGHTEEN

I t was a glorious day given it was the beginning of spring. The air was fresh but the sky was clear and the sun shone giving a feeling of newness and anticipation. An entourage had arrived from Europe hoping to interest Duke Richard in a new model crossbow, which hadn't really taken England by storm as it had over there. Basically they were salesmen, but Richard was feeling particularly generous as Alice had just presented him with a daughter, Eleanor, so he decided to organise a display and a competition against his longbows.

On the morning of the event the castle was filling with visitors and competitors so Hilda and I readied ourselves and escaped to the village. There was great excitement, not only for the chance to meet and greet people after the restrictions of the harsh winter, but Jon Archer, Maggie's husband was taking part. He had left early to prepare so we helped with the children, Jon Junior, who we called Jojo and Ellie, both who were right little wrigglers and quite a handful. Fortunately there were always willing hands in the village and the other children would play with them and keep them entertained.

We sat outside the cottage and ate some lovely fresh bread and cheese and more villagers joined us, all jolly and chattering. There was quite a crowd of us as we set out just after noon to leisurely climb the hill to Wyvern. The practice field had been prepared for the event. Along one side, benches had been brought from the Keep and arranged for spectators. The seating for Richard and the VIPs had a canopy draped overhead with colourful streamers fluttering in the breeze. Opposite along the other long side was the area for the villagers and serfs, there were a couple of benches but mainly they would sit on the grass or stand. On the course were two large targets made of straw with bullseyes and rings painted on them. There were also various other targets dangling from a crossbar.

It was very busy when we arrived with most of the seats taken, but Hilda and I turned to the villagers' area with Maggie and we were promptly offered a place on one of the two benches. It was very noisy with excited chatter and the children running about the field behind us. I had Jojo on my knee and he was squealing with delight as I sang 'gee up horsey to the fair' and jigged my knees in time with the rhyme. Several of the children had found a couple of early spring flowers and insisted on twining them in the cord securing my veil. It was a lovely atmosphere and it was lifting everyone's spirits.

I was just passing Jojo to the next pair of eager hands when I saw Hilda raise her hand to her breast and heard her give her embarrassed little giggle.

"Who are you flirting with now, Hilda?" I teased.

She giggled again and raised her hand in greeting. As I followed her line of vision I saw the crowd under the fluttering canopy. Could that be…? I shielded my eyes and squinted, not believing my eyes, there sat Robin. He was just lowering his hand from greeting Hilda but when he saw me looking, he raised it slightly again to acknowledge me. I was flustered and really not conscious of my actions but found myself waving. Unfortunately Sir John had squirmed in beside him and assumed the greeting was for him. He stood and bowed and I cringed in embarrassment. Robin starred at him with a confused expression and then back at me. Sir John took his seat and leant over and said something to Robin, he continued to do so for the rest of the event.

Fortunately, to watch the archery I needed to look in Robin's direction and could keep him in my peripheral vision most of the time. I heard nothing of the demonstration and only took notice of the proceedings when Jon Archer's name was mentioned. He put on an exceptional performance and there was great cheering particularly from our side of the field. The crossbowman was skilled and hit his mark consistently but he was only able to release two bolts per minute whereas the longbowmen could release as many as a dozen under pressure, in the same given time. The crossbow, however, could penetrate the metal targets more efficiently.

I wasn't sure if Richard would agree to purchase the crossbow for his men. He was a thrifty man and use of the weapon would be expensive. The actual equipment cost more and extra soldiers would be required to protect the archer due to the time taken to prepare for each shot. I heard someone say that the bow was susceptible to rain damage, whereas a longbowman simply unstrung his bow for protection. Whatever the outcome, great fun was being had by all.

My eyes kept straying across the field and I saw Sir John repeatedly engage Robin in conversation. The only benefit to this was, he demanded more of Robin's attention than Isabelle and she looked furious. The afternoon had been a success and Richard decided to prolong it by announcing an 'all comers' display. Anyone could take a shot with either crossbow or longbow, not for reward but simply for entertainment. Some of the village farmers tried their hand to varying degrees of success, mostly wanting to try the new crossbow. Finally, Richard stood and thanked everyone for their attendance and asked if there was anyone else willing to try their hand before he closed the proceedings.

I am not sure what the thinking behind my action was; looking back I don't think I actually did give it any thought, but I found myself slowly rising to my feet and raising my hand.

"My lord, I should like to give it a try."

There was stunned silence and then a few titters could be heard in the crowd, followed by some words of dissent. Richard was caught off guard and looked to those sitting near him for support, but I stood my ground.

"I would really like to try, sir, but if the gentlemen present feel threatened by my actions I will not participate, if it is your wish."

I saw Robin discreetly cover his mouth to hide what I hoped was a smile. My words had the desired effect and most of the men assumed I would make a fool of myself so prompted Richard to allow me to take a shot. I saw Sir John stand as if to come and escort me onto the field but before he could leave his seat Jon Archer stood at my side. He walked me to stand before Richard where I curtsied politely and waited for his decision. He smiled then in his easy-going manner.

"Well Mistress Evelyn, if you feel you can use the bow without detriment to yourself; I wish you the best of luck."

I heard Isabelle comment very loudly that it was a most unladylike action on a par with the lower classes. This spurred me on even more; I was just sorry I could not use her as the target.

"Which bow is your favoured weapon, mistress?" he asked.

"The longbow, sir," I replied.

This caused a stir amongst the spectators for I think most were of the opinion I would chose the crossbow which someone would cock for me and my only participation would be to pull the trigger.

"Very well," he continued. "Would you like to stand closer to the target?"

"Oh no, my lord, I will abide by the same rules as the men."

I then turned to Jon. "Will you allow me to use your bow please?"

He nodded his agreement and took me to the range. As we walked he whispered out the side of his mouth, "I hope you know what you are doing."

"So do I," was my reply, "or I am going to look very silly."

As I took my position he made a show of giving me instruction, but as soon as I took his bow he knew from experience that I had handled one before. He gave me a knowing look and after handing me an arrow took his position behind me. I was trembling a little so I took my time; closing my eyes and concentrating I could feel Grey Feather moving my body into position and as soon as I was calm I took aim and shot. There was a collective gasp as my arrow embedded itself right on the edge of the target. I heard some laughs and a few cheers but looked at no one. Jon stepped forward with my second arrow.

"Why did you do that?" he asked. "You were perfectly lined for that shot, I could see right down the arrow and then at the last moment you moved."

"Did I?" I replied giving my most innocent look. "I must have been nervous."

He raised his eyebrow and grunted, he didn't believe me for one moment. Once again I composed myself and took aim. I held my breath and then released the arrow. I maintained my position until the arrow plunged into the target with a thwack. It was a bullseye, not the dead centre, but a bullseye nonetheless. This time there were plenty of cheers and applause. Jon escorted me to stand before the Duke who heartily congratulated me, jesting that perhaps he would benefit from employing me as one of his archers. Isabelle tossed her head and refused to look at me, Sir John looked a little confused not realising to the full extent what taking me on as a wife might entail, but the sight that made my heart leap was Robin standing clapping his hands and beaming at me.

My achievement kept me buoyant for the remainder of the day

and throughout supper I maintained a radiant smile, although every time I glimpsed Robin my stomach somersaulted because he seemed to have taken on a rather serious mood. He approached us at the end of the evening, looking dashing, this time clothed in a dark blue, his hair swept back but the same unruly lock falling onto his brow. He went to Hilda first as was his custom, taking her hand and then kissing both cheeks. He spoke softly and complimented her which always made her glow.

When he turned to me he hesitated. Finally I saw him force himself to relax and fixing a smile on his face he took my hand and kissed me briefly on both cheeks.

"Evelyn." He stepped back, releasing my hand. "What a marvellous performance you put on this afternoon."

For a moment I wondered if he was being sarcastic but I put that thought to one side as he continued.

"You are skilful with the bow and I am sure you have made a favourable impression on quite a few of the spectators. Why, Jon Archer has told me he intends to teach his daughter the longbow as well as his son, after seeing you shoot this afternoon."

It was obvious he was making small talk; he seemed uncomfortable and didn't make very much eye contact.

"Well that is encouraging to hear. I have always believed girls should be given the same chances in life as the boys."

"Yes, quite."

Once again he hesitated; he had something to tell me which he was uncomfortable about. The colour drained from my face; was this where he tells me he has decided to take a bride? I didn't want to hear it, not here or now, so I launched into an informal conversation.

"We were all very relieved to hear of your success in recapturing DeLacey Manor. I trust there were few casualties. Is Sir Godfrey well?"

"Sir Godfrey is very well and sends his regards to both of you ladies. He has returned to his residence but will no doubt be a regular visitor to my manor. His support was invaluable and we have forged a great friendship."

"That is very good to know. Do you have much to achieve at the manor?" asked Hilda. She seemed to sense the awkwardness between us.

"A great deal, Hugo did nothing to develop the land or organise the serfs. He lived off William's wealth and now it will take much to return it to what it once was. For that reason I must return in a couple of days."

A quietly whispered 'oh' escaped my lips. Robin finally looked into my eyes.

"It seems much has happened in my absence and I have business to attend here too."

I kept quiet and held his gaze with difficulty.

"I must say, Evelyn," still he avoided my nickname, "I was surprised to find you here still and it appears you are to be married."

"What?"

My response had erupted from me and I was angry. Several people had turned to stare at the commotion so Robin ushered us from the main hall. Hilda made as if to leave but I grabbed her arm to make her stay. So that's what all the conversation between Sir John and Robin had been about.

"How dare you?" I screamed at him. "Only I will choose who I will marry and no one else."

How could he give his permission for me to marry Sir John? Obviously he had lost all feeling for me. I was angry with Richard for giving Sir John false hope and not telling him immediately of my refusal. I was angry at Sir John for telling Robin he was going to marry me, or so he thought, and I was furious Robin had given his permission. I was furious with everyone if truth be told. Robin's eyes were wide, obviously not expecting my outburst. He opened his mouth to speak but I rounded on him once again, cruelly wanting to inflict pain equal to the pain I was feeling.

"I am sorry to have been such a burden to you," my words dripped with sarcasm, "but fear not, I am leaving this time. You can take your sarcastic, bitchy, selfish little teenager and go back to your manor and I hope you regret it for the rest of your life."

Spinning around I headed for the steps dragging Hilda with me. She tried to calm me but I was moving swiftly and she was having trouble catching her breath. Robin gave chase catching me by my wrist and spinning me around, but I was prepared and brought my other hand round and gave him a hearty smack.

"Don't you ever touch me again."

He was so shocked he released me and I fled to Hilda's chamber. By the time she caught up with me I was in a heap, sobbing on the bed. She tried to hold me and soothe me but I was having none of it. I started ransacking the room looking for my belongings, dragging my canvas bag from under the bed. I shook the bed post trying to dislodge the package we had replaced in the headboard. It was proving stubborn and I was getting frustrated, grunting and straining like an animal until it finally fell onto the floor. Snatching it up, I pushed it into my bag.

"Hilda we must pack our things and go to St Winifred's at once."

Poor Hilda was practically chasing me around the chamber, fretting and trying to calm me. My veil had come off and my hair was wild and in my eyes. My nose was running and the tears had left streaks down my cheeks, not a pleasant sight I was sure but I didn't care. The last straw had finally broke the camel's back; I no longer wanted to be the delicate medieval female beholden to the male sex, I wanted to be the twenty-first-century independent, outspoken female in charge of her own destiny.

Suddenly Hilda grabbed my shoulders and gave me a teeth-chattering shake. It totally stopped me mid-rant, flabbergasted that someone of her stature and temperament was capable of such an action.

"Do not make me slap you, young lady," she threatened. "I will I promise you, acting in this manner when all of this could easily have been avoided."

I stood gaping at her, breathless from my tantrum. Seeing that I had finally stopped acting poorly she released my shoulders. She stepped back, adjusting her dress and veil which were rather dishevelled after our tussle. I was standing stunned, impersonating a goldfish.

"Are you saying it is entirely my fault?" I asked between dry sobs.

"Not all your fault, no," she clasped her hands in front of her still looking quite stern, "but you could have put a stop to all," she waved her hand about as if grasping something from the air, "this."

"How?"

She softened and smiled. "By telling him how much you love him."

Well, that started me crying all over again but this time I allowed her to comfort me. She took my hand and made to guide me to a seat but as I turned I became giddy and stumbled slightly. I pressed my hands to my temples to try and stop the thumping as the blood pounded through my veins. Hilda sat me on the side of the bed and pushing my bag aside managed with some difficulty to raise my legs and lay me down.

"See what a state you have gotten yourself into." She adjusted the pillow and stroked my hair. "Now just rest and we will sort this problem in the morning."

I lay as still as I could with my eyes tightly shut and the pounding eased, but as soon as I lifted my head I became giddy and nauseous. I asked Hilda if she would find me some tablets but she seemed reluctant to look into my bag.

"Hilda, you know all my secrets, there is nothing in there that I want to hide from you," I whispered, not having the strength to speak louder.

She patted my hand and smiled sympathetically. It took her a few minutes to find and she tried to be cheerful, hiding the worry which was etched on her face.

"My goodness, the contents are endless, it holds everything."

She looked puzzled when I muttered, 'Even the kitchen sink,' under my breath.

I fell into a fitful sleep but woke when it was still dark, needing to be sick. I tried to reach the wash basin but had no sense of direction or balance. I knew where I wanted to go but my body refused to obey and I stumbled nosily. Once again Hilda came to my rescue, holding me as I vomited and then somehow managed to get me back on the bed. I lay exhausted when the buzzing started in my ears and I became afraid. I reached out, repeating, "Bag, give me my bag," and Hilda wrapped the strap around my wrist. Our eyes met briefly and I knew she realised what might happen.

I lost all sense of time; I lay where she had managed to push me on the bed. My eyes were closed but I sensed her straightening my clothes and brushing my hair from my face. A cover was gently tucked over me and I heard her moving around the room. There was whispering, to whom I did not know, but I heard instruction to remove the basin and return with a clean one and fresh linens, so perhaps it was Avis.

Drifting, I realised that my head no longer hurt but I could detect the buzzing quietly in the background. Someone was washing my face; it felt good but my eyes remained closed. When next I was conscious Hilda was shaking my shoulder but my body did not respond and my eyes were far too heavy to open.

"Avis, find Sir Robin and tell him he must come immediately. Whoever he is with or whatever he is doing he must come. Tell him Mistress Evelyn is very ill."

There was urgency in Hilda's voice and I heard scurrying footsteps leave the room. She was by my side begging me to wake, holding my hand and patting my cheek but my body would not respond. Presently the door opened and Hilda dropped my hand and I heard her skirt rustle as she crossed the room.

"Oh Robin, thank goodness you have come, I fear the worst. She is totally unresponsive. I think perhaps she is… leaving us again."

She sent Avis away and the two of them came to the bed and held my hands. I could feel Robin's strong hand holding mine but he was strangely silent.

"You know about…" he hesitated, "where she is from?"

"Yes I do," was the reply, "when you left she was unhappy and confused and she turned to me."

Once again there was silence; I could feel Robin brushing his thumb gently over the back of my hand and then heard a sharp intake of breath as if he was about to speak, but he could not find the words.

"You must try to stop this," she said anxiously.

"What can I do?"

"Speak to her. Declare your true feelings."

"How can I, Hilda?" He sounded agitated, almost angry. "She is to be wed."

Hilda scoffed. I sensed her raise he hand in the air and then let it fall back onto the bed.

"Who says this?"

Robin was quick with his reply. "Sir John." It sounded very much as if he spat it through clenched teeth.

"Sir John never once approached Evelyn but went directly to Duke Richard. She turned down the proposal and was very annoyed he would not pass on her decision, but Richard thought it was silly of her to decline the offer and said he would delay her response until you talked some sense into her."

I heard Robin sigh heavily, obviously angered by what he had just been told.

"Sir John informed me that Richard was very pleased with the match, but out of respect for me Evelyn would not proceed without my blessing. I see I have been fooled."

"I think Richard was acting with good intentions," Hilda said. "He saw it as security for her, quite fortunate for one with no dowry or possessions."

"Perhaps, but what can I say? Will she even hear me?"

I felt Hilda rise; she carefully laid my hand on the coverlet and patted it affectionately.

"I do not know, Robin, but you are the only one who can bring her back to us."

And with that she left the room. Robin sat quietly beside the bed; he lifted my hand to his lips.

"Can you hear me, Evelyn?"

I wanted to scream 'yes' but I was paralysed. I could not speak or move or look at him, but I was here at Wyvern with him and somehow I had to stay.

Robin sat quietly; he smoothed my hair and gently stroked each finger of my hand which lay in his palm. Periodically he would catch his breath and then sigh; he didn't know what to say. I wished I could squeeze his hand to encourage him but it was impossible. I lay motionless, breathing evenly, willing him to just be himself and talk, talk about anything. Eventually I felt him rest his elbows on the bed and hold my hand with both of his. I imagined him staring off into the distance as he started to reminisce.

"Do you remember the first time we met, Evie?"

My heart leapt; he had finally used my nickname. Did this mean we were on a path back to the relationship we once both enjoyed? There was just the two of us and it was quiet and peaceful and I lay and reminisced with him.

"You resembled a monk who had been fighting. Your hair was still stained with blood and you spoke strangely. I could hardly believe the transformation when you came to supper that evening. Your gown reflected the colour of your eyes, you were tall and striking. When you beckoned me over to thank me for helping when you were attacked, my stomach knotted and I was worried you would detect my blushes. It was when you called me your champion and held out your hand that I lost my heart."

A soft chuckle escaped his throat and he gave my hand a squeeze. He was beginning to relax and his words started to flow more easily.

"Your actions caught the eye of many at the castle, including William. He finally started to emerge from the gloom that had surrounded him for years. He was falling in love with you too and I knew my love stood no chance compared to his. When he was called home and he left me behind to watch over you, I was thrilled with my task. But you were stubborn and outspoken and a headache."

He said it good-humouredly and I could visualise him shaking his head in despair.

"You treated me well, as a friend and an equal and my love grew but you were aware of the age difference between us and I felt like your younger brother. I did not mind for at least I was with you and I hoped that you cared for me.

"After the execution we returned to find you gone. We searched the castle and went to the Priory but you had vanished as if by magic. Lady Hilda was beside herself and was convinced you had been taken and that you would not have run away. We hoped that it was so, for we could search and find you and bring you back. We journeyed many miles but eventually we had to admit that you were lost to us."

I could feel the sadness in his words and was sorry to have caused so much sorrow, but Hilda had been correct, I would never have left of my own free will. Robin remained quiet for a time, immersed in his private thoughts.

"I was sad and lost when you went but then I have to confess I became very angry. I hated you for not having said goodbye or at least having told me you were going. William and I went across the sea to fight. I told you he was reckless and threw himself into the fighting to forget you, but in truth it was I who chased the battles. I took risks and always led from the front with William hoping death would put me out of my misery.

"Time passed and still there was no word from you. I knew various women but my emotions were locked away and it was just a physical act. I doubt you would have approved of them or my behaviour."

He was silent for a long time, I wondered if perhaps he had fallen asleep but once in a while he would stroke my hair or raise my hand to his lips. As I lay there on the bed I was amazed how strong my feelings were for him. After the death of my husband back in my time I wanted no other. We had been a perfect match and I didn't believe that happiness could ever be replaced. Robin was nothing like him, he was unique, not a replacement. Our friendship had grown and blossomed and I felt confident that we could be happy together and I was ready to take that chance, but maybe it was too late.

Robin stirred.

"Evie, can you hear me? For seven years I hoped I would find you and now I might lose you again. Not a day passed that I did not think of you. When I was in France I thought William might die and I prayed for his return to health, I prayed for some relief from my torment and I prayed for you. God must have finally heard my prayers for suddenly there you were. As I entered the square in Rouen I saw you, I could not believe my eyes. So many times I thought I had seen you only to be disappointed, so I waited and watched.

"Your clothes were ripped and your skin was burnt by the sun and I thought perhaps you had been held captive and had escaped. Your hair was longer and you walked with such a confident air even though you looked in less than a good situation. I watched, hoping, but finally I thought my eyes were deceiving me once again, for you had not aged in all that time. I was about to move on when you started to scuffle with some drunken men, you handled yourself quite well and when you started swearing at them I had no doubt it was you."

He laughed quietly to himself and I was a little disappointed that it was my swearing that had identified me. I rarely swore but in a dangerous situation I think I could be excused base descriptive adjectives.

"When we hid in the alley and I held you close it felt so right, we fitted together perfectly. I had dreamed of such a closeness, to hold you and make love to you. I was engulfed in the aroma of your hair; your hair had always been so fragrant, and I was lost in the moment. Years of yearning for you had culminated in that moment and it was too much to control myself, until of course you hit me and I knew without doubt it was definitely you."

Once again he withdrew into his own thoughts.

I hated the silence. I could feel my blood pulsating in my temples and the buzzing in my ears steadily growing louder to a roar, like an old radio in need of tuning. Robin remained silent, occasionally adjusted his position on the stool or absently fiddling with something around his wrist. Could it be the friendship braid I had tied there years ago? His breathing was soft, not nearly loud enough to drown out the noises in my head. I silently pleaded for him to speak or make a noise, any noise.

"I did not expect William to make me his heir," he began again to my relief. "He did speak of you though, still caring for your needs although he was in pain and near to death. He asked me to take care of you, to protect and provide for you, as if I needed asking."

He snorted quietly. "All I had ever wanted was you by my side. I thought as we journeyed home you might want it to, but not long after setting foot on English soil I failed you miserably."

His voice became husky and he swallowed repeatedly.

"When you confessed to me where or should I say when you were from, I turned my back and walked away. I deserted you, not considering how I must have wounded your feelings. I am ashamed of my actions, can you ever forgive me?"

He had wounded me. I had felt my heart ripped in two but I still didn't understand why he left if he had loved me. Perhaps our differences were too great, I should have remained quiet.

"I thought long and hard about the things you had told me, unbelievable things: things beyond my comprehension, but in the end I knew it would not matter if we loved each other. There was only one thing I was afraid of and that was if you left again. When you left the first time I felt my life was over and I needed you to tell me you would stay. The loss would be unbearable if we married and enjoyed each other's bodies or you had our child, I feared even to think such thoughts, but you confessed you had no control over staying or going. Sometimes in dark moments I wished you had lied to me and said that you would stay forever, but I know lies do not come to your lips."

He sounded so forlorn, I wished I could comfort him but at least now I knew the torment he had suffered. His pain was as great as mine; even greater for he was the one who had considered the future and what pain it might have held for us.

"I thought going to Delacey Manor would help me forget. My hours were filled with fighting and building, all manner of things, but you were always with me. It was a long cold winter but I had Sir Godfrey for company and he gave me good counsel. He said nothing was certain in love, that you had to surrender yourself to each other in trust and grasp every precious moment and he is right.

"My heart leapt when I saw you on the archery field smiling and chatting to those near you while you balanced the baby on your knee. I think you were pleased to see me too and your archery skill was amazing. The day was fine and I was so optimistic until Sir John started chewing my ear. I had lost my chance at happiness; foolishly I had left it too late and you were to marry another. I watched you during supper and I decided I was going to fight for you, I had to have you and I could halt the marriage if I wanted but you spouted pure venom when I spoke to you. I was taken aback and had no notion you thought I was to marry Isabelle. Heaven forbid, her vanity and incessant chatter would drive me insane."

He drew me closer to him, cradling me in his arms. It felt natural exactly where I should be.

"Goodness, Evie, do you not know me at all? We should have

been more open with one another; will you give me another chance? Please come back to me, Evie. I love you with all my being."

Finally, the words I so wanted to hear. I wanted to laugh and scream and dance around like a woman possessed but all I could do was lay there, I couldn't even look into his eyes.

As he lowered his head, I felt his hair brush my forehead and his breath on my face. His lips were soft on my cheek and then slowly, tenderly his mouth was on mine. He lingered there and I could feel my heart start to race in response.

'...Prince Charming gazed at the Sleeping Beauty; he gently kissed her lips eager to wake her from her slumber...'

Was this my happy ever after? Fireworks sky rocketed in my head and then... darkness.

*

I could open my eyes; they slipped open effortlessly but everywhere was still blackness. Perhaps it was night time. I was comfortable and warm and so, so sleepy. Closing my eyes I drifted back to sleep.

I don't know how long I slept but I woke very conscious of my body. My head was clear and there was no pounding, blood rushing through my ears or buzzing noises. My body felt fit and well, in fact totally refreshed but I was afraid to open my eyes. I didn't want to discover where I was, or start a new adventure, or meet interesting new people. This time I had not wanted to leave. I had wanted to stay, to remain with Robin and Hilda, to manage without indoor plumbing, or hairdryers, to endure bumpy rides on smelly carts or astride cantankerous horses. I no longer yearned for chocolate or cream teas. I could even cope without the instant communication provided by my mobile phone. I wanted the chance of happiness that Robin's words had promised.

I was aware of lying flat with a heavy weight holding me down, and that heavy weight was breathing in my ear. I could smell tallow and smoke so I assumed I had not returned to my own time. I cautiously cracked my eyelids and saw daylight filtering in through high slits in a stone wall. I knew this place; opening my eyes in wonder I recognised Hilda's chamber. I had not travelled; I was still lying on her large bed. Perhaps the heavy weight had prevented me leaving. Dare I hope that the heavy weight might be Robin? I could barely move my head because my hair was held down by his head buried in the crook of my neck. I glimpsed unruly muddy blond hair and casting my eyes down saw the familiar dark blue tunic.

Tears of joy were welling up into my eyes. There was the merest sound at the door and I tried to focus as first a hand and then the worried face of Hilda appeared. On seeing me awake she clasped her hands together and brought them to her lips to stifle the surprised gasp. She was very emotional and stood several seconds before she could bring them under control. She smiled and pressing her index finger to her lips quietly backed out of the room.

Now that I was fully awake I wanted to move but found it almost impossible. Robin lay on his side facing me, his leg thrown across my hips and legs so I could only wriggle my toes. His arm stretched across my chest and gripped the top of my arm, the weight of his chest pinning my other arm and shoulder to the bed. He really had no intention of letting me leave this time. I wriggled slightly and he adjusted his head, pushing his face into my hair. Trying to rouse him as gently as I could didn't work and I was hesitant to jab him in the ribs as it would cause him too much of a shock to find me awake and well. I managed to raise my arm and grip his sleeve.

"Robin, wake up."

His breathing altered slightly as he started to wake.

"Is my company so boring you fall asleep?" I teased.

His head shot back, surprised to hear my voice and then he raised himself on his elbow enabling him to see my face clearly. The look of shock melted into the biggest smile and he hugged me to him crushing the air out of my lungs. He pulled back and examined my face hardly daring to believe it was me.

"You stayed!"

I grinned and nodded, not understanding how it had happened and frankly at that moment not caring. We embraced and his kisses were gentle and loving but soon they became wilder and searching. We clung to each other, lost in the moment, the moment we had both waited so long for. My body had a mind of its own and readily responded to his lips and touch, wanting him so badly. Suddenly he pushed away from me and almost slid off the edge of the bed. We were both breathless and I wondered what had caused our love making to come to a halt so suddenly.

He stood next to the bed trying to adjust his tunic and pushing his hands through his hair. Reaching for my hand he practically dragged me off the bed and headed for the door.

"We need to be married. I will not risk losing you again."

I stumbled after him and fell against him as he abruptly stopped at the door and turned to face me.

"Evie, you will wed me will you not? Be beside me always?"

I held his face and gazed into his eyes which were afire. I kissed him gently.

"Of course I will, but could we sup first? I am absolutely starving."

ABOUT THE AUTHOR

Becoming widowed relatively early in life I was apprehensive as I approached retirement. After raising three children and working over twenty years for the NHS and enjoying my work, I feared a sense of emptiness due to the loss of routine and interaction with others. Finally taking the plunge I felt a certain pressure to be productive. I had always wanted to write but never made the time; now I had no excuse.

Writing has become the creative outlet I needed and my first book allowed me to express the anxiety many people suffer being out of their comfort zone and experiencing new situations, no matter what form it may take.

I reside in Northamptonshire with my family close by and now wonder how I managed to fit a job into my life.

Printed in Great Britain
by Amazon